"I remember you," Rebecca said, sliding in next to Brooke in the chair across from the sofa. "You're the man from the park with the funny hair."

Damon smiled, running his fingers through his silky dreads. "How are you?" He was nervous, but delighted to meet his daughter. He glanced at Brooke. Her expression reflected worry about how Rebecca would receive him, and how he would handle it.

Brooke tucked Rebecca's braids behind her ears. "I told you about Damon, remember?"

Rebecca looked up at her, clearly confused.

"The dad who helped me make you," Brooke clarified.

He watched the interaction, questioning how much Rebecca really understood. At five, she was still a baby, not able to grasp adult concepts of heritage.

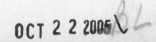

SWEET REPERCUSSIONS

KIMBERLEY WHITE

Genesis Press Inc.

Indigo Love Stories

An imprint of Genesis Press Inc.
Publishing Company

Genesis Press, Inc.
P.O. Box 101
Columbus, MS 39703

ISBN: 1-58571-159-4
Manufactured in the United States of America

First Edition

Visit us at www.genesis-press.com
or call at 1-888-Indigo-1

CHAPTER 1

Brooke Foster began to run before her feet hit the wet pavement. She didn't open her umbrella—too much of a hassle. She prayed her hair would hold up against the heavy rain. She aimed the keyless remote at her car, waiting to hear the chirp. *Ching, ching.* She darted around parked cars; afraid she would slip off the three-inch heels and land in a muddy puddle. If she did fall, maybe Neal would have pity and spare her the scolding normally reserved for a child. She pushed the strap of her brown Coach bag up on her shoulder, her mind rehearsing an apology as she sprinted across the wet pavement.

"Thank you," Brooke called over her shoulder, rushing past the white-haired man holding the door open for her. She burst into the posh restaurant, making a spectacle of herself. She dropped her eyes and quickly disappeared into the ladies' room to put herself back together. That's what he always said, "I like my woman to keep herself *together*. You have to keep yourself together, now."

Fully composed and dry, Brooke approached the maitre d'. With a flick of his wrist, he pointed out her dinner companion. The early evening crowd was beginning to thin. She weaved around the circular dinner tables covered with black tablecloths and elaborate decorative settings of sterling silver.

Still handsome and distinguished at fifty-two, Neal Kirby sat alone near the back of the restaurant. His eyes followed her across the room. She couldn't help feeling he was imagining her in one of the compromising positions from their past. She pulled the edges of her jacket together to cover her ample breasts.

"I'm sorry I'm late, Neal. I had a hard time getting away from work."

He stood and pulled her chair out. "I was a little late getting here myself," he offered as a way of granting forgiveness. "How is the wedding planning business?"

"I'm more than a wedding planner." He knew as much, yet it had always disappointed him to see his favorite student had not done more with the education he had provided.

"Yes, you are. You design conferences, too." He signaled to the waiter. "The lady will have a chicken Caesar salad and white wine. For myself, the shrimp and fettuccine dish."

She should have been impressed by Neal's remembrance of her favorite food at the swank restaurant, if not for his backhanded comment about her job. That he had ordered for himself the shrimp and fettuccine dish he often raved about should have put her at ease, but it didn't. She sensed a problem brewing. His demeanor seemed tense, his wide shoulders straight and stiff. The silence between them grew awkward. Neal was never a man of many words, but he was uncharacteristically quiet this evening. Very decisive, he revealed his wishes only after contemplating his wants and needs from every angle.

She balled her toes inside the high-heeled shoes and then released them, trying to relax. Being the convention services manager during a computer sales conference did not allow much time for sitting down. She wanted to get home and sink into a nice hot bath. She pushed the conversation along when the food arrived and he still had not mentioned the purpose of their dinner. "Did you want to change your visitation with Rebecca?"

Neal shook his head. He wiped away the sauce tangled in his graying mustache. "No, I'm looking forward to seeing her this weekend. I thought I'd take her to the carnival downtown." He tossed the linen napkin on the tabletop.

"She'll like that." Brooke speared parmesan-covered lettuce onto her fork.

"We have a good time during our visits." He watched her for a long, unnerving moment. "However, I did ask you here to talk about Rebecca."

The no-nonsense tone of his voice demanded her attention. "What is it?"

"I want a paternity test."

He caught her mid-chew and her mouth fell open in disbelief, almost losing the half-chewed lettuce inside. "A what?"

"I want Rebecca's paternity to be tested." He ignored her horrified expression and rushed on. "I went to college with several physicians, any one of whom will perform the test discreetly at my request. I'll cover the cost. I think we should get it done as soon as possible."

She held up her hand, stopping his rambling. "Wait. You want a paternity test after five years? Why?"

"There are several reasons." He lifted his wine glass and took a long sip, making her wait to find out what had prompted such a rash decision.

Always has to be in control, Brooke thought. She watched his every move as if she were back in his economics class, taking notes for the big final. She waited as long as she could stand before she asked, "What reasons?"

His stubby hand fingered the linen napkin. "The last weekend I had Rebecca she mentioned something I found quite disturbing."

"What?" *This decision had been two weeks in the making.* For two long weeks he had stewed on something Rebecca had said and come to this rash decision—a paternity test. Neal made many unreasonable demands when it came to his daughter, but Brooke tolerated his actions because he was an involved and loving father. But a paternity test? Now? "What did she say, Neal?"

"She mentioned something about Kurtis becoming her 'real daddy.' Do you know what she was talking about?"

She hated being on the defensive with Neal. She had never learned to see him as an equal. He would always be the older college professor who had taken a naïve girl under his tutelage. She especially hated being on the defensive about something Kurtis had said. Neal and her fiancé had not gotten along from their first meeting. Since she'd started dating Kurtis seriously, the two men had been in a constant power struggle over how she would live her life, neither having the authority to exert power over her will.

Kurtis's tendency to make unilateral decisions about her life often caused trouble with Neal. If Kurtis had consulted her, she would have forbidden him to talk to Rebecca about his desire to adopt her once they were married. The wedding date had not even been set, and incidents like these were causing Brooke to take a second look at their relationship. He was premature in even *thinking* about adopting Rebecca.

"Brooke? Was Rebecca right? Kurtis wants to adopt her?"

She didn't lie. "He mentioned the idea."

Neal leaned forward, and between clenched teeth he said, "I doubt it was as casual a statement as you're trying to make it seem." He sat back and took the no-nonsense tone again. "I hope you told Kurtis adoption is not an option. Rebecca is *my* daughter, and there is no way I'm forfeiting my legal rights." He straightened his tie in an attempt to regain his composure.

"Kurtis mentioned it. I would never agree to anything that would alienate you, or challenge your relationship with Rebecca. No matter what happens between me and Kurtis, you'll always be Rebecca's father."

He continued on as if not hearing her. "I should have made certain my parental rights were established long ago, but under the circumstances... Now things are different and I want my paternity authenticated."

"You can't demand this out of the blue." Her voice rattled, betraying how upset she was.

"Oh, I can demand it, and I am demanding it."

"You need my consent before testing Rebecca and I won't give it. You can't throw me an unexpected curve like this. It's unfair. I won't be bullied into this." Her emotions were fleeting, jumbled, her first response being to defend her child. Nothing good would come of the stance Neal was taking. If she gave in, he had be winning again. As he always did when it came to making decisions about Rebecca. Kurtis would flip, arguing Neal was up to his old tricks, trying to find new ways to control her. And poor Rebecca, who was terrified of needles, would be stuck in the middle of two grown men who were playing power trip games with her life.

"You say my parental rights are safe," Neal said, building up steam to support his argument. "You claim you won't let Kurtis take Rebecca away from me. Then why the resistance to a paternity test?"

"Because you're overreacting. You sprang this on me without any warning. I need time to think about it."

"There's nothing for you to think about, Brooke. I've already decided."

"*You've* decided? I'm her mother."

"And I'm her father and I've made *my* decision." He raised his voice to the stern tone that always made her agree to things she didn't believe in. "Now we can do this the easy way—my way. Or I can go before a judge and get court orders and that sort of thing. However, this will be done. Either way, Brooke, you decide."

—— ∞∞ ——

Brooke had been sitting on the side of Rebecca's bed for the last thirty minutes, watching her sleep. Kurtis stood in the doorway, arms folded across his chest, frowning. He knew something was wrong—she always retreated to Rebecca's bedroom in times of crisis. He shifted against the door frame and she spared him a glance. His vanity forced him to wear sweaters to hide his love handles even in the summer. At forty, Brooke would have expected him to have a little excess cushioning, especially being a CPA who sat behind a desk for most of his waking hours. Sometimes in the middle of a jealous tantrum, he'd admit his vanity was connected to his worrying about the twelve-year age difference between them. She'd done everything she could to convince him age didn't matter, but it was always a sticking point with him.

"Brooke, let her sleep," he quietly prompted.

She stroked Rebecca's hair.

"C'mon." He stepped into the darkened room, touching her shoulder.

She kissed Rebecca one last time before brushing past him without acknowledgment.

He flipped the light switch and followed her across the thick green carpet into her living room. Gathering his slacks at the thigh in an attempt to keep them from wrinkling, Kurtis sat down next to her on the sofa. "Are you mad about dinner Sunday? You know I hate missing dinner at your

Aunt Foster's. I'm still trying to win her over. I had pressing problems to clear up at work."

"You always miss dinner. Unless it has something to do with a promotion, you can't fit anything into your schedule."

"That's not true."

She threw him a skeptical look.

"Work does consume a great amount of my time, yes. But the only reason I took on this extra client was to pay for our wedding."

"I never asked you to. A small wedding with a few of our friends and family is fine with me. It's your mother who wants to put on this big show. I don't know if I'm cut out to be a corporate wife. Having my husband at home is more important to me than having a fat bank account." She dropped off the sofa to her knees, picking up Rebecca's stray toys.

"It's plain to see by the way Aunt Foster pinches her lips together whenever I come around that she doesn't like me. But she will. After I marry you, and give you the life of a princess, Aunt Foster will see how wrong she was about me. In order for me to do this, I need to pick up extra clients and work long hours, but it won't last forever."

"So you're doing it to impress my aunt?"

"To impress you, too. And to make you and Rebecca happy. Where's all this hostility coming from? Are you really that upset about me missing dinner at your Aunt Foster's? With her not liking me, the dinner should have been more enjoyable without me around."

She dropped down on her bottom, clutching one of Rebecca's dolls to her chest. "Does everything have to be about you, Kurtis?" Her large eyes were fixed on him, her bottom lip twitching.

"What is it?" He gathered the crease of his slacks and slipped off the sofa. He sat facing her, his hand on her knee. "This is about more than dinner."

"I needed your support today."

"Did something happen between you and your aunt?"

She shook her head, plucking at the doll's head of black yarn. "Dinner was fine." She tossed the toy aside.

"You needed my support because..." Kurtis prompted.

"I had dinner with Neal today."

"I should've known this had something to do with the pompous professor. Neal is a constant source of trouble. He's full of drama. He's trying to put a wedge between us by pushing his importance in your life—even if he has to use his child to do it."

"That's not true, and you know it. Neal loves his daughter. Don't start this fight today." She said the words to stop Kurtis's endless argument before it started. With his recent paternity test demand, she too had begun to wonder how devoted Neal was to Rebecca.

"Tell me why you went to dinner with Neal. Was it his idea? What did he want?"

"He wants a paternity test."

His eyes nearly bucked out of his head, and Brooke wondered if she'd looked the same way sitting at the expensive restaurant. "He wants a *what?*"

"Your reaction tells me it is as bad as I think it is. I wasn't sure if I was overreacting."

"What did he say, exactly?" Kurtis listened in horror as she choked out the details of Neal's latest demands. "This is just another one of his power plays to control your life. Is he planning to block the adoption?"

"I've never agreed to you adopting Rebecca. We never seriously discussed it. You shouldn't have said anything to her. It wasn't your place."

"Not my place? I'll be your husband soon. And I was very serious when we talked about it. What did you think I meant when I said I wanted us to be a real family?"

"You mentioned it, and I said we'll talk about it later. Nothing more. Neal has the idea we've met with lawyers to file papers and a court date will be announced soon."

"It's not my fault if he's a melodramatic old fool. All I did was ask Rebecca how she felt about me becoming her dad. It's a fair question since we're getting married—with or without me adopting her." He moved to place his arm across her shoulders. The gesture was meant to comfort her, but she wanted to slink away from his touch. More and more she'd needed time away from his stifling presence. She'd started questioning their relationship and their future. The man she'd once thought of as gentle and kind had become pushy and annoying.

"Is he going to fight the adoption?" he asked.

"No, there won't be a fight because once he establishes paternity you won't be able to adopt Rebecca. Neal made it clear he'd never allow it."

"So, you plan to lie down and let Professor Neal Kirby tell you what to do as always?"

"I don't have any other option. I tried to reason with him."

"I won't let Neal ruin our plans. Rebecca is part of our family. I'll call an attorney and see just what our options are. We can fight Neal and win."

"You accuse Neal of always telling me what to do, but again, you're making decisions about my life without consulting me. Neal is a good father. I don't want to sever his parental rights. There's no reason for it."

"Are you saying I haven't treated Rebecca like she was my own?" A frown appeared on his face while anger flared in his voice.

"You're great with Rebecca, but I can't exclude Neal from her life when we get married." "What are you saying, Brooke?"

"Neal doesn't want to lose his daughter. The three of us will be living in the same house, and he's afraid she'll be closer to you since you'll be with her every day."

"I bet he'd love the chance to move me out, and himself in."

She bit her bottom lip, not wanting to engage in the 'Neal still loves you' argument. She assuaged Kurtis's anger by stroking the area above his flat nose. The gesture calmed him, and made a lump form in his pants. This was another part of their relationship she'd been avoiding lately. Sex with him was mechanical. None of her emotions were engaged in the process. It had become her duty and not her pleasure, so she'd been shying away from his advances. So far, he'd understood, not wanting to jeopardize their entire relationship, but Brooke knew it was only a matter of time before his patience ran out. When he leaned toward her, she gave him a peck on the lips, not wanting to encourage intimacy.

Kurtis accepted the kiss, but continued the argument. "Neal wants you back. He'd try anything to steal you away from me. And don't tell me the argument has no merit."

"Neal and I never were a couple, and he's happily married now. The only contact we have is through Rebecca. You're jealous. You can't see the situation rationally."

"You're the one who can't see it. Or don't want to see it. I don't know which, but I'm a man and I know when another man is trying to sneak in the back door. He put his precious job as a college professor on the line to have an affair with you. He knew dating a student would cost him his career, but he didn't care. Nothing is more important to *Professor Neal Kirby* than his status at the university, yet he was willing to risk it all to be with you…and you don't think he still wants you?"

"What happened between Neal and me happened a long time ago. And you're making it sound more romantic than it actually was. He was my professor. I was his student. We worked a lot of hours together. It happens."

He watched her skeptically. "You don't believe that, so don't try to feed it to me. You had a boyfriend at the time. If it just 'happened' and meant nothing, why did you break up with your boyfriend to be with Neal?"

Damon Richmond. She hadn't thought of him in…who was she trying to fool? Memories of their time together lived in her heart, which was one of the reasons she could never truly give herself to Kurtis—or to any man. Whenever she saw a loving couple, she wondered what her life would be like if she hadn't pushed him away to be with her handsome, unattainable professor.

As Kurtis rambled on, Brooke wished she hadn't told him the details about her relationship with Neal. At the time their relationship was stellar, and she'd thought this was the man she'd spend the rest of her life with. She'd had no way to know Kurtis would erupt like a volcano in molten jealousy. The argument always went the same way. Kurtis presented the evidence to support his belief that Neal still wanted her. She'd counter with facts about Neal's recent marriage. Her naiveté frustrated him until he would have a tantrum. They would go back and forth until he stomped out of the house. It was emotionally tiring, and this night played no differently.

"How can I make you realize how much I love you?" Kurtis asked as he stepped out onto the porch. "I've been asking myself this since the first day I saw you."

Famous parting words, Brooke thought. The sad expression and down-turned mouth used to make her remorseful about her behavior, and appreciative of his feelings for her. Lately, the words had little effect. Truthfully, she was glad when he stomped out of her townhouse and she heard his car race away. She needed to de-stress and she couldn't do that with Kurtis there, demanding she see things his way. She had hoped he would be supportive and reassuring, helping her to remember why she'd fallen for him. Instead he took her crisis and made it his own.

When Kurtis got home, he'd be regretful about their argument and give her a call to apologize. He'd say his jealousy made him say things he didn't mean. He'd hate himself for raising his voice over hers. "You're the most beautiful thing in my life," he'd say. "I can't lose you."

Brooke had lived through the dramatic episodes enough to know every emotional card Kurtis would play. She crawled into bed just as the telephone rang.

"My gut tells me this is the start of something bad," Kurtis said. "Once we're married, Neal will always have his nose in the middle of our household."

"Kurtis, I'm really tired." She couldn't pacify him right now. *She* needed support. Yes, Neal was being unreasonable, but he was Rebecca's father and it gave him the right to have the fact acknowledged legally. It didn't matter if his efforts were five years too late in her book. No matter the motive behind his decision, he'd decided to assert his rights. Coming to this realization had prompted her to give in to the paternity test.

"I'm in your corner, watching your back, and looking out for Rebecca. I'm sorry for my jealous behavior. You don't need that right now. I love you and Rebecca so much. I don't want to lose you."

"This test doesn't change our relationship."

"I know, I know. Do you forgive me?"

She hesitated. It couldn't always be about him and his needs. Aunt Foster had warned her to put her foot down now—before they were married. But it was late and she was emotionally tired, and selfishness was a big topic to tackle with Kurtis. She exhaled into the phone. "No, I'm not mad at you, but you have to stop this. I can't take all the arguing."

"I know. You're right. I'll make it up to you. I'm going to support you through this."

"If you want to support me, I need you to go along with what I've decided without trying to make me see things your way."

He hesitated, but knew he really had no choice. "All right. What have you decided?"

"I'm calling Neal in the morning and telling him to schedule the test. He'll have legal proof of his paternity, which will make him feel better. I'll assure him we aren't actively pursuing adoption, which will put him at ease. In a couple of weeks, this will all blow over."

"All right," he ground out with some difficulty. "I'll drive you to the clinic and wait while—"

She assured him his presence was not needed. "Neal might be there, and you two will fight. Right now, we want him to know we're being cooperative. I just want this to go away."

Four days later, when Brooke and Rebecca stepped out onto the front porch of her townhouse, Kurtis stood there wearing a sheepish grin. "I wanted to support you," he simply said.

Another decision about her life he felt he could make better than she could. She fought the urge to send him away. Truthfully, she didn't want to go to the clinic alone. Kurtis was there, trying to prove he was a supportive fiancé as he'd been doing since their last argument.

"If Neal shows up for some reason, you'll leave without any debate?" she asked.

"I will. I only want to be there for you."

At the clinic, Kurtis held her hand in his lap as they waited to be called into the exam room. She studied his profile as he laughed at *Regis & Kelly* playing on the television suspended from the ceiling. His laugh began as a deep rumble below his belt, and trickled upward through his chest until it escaped past dentist-made-perfect-teeth. It was times like these that she appreciated him. When he could be with her without making unreasonable demands. When his focus was on being a strong presence in her life. When he tried to be a role model for Rebecca. When he gave her unwavering support, he helped her remember why she planned to marry him. He was ambitious and wanted to please her. He cared for Rebecca as if she were his own daughter. He wanted to give them a perfect life. What more could she ask for?

"I'm glad you're here," she confessed.

He smiled, gathering her into his arms.

"You have the most wonderful laugh," she told him. "It's one of the things that first attracted me to you."

"You're feeling sentimental today. Your sentimentality is one of the first things that attracted me to you." He caressed the back of her hand. "Don't worry. Rebecca'll be fine. Everything is going to work out."

She knew what the results would be, but she couldn't shake the feeling that this paternity test would open a Pandora's box in her life. "I know you're right."

The sadness in her voice made him hold her tighter. "The nurse called your name."

She rose and gathered Rebecca from the play area. She couldn't shake the feeling of doom. The most ill timed question jumped into her head. She pushed it away. Usually her thoughts of him came late at night, or when some small thing jogged a memory of their time together. That Damon Richmond would come to mind now made no sense and she refused to acknowledge his presence in her head.

"Do you want me to come?" Kurtis called as she moved down the hallway.

"No, we'll be fine." She smiled, looking down into Rebecca's dancing eyes. "This is going to be a piece of cake."

CHAPTER 2

Damon Richmond took a break from the paperwork stacked in front of him only long enough to remove his glasses and rub the bridge of his nose. Replacing the glasses, he returned his attention to the work at hand. He had just recently acquired the need for specs. The optometrist had blamed his failing vision on the number of hours he spent at his computer screen and trying to decipher unreadable handwriting. He thumbed through the stack of documents counting how many pages he had to examine before he could go home for the night.

Mrs. Friedman suddenly appeared in front of his desk. The petite old woman moved with the quiet ease of a house cat. He never heard her coming, but she was always there. Always around when he needed her.

"I'll be leaving for the night if there's nothing else." She tossed her wheat-colored hair over her shoulder. The shade was distorted by the underlying gray-whiteness fighting to take over.

"No, there's nothing else. I appreciate you coming in on a Saturday to help me get caught up."

"I'll add an extra day to my vacation time over the summer." She chuckled as she left the office. "You should be leaving, too."

Damon watched the woman's fragile frame disappear from his sight. Going home was not what he wanted to do. Home was not a peaceful place anymore. He fanned through the papers again. With all the fighting, it was better to spend as little time at home as possible.

The phone rang four times before he heard Mrs. Friedman's voice ring out announcing Employment Network Unlimited was currently closed. His business hours were announced, followed by the prompt to leave a message. Before he left, he would roll the phone lines over to the answering service until Monday. He listened intently for the caller's message. His business was solid, but he needed to acquire more contracts to obtain his ultimate dream. One day he'd like to be able to run his business from home with the help of an executive board. He'd spend his days golfing, or on vacation in exotic locations.

Barbara would be happy when that time finally came, too. His wife was already leading the life of the *Rich and Famous*, which was another reason he needed to be in the office every Saturday. Supporting Barbara and his two stepchildren was draining his bank account. He'd asked her to pick up a part-time job, but she'd stared at him like he had lost his mind. She had married him so she wouldn't have to work, she calmly informed him before pulling out a clothing catalog.

He tried to refocus his attention on the work piled at his fingertips. He shouldn't enjoy his time at the office more than he did being at home, but he did. There was too much turmoil at home. The kids ran around unsupervised. Barbara spent too much time nagging him to spend money they couldn't afford to spend. The cook she'd insisted on hiring had quit within a week because the kids kept tormenting her, which meant there was never a warm meal awaiting him. He sighed long and hard, comparing his marriage to his parents' perfect life together. Never had he thought he'd end up one of those men who dreaded going home.

He squinted his eyes together, pinching them with his fingers. His eyes were aching, so regretfully, he shut down his computer and switched the telephone lines over to the answering service. Maybe if he had a better attitude, things at home would be better. If he looked at his wife with new eyes, maybe things would go back to the way they were when he'd first met her. He held onto this hope during the long drive home.

He had wanted to live in one of Detroit's new urban neighborhoods near downtown, but Barbara had wanted to be a suburban housewife—a soccer mom—so they'd moved to a suburb almost an hour away from his office. And neither of the kids played any kind of sports.

He rolled into his driveway but was unable to pull into the garage because of the bikes blocking his path. As usual, his home was the neighborhood kids' hangout. He entered the house and stopped to turn off the blaring television no one was watching. He found his wife in the kitchen on the telephone talking loudly with one of her girlfriends. She finished her conversation before acknowledging him.

"The kids left their bikes in the driveway again." He rested his arm on the top of the refrigerator door while he pushed around bottles and jars to find a can of soda.

"I'll tell 'em to move them later."

"Why is it so hard for them to keep the driveway clear like I asked?" He shut the refrigerator door and turned to his wife.

"I said I'll have them move the bikes later."

"Will you go out and move my car?"

Barbara ran her hand through her short-cropped hair. "Speaking of cars, I picked out a new one today. The salesman said I just need you to sign these papers and I can pick it up in a day or two unless the custom features might delay delivery." She waved the contract at him.

"Wait a minute. I never said anything about buying another car." He walked over to the stove, hoping to find dinner even though he didn't smell anything cooking.

"I thought we'd go out for dinner." She crossed the long, shapely legs that had led him down the aisle. "The car is for me. I need another car. The Mercedes just isn't what I thought it would be. I'll be happier in an Audi."

"The Mercedes is less than six months old. We can't buy another car right now. We're extending over ourselves."

"You always say that, Damon. We have plenty of money. And while we're on the subject, I don't like having to beg you for money every time I want any little thing."

Any little thing? The house and the Mercedes had all been purchased within the last six months. The Land Rover sitting in the garage was a year old and Barbara had driven it exactly two times—once being on the way home from the dealership. The Lincoln he was driving was only two years old. She had two walk-in closets bursting with new clothes and shoes. Her children had everything they wanted, and more stuff than they'd ever need.

When they were married three years ago, he'd put Barbara in charge of their finances. He had thought he would be demonstrating trust by giving her the freedom to manage the household as she saw fit. Besides, he was absorbed in planning and opening his new business. Within three months of opening Employment Network Unlimited, angry employees whose payroll checks had bounced were pounding on his door. He'd quickly learned his wife had a talent for spending his money, but an allergy to making any of her own.

"No more cars. We can't afford it right now."

"Don't bother looking in the oven," Barbara huffed. "We're going out for pizza."

"We had pizza last night." His complaint fell on deaf ears— Barbara was already leaving the kitchen.

"I'm going to change."

As Damon watched her sashay out of the room, a frightening thought assaulted him. He wasn't happy, and hadn't been in a long time. Everything he needed, he wasn't getting. He wanted a warm, loving family to greet him when he came home from a long day at work. He wanted a successful business that enabled him to do the things in life he'd always dreamt of doing. He needed to be on the same page with his wife—both of them working toward the same goals with the same aspirations. Family and financial security should be important to them both. He shouldn't feel he was carrying an unmanageable burden for a family who didn't appreciate his efforts.

He wasn't a chauvinist. He understood Barbara needed interests separate from his, and a life of her own. He would definitely support Barbara's career if she chose to enter the workforce, but he would demand they put uninterrupted time aside to spend quality time together.

Part of the responsibilities of being a parent was disciplining your children, and making them responsible citizens. His children should be orderly and have good manners, not completely out of control. Family vacations should be a fun time. After the last disaster, he had found excuse after excuse not to take another one this summer.

Although his business was doing well, his family was not as he wanted it to be. There was an emptiness in their house, and he seemed to be the only one noticing it. He remembered his pledge to make his relationship with Barbara work and pushed away all the negative feelings tied with the past. Dutifully, he gathered his family and took them out to dinner; hopeful tonight would give them a new start.

⸺∞⸺

"Stop it, stupid." Roger pushed Lisa's plate, knocking over her glass of fruit punch.

"That's enough!" Barbara shouted across the table. Her voice went unnoticed in the crowded pizza parlor. "If you two keep it up, Daddy and I will *never* take you out to eat again."

Damon bit down into his slice of pizza. He had given up trying to teach the kids manners after they slipped under the table and used their soda to make a slippery trap for the waiter. The man left early for the day, vowing to sue everyone in the restaurant for his hurting back. No wonder Barbara calling him "Daddy" made him cringe. The thought of having children was scary enough without being placed in the position of being stepfather to the unruly brats sitting across from him.

They had been such good children before he married Barbara. Once they all moved in together, things quickly changed. They never followed the rules he set down. They were disorderly and loud. And like their mother, they spent too much money. He had tried to persuade Barbara to get the kids in line before they were too old and too out of control to handle. At eight and ten, Roger and Lisa's behavior could still be managed—with the right adult supervision.

Their father had never married Barbara. He had said he wasn't ready for commitment. Some men just couldn't connect the dots between sex, fatherhood, and commitment. Damon had stepped into Barbara's life fully prepared to take responsibility for her two adorable children without a second thought.

Damon glanced up at his wife. *Boy, how quickly things changed.* Too much lately, he kept asking himself what he'd been thinking when he had asked her to marry him.

A beautiful, challenging woman had walked into his life, and he'd snatched her up and placed a ring on her finger. He'd been left so many times in his relationships; he refused to let Barbara get away. He was tired of being alone, left trying to figure out what his big mistake had been.

Barbara was still very beautiful, but not at all the woman he had dated. Her quiet agreeable nature had been replaced by expensive demands. Her pampering of him had changed into a lack of consideration for his wishes. Making love every day had become him begging for sex once a month. There were no more candlelight dinners—they were now regulars at the pizza parlor. The clean comfort of her apartment disappeared the day they were married and he moved in with his new family. The kids had run off the maid he'd hired after they moved into the house. So if he didn't clean on the weekends, their house was always a mess.

Lisa and Roger continued to bicker.

"Lisa," Damon said, "Roger is your little brother. You shouldn't talk to him like that. You're supposed to set an example for him."

Lisa spared him a glance. She did quiet down—for a hot second, and then they were at it again.

Barbara ignored the scene. She knew their behavior would embarrass him, but she didn't intervene. She was mad about his refusal to buy the Audi. She could always get a job, make her own money and buy the car she wanted. But that would be too foolish for her to consider. What would be the point of being married if you still had to work and support yourself?

"Barbara." Damon waved his fork between the fighting kids.

She raised an eyebrow.

"Can you help me out here?"

"They're kids. They're supposed to be noisy." She went back to her pizza, ignoring the ruckus her children were making.

Intent on making an effort to be happy with her again, Damon reached across the table for Barbara's hand. "Remember that nice French restaurant we used to go to all the time when we were dating?"

Her glare flew to his hand. She looked up at him apprehensively—no love there, just suspicion of his motives.

"We should leave the kids with your sister and go there tomorrow night. Maybe catch a movie." He gave her his most seductive smile. "Come home afterwards and make love." Tossing their almost nonexistent sex life into the deal had been risky, but he was a healthy thirty-year-old man who wanted to make love to his wife. It wasn't just about physical needs. If their marriage was going to survive, he needed to share this ultimate closeness with Barbara.

She pulled her hand away. "My sister's out of town, and I'm playing bingo tomorrow with my friends. I told you about this earlier in the week. You're keeping the kids. Don't try to get out of it."

Roger and Lisa's fight had escalated into a salad toss. Roger flung a forkful of lettuce across the table, hitting Damon in the face. The kids broke into hysterical laughter.

Barbara giggled, too. "You need a haircut, Damon," she said, not reprimanding her kids, but belittling him.

CHAPTER 3

Brooke left work early, eager to start her weekend. Rebecca was spending the weekend with Neal, and Kurtis would arrive at her townhouse any minute so they could begin making wedding plans. She put dinner in the oven and then sank into a hot bath with a glass of wine.

Kurtis had been making a real effort lately to be supportive of her needs, and tonight she would put forth an equal effort with planning their wedding. As she relaxed in the tub, she listed his good qualities, remembering the things that had attracted her to him. He was a little nerdy, bossy, absorbed with work, and still under his mother's thumb, but he had good qualities, too. He loved her. He took her to nice places. He cherished Rebecca. He was good company when she was lonely.

Cataloging the reasons she was going to marry him came harder. Aunt Foster's numerous warnings rang in her head. Aunt Foster hadn't liked Kurtis at their first meeting when he came on too strong, trying to her win approval. He tended to rub people the wrong way. Brooke discounted her aunt's assessment of him, because Aunt Foster never approved of the men she dated—few as they were. Lounging in the tub, Brooke convinced herself she wanted to marry Kurtis because he was a good man—not because he filled the emptiness left by the loss of her parents.

True, they had their issues, but they could work everything out. Lately he'd been hinting at wanting her to quit her job. He wanted a baby as soon as they were married, and thought her becoming a housewife was the best way to make it happen. Although it had been Neal's drastic reaction to her pregnancy five years ago that had pushed her into taking the position at Vintage Suites, she couldn't imagine losing the independence of having a career. She had no desire to be a house-wife and full-time homemaker.

Afraid he'd lose his job at the university, Neal had blown his top when Brooke announced her pregnancy. He had smoothed over his harsh reaction. "If I'm unemployed it'll be impossible to give you the things you'll need during the pregnancy," he'd said. Even as he gave her the explanation, her instincts had sounded a warning.

In a vain attempt to put him at ease, she'd accepted the position at Vintage Suites. With a lot of hard work, she'd moved up into the convention manager's position. The work was fast-paced, and though dealing with celebrities could be a hassle, she loved what she did. She made a good salary, and the perks were even better. No, she wasn't ready to give up her job or her independence in order to be married to Kurtis.

Brooke was searching for her favorite pair of jeans when the doorbell rang. "Come in." She slipped into her robe and went to greet Kurtis. She stopped short when she entered the living room. Neal was sitting in the green recliner nearest the front door looking very unhappy.

"Where's Rebecca? Is she all right?"

"She's at home getting ready for bed." He slowly, painfully turned to face her.

She pulled the edges of her robe tight, belting it at her middle. "Why are you here?" She took a seat near him on the sofa.

"We need to have a talk." His voice was icy. "Just the two of us, without Rebecca around."

Kurtis was right about a few things when it came to her relationship with Neal. He had a tendency to become melodramatic when it came to Rebecca and any issues surrounding her.

"Is there a problem?"

"There certainly is," Neal answered tightly.

"What is it?"

"I have the paternity test results." He pulled the white envelope out of the breast pocket of his suit.

"I told you I'd never allow Kurtis to adopt Rebecca. I don't need to see the results of the blood test. No one will interfere with your relationship with your daughter. You're Rebecca's father."

"No!" Neal leapt to his feet. "Rebecca is not my daughter!" He threw the white envelope in her face.

She scrambled to catch it. "What are you talking about?"

"The test is 99.98% positive Rebecca *is not* my daughter."

"You must have read it wrong." She opened the envelope with trembling fingers and confirmed Neal's words. She looked up at him helplessly. "This can't be right."

He stomped away from her. "All these years! All this time I thought Rebecca was mine! I've loved her as if she was my daughter." He rushed up to her as she reread the letter for the third time. "Did you know this all the time? Were you laughing at me because I was such a fool?"

"This can't be true, Neal. Rebecca *is* your daughter." Her eyes filled with tears of confusion.

He stood over her, staring, searching for the truth. "Did you know?"

"There's nothing to know! Rebecca is your daughter."

He balled his hands into tight fists. His temper flashed out of control. "Five years!" he shouted. "Have you known all this time Rebecca wasn't my child?"

"She is your daughter."

"Stop saying that!" He snatched the paper out of her clutches. "Look at the test results, Brooke!"

"The test is wrong."

"I had them run it twice. Rebecca is not mine."

"Stop saying that!" She tossed his words back at him, standing up to face him head on.

He pushed her back down on the sofa. When she scrambled to stand up again, he pointed a finger at her nose. "Sit down!"

She couldn't remember ever seeing him angry before. He used manipulation to get what he wanted. The man standing in her living room was so mad his body trembled. Neal never shouted, and he had never put his hands on her. His actions surprised him as much as they did her. He took a staggering step back.

"It's not true," she sobbed.

He backed to the door. "I can't talk to you right now."

Their eyes locked, and she tried to send him a silent message. *Rebecca is your daughter.*

"I can't even look at you." He flung the door open. "I'm afraid of what I might do."

"You won't say anything to Rebecca, will you?"

"Of course not," he spat.

She let him go. They would never have a rational discussion with his anger being so intense.

Neal brushed past Kurtis as he stormed out of the townhouse. Kurtis spun around in a complete circle, mocking Neal's dramatic exit. His mouth dropped when he saw her, naked beneath her robe. "Why the hell are you dressed like that while he's here?" His eyebrows knit together. "What is he doing here at this time of night anyway? Where's Rebecca?"

She tore her gaze away from the front door and moved them to Kurtis.

"Did you hear what I said?" He closed the front door, and turned, ready to start a huge fight about her being with Neal.

"Brooke? Are you crying? What did he do to you?" He rushed to her side, dropping down next to her, accidentally sitting on the crumpled letter Neal had torn from her grip. He pulled it from beneath him, and seeing the official letterhead, began to read it.

She didn't want him to know about the results yet, but she was frozen, unable to stop him. She needed time to process what she had just learned, and figure out how she would handle it. He glanced at her, then reread the letter.

"It's wrong."

The truth being revealed, he met her eyes again.

"There has to be some mistake," she mumbled.

"How can Rebecca not be Neal's daughter?"

"The test has to be wrong. The blood tubes must have gotten mixed up. Or the lab made a horrible mistake." She needed to convince herself more than Kurtis.

He shook his head. "It says here the test is 99.98% sure Neal can't be Rebecca's father."

"I know what it says!" She stood and crossed the room, moving away from him. "It's wrong. We'll just have to repeat the test."

"Brooke, this is real. This isn't a TV movie-of-the-week. A 'ghastly' mistake isn't going to be uncovered at the end of the movie. Rebecca *is not* Neal's daughter."

Her legs went weak. Kurtis was there in a flash, gripping her arms to keep her from falling. He swiveled her around and lowered her to the sofa. He sprinted into the kitchen, returning with a glass of water. "Drink this." He wrapped his arm around her shoulders and held the glass to her lips. "This is not good. Everything is getting ready to fall apart for us."

She pushed him away, refusing to let him make this about him.

He put the glass down and turned to her. "What did Neal say to you?"

"He's upset. He thinks I've been lying to him for five years." She turned pleading eyes to him. "I haven't been lying. Rebecca *is* his daughter. I would never do something like this to anyone."

Kurtis took her hand in his. He spoke slowly, in a soft tone. "These tests are sophisticated." Guiding her through a crisis gave him the opportunity to shine. He liked being the rational one in their relationship, taking control. "Rebecca can't be his daughter. We have to face that fact."

She shook her head.

"Who else could be her father?" He asked the question as casually as ordering a cup of coffee. Did he not see her life was on the brink of crumbling? She couldn't accept the accuracy of the paternity test yet. She wasn't ready to face the inevitable.

"Neal," she answered. "It could only be Neal."

"This is a shock. I know you're upset, but let's be realistic. The test is 99.98% sure Neal Kirby is not Rebecca's father."

"Why can't you take my side unconditionally?" It angered her that knowing the implications of the paternity results, he forged on into threatening territory.

"I want to get to the truth." He tried to calm her by stroking the back of her hand.

"And I don't?"

He ignored her attitude. "One step at a time. You didn't know Neal wasn't Rebecca's father. If you had, you would've done the right thing. But now we know the truth, and you have to step up." He paused, trying to read her. "Who could be her father?"

"There's no one else."

"Okay." He pulled her against his chest.

"Neal is Rebecca's father. The test is wrong."

"This is going to be all right," he whispered.

She could hear in his tone he was planning to use the situation to his advantage. She would convinced him the test was wrong. And he believed it because it benefited him to do so. She let him become her safety net while she tried to absorb everything.

"I don't know what Neal's game is, but it doesn't matter," Kurtis told her. "I'll take care of everything. We'll be married soon, and Rebecca will be *my* daughter. I'll adopt Rebecca. As far as I'm concerned, she's my child."

------ ∞ ------

Brooke couldn't sleep that night. She cuddled up in her favorite chair, her mind frantically trying to accept the truth.

Kurtis could be right. Neal might have cooked this all up to upset Kurtis's adoption plans. The physician friend of his must have doctored the test results. Even as she imagined an elaborate scheme, she knew it wasn't in Neal's character to do such a thing. *How would that help him anyway?* It wouldn't. The only way to keep Kurtis from adopting Rebecca was for Neal to prove his paternity and refuse to give up his parental rights. *What could he be up to?* There had to be an explanation.

Brooke thought back to the days of her love affair with Neal. Her life had been such a mess during that time. She still hadn't gotten over her parents' death. Her finances were tight, but Aunt Foster couldn't offer much help. She'd had to work meager part time jobs to pay tuition. Her classes were so challenging. Graduation was coming and she had to plan for her future. Despite living away from home in the campus dorms, she had led a sheltered life and was still very naïve. Professor Kirby was the role model she'd needed. He had been confident and knowledgeable about the world while she was young and inexperienced. Completely in awe of him, she had been vulnerable to the attention he'd lavished on her.

Brooke closed her eyes, squeezing them tight against the truth. She had blocked out a large portion of her college years because of the pain associated with it. She never thought about *him*. There was too much hurt associated with the memories.

She'd been so sure back then that Neal was the father that she'd never considered the other possibility.

But know she knew the truth. It was staring her in the face.

She glanced at the letter discarded near the sofa. The indisputable truth was written in black and white: *Neal Kirby was not Rebecca's father.*

Mrs. Friedman helped Damon slip into the jacket of his suit. "Your students are waiting."

"Thank you." He began buttoning his jacket. "What does the class look like?"

"There are twenty students, mostly female, all African-American. Cathy finished up the registration. They have all of their books, and are finishing up their break."

He turned to the older woman with a broad smile. He held his arms out from his body to allow for an unobstructed final inspection. "Do you think they're ready for me?"

"They won't know what hit em." She handed him a stack of materials he would need to instruct the class.

With that, he moved down the private corridor to the passageway leading to the conference room. He detoured to the cubicles where his employees were making deals and tracking employment trends. He said good morning, confirmed a lunch meeting, and continued down the hall. As he passed the group of females standing in the hallway waiting for class to begin, the chattering stopped. It always did when he appeared, shattering their expectations of a white-haired, and aging instructor.

He enjoyed taking a break from running his company to substitute for one of his employment counselors. This seminar would focus on how new college graduates could best impact the job market. The city was funding the seminar for this group of "at-risk" graduates. They were considered underserved and had completed their community college educations with the financial assistance of the state. They were now competing with thousands of their peers who had more prestigious educations and unlimited financial support. They needed any advantages they could get, and this seminar would help them realize they were equally qualified for high-paying, upscale jobs. The seminar always brought lively discussions and heated debates.

At the completion of the four-hour lecture, Mrs. Friedman met him outside the conference room. "Your lunch meeting has been canceled. I already let everyone involved know." She smiled smugly. She knew her job well.

"Any important calls?"

"There were several I transferred to the counselors. A new company is interested in meeting with you about a possible contract. The message is on your desk."

He always met with prospective clients himself, giving them personal service. "I'll have lunch in my office. Can you order in?"

"Lunch is waiting on your desk, Mr. Richmond," she answered, almost annoyed he felt the need to prompt her on doing her job. "There was one particular call, from a Brooke Foster; I wanted to bring to your attention." She handed him the slip of paper containing the message. "She wouldn't say what the call pertained too, but did say it was important you contact her as soon as possible."

He stopped and studied the paper. "Brooke Foster?"

"Yes, sir."

"Hmm." He raised his eyes to Mrs. Friedman's inquisitive expression. "Is there anything else?"

"No, I'll be leaving for lunch now."

Brooke Foster. His body warmed with forgotten memories. Brooke Foster—his first love. His smile was quickly chased away by a frown. That was a long time, and a lot of hurt ago. *Why would Brooke be calling me after all these years?* He read the message again. The urgent box was checked. He tucked the paper inside his planner, hurrying to the privacy of his office to return her call.

———❦———

Damon removed his reading glasses and checked his watch. Brooke would be arriving in minutes. Things hadn't ended well between them, but he wouldn't relive any of it with her today. She'd suggested they get together for lunch. Even as he accepted her invitation, he'd questioned his loyalty to Barbara. He'd gone home that evening, trying to seduce his wife with flowers. She'd turned a cold stare on him, reminding him about the contract he needed to sign for her new car purchase.

The click-clack of heels crossing the restaurant made him look up. He did a double take. The woman standing with the hostess was every bit as gorgeous as he remembered. Her eyes were as dark as the night and as big as saucers. Her pecan complexion was smooth, flawless. He suddenly missed her. He remembered an easier time in his life with long kissing sessions in the park, holding hands at R&B concerts, and long drives in his beat-up old car.

The hostess checked her seating book. He could have called out, but he suddenly became anxious. His thoughts were inappropriate for a married man. The hostess pointed in his direction. A lopsided smile filled Brooke's face. He chastised himself for admiring her beauty, and stood to greet her. His nerves were firing twice as fast as normal. He watched every stride that brought her to him. When she reached the table, he offered his hand. They touched, and it was as if six years had not passed since he'd last seen her.

"Brooke," Damon breathed with smoky familiarity.

He was bigger than life. His face had matured, his body solidified into chiseled manly features. His skin, a milky combination of his white mother and black father, didn't hide his blushing enthusiasm. His cheekbones were prominent, his thin-lipped smile wide. His hair was styled in short, silky twists of jet-black dreads. Though different from the short waves with "lines" she remembered the new style suited his strong facial features.

One thing that hadn't changed about Damon was his beautiful hazel-green eyes. Depending on his mood, his eyes reflected more hazel or green. She had learned to read his eyes even before they spoke their first words to each other. When she looked into his eyes she found the meaning of her existence. She knew herself through his eyes. He had a direct line to her desires through his gaze.

Her hand quivered inside his.

"Brooke." He peered down at her, excited to see her.

She didn't know what she had expected to experience when she saw him again, but not this. Not this overwhelming nostalgia. Every emotion ever evoked by him rushed at her. She felt flushed, and heated, and overwhelmed by his single-word greeting.

She didn't trust her voice. Her throat was dry. She didn't know what to say, but needed to say something. "Hi, Damon." She took her seat, and immediately reached for a glass of water.

The waitress appeared, asking, "Do you need a minute?"

Brooke welcomed the interruption. Her speech, so well thought out, escaped her. Before seeing Damon, she had thought the hardest thing to do would be telling him about Rebecca. She hadn't accounted for how strong dormant emotions could be. She ordered, forcing Damon to take his gaze off her and focus on the menu.

"I can't tell you how surprised I was when you called," he said once the waitress left them alone. "How long has it been?"

"Almost six years."

He ran his fingers through the short twists in his hair. "Yeah, you're right. Six years. I hate to ask an obvious question, but what made you look me up after all these years?"

Leading with the truth would be callous. She had to set the stage. She'd forgotten everything she rehearsed, so she improvised. "My aunt was talking about you the other day, so I decided to look you up."

He threw his head back with laughter. "Aunt Foster. How is she?"

"Good."

"We sure gave her a hard time." He watched her inquisitively. "How have you been? What have you been up to? Where are you working now?"

She gave generic answers to generic questions, unsure if finding him had been the right thing to do. He fired questions at her, trying to fill in the gaps since they had last seen each other, completely oblivious to the seriousness of the situation and how his life would be changed by what she needed to tell him.

"Are you married?" he asked.

"No, but I have a beautiful daughter."

"Pictures?"

She pulled out her wallet and showed him kindergarten pictures of Rebecca. She watched his face for a hint of recognition, but found none.

He smiled and returned her wallet. "She is pretty."

"How about you? Are you married?"

He nodded and retrieved his wallet. She'd never considered he could be married, and have children—with his wife. Panic swept over her, pushing her to run from the restaurant. Telling him about Rebecca could destroy his family. What she was about to do affected more people than she had imagined.

She had to digest the newly found out information and rethink telling him about Rebecca. Doing the right thing would be harder now that she knew the details of his life. He told her about his wedding three years ago, and his spirited stepchildren, Lisa and Roger. He described his new house and told her about the success of his new, but growing business. She listened to the details of his life, wondering how having a daughter would change what he had built. She weighed Rebecca's needs against Damon's, and even her own, trying to determine if selfishness played any part on her decision. She sat through lunch, distracted but holding up her end of the conversation. She needed more time to decide what to do.

Damon insisted on paying the check. "It was nice of you to call. We should do this again. I don't keep in touch with anyone from school."

"I'd like that." She plastered on a smile as they stood to leave, knowing she had probably never see him again.

He shook her hand, enveloping it in the warmth of his touch. His eyes sparkled translucent green. "How about lunch next week?"

CHAPTER 4

Do I tell Damon he's Rebecca's father, or do I keep it to myself, and let Kurtis adopt her as he wants to?

Brooke needed to cancel her lunch plans with Damon until she decided what to do. She dialed his office, but froze when a woman's voice sang out, "Employment Network Unlimited. How may I help you?" She hung up.

What in the world were you going to say?

"Can I please speak to the father of my child? He won't know who I am because he doesn't know he has a child by me. It's a long story. A six year story. Where should I begin?"

She had been weighing the positives and negatives of the issue since her lunch with Damon. It would have been much easier if he weren't married with a family. It would have been easier if she'd never ignored the possibility of him being Rebecca's father five years ago. She berated herself, fully willing to take responsibility for the mess she had made. Knowing wallowing in regret didn't help anyone, she tried to take an objective look at the situation. Was there an objective way to see impending disaster? She debated several possible scenarios, but in the end she had to do what was best for Rebecca.

Kurtis's midday phone call was a welcomed distraction. "Can you get away for lunch?"

"Only if you take me for Mexican *and* if you promise to make it an extra long lunch."

"I'll be at the hotel in ten minutes. Pick you up out front?"

The sky blue Coach saddlebag and matching leather pumps Brooke wore contrasted perfectly against her dark blue suede skirt suit. Her salary at Vintage Suites allowed her to indulge her weakness for expensive clothing. Growing up, Aunt Foster could only afford to buy her secondhand clothing. She'd always had clean clothes, but it had embarrassed her to know someone else had worn them before her. The kids at school knew too, teasing her because she never wore the latest designer names. It had taken Damon's kindness to help her learn what was inside her mind was more important than wearing designer labels.

Brooke was waiting out front when Kurtis whipped his black Stealth around the hotel's circular driveway, stopping short where she stood. He leaned across the seat to push the door open for her, and mashed the accelerator as soon as she climbed inside. Classical music played too loudly over the digital sound system. He gave her the details of his day, unconcerned about how her day was going.

She remembered a time when he would have gotten out of the car and held the door open for her. Aware she hated classical music; he would have had her favorite R&B CD playing. He used to insist she give him every detail about her workday, including a full character description of everyone she'd encountered. She wondered how their relationship would change once they were married.

———

"Have you heard from Neal?" Kurtis asked at the restaurant. He dipped a white corn chip into the extra spicy salsa.

"Nothing."

A skeptical look marred his face. "Think you should call him?"

"No, I'll wait for him to come around. He was very angry. I've never seen him that way before." She sipped her water, hoping to circumvent the conversation.

"It's understandable, but this has to be settled." He reached across the table and ran his thumb beneath her eye, capturing evidence of sleepless nights. "You haven't been sleeping much. Wouldn't it be better to meet this head-on? Everything will get back to normal that much sooner."

She avoided making an observation by taking a sip of her cola. Kurtis would push until he got his way. She wouldn't allow him to take charge of handling Rebecca's paternity. He had been trying to be supportive later, and she appreciated it, but how this situation was handled would affect Rebecca for the rest of her life.

Kurtis continued to push. "Since you haven't been sleeping much, I assume you've been doing a lot of thinking. Have you remembered anything?"

"What do you mean, 'anything'?" She dipped another chip in the salsa.

"Who's Rebecca's father?"

"I don't want to talk about this. Not here. Not now."

"I'm not judging you, Brooke. I know this happened before you even met me. I'm interested because I need to know how to proceed with Rebecca's adoption."

How many times and how many ways could she tell him she *did not* want him to adopt Rebecca? Maybe after they'd been married for awhile, maybe then she'd consider it. Right now, especially with the new confusion surrounding Rebecca's father, it wasn't possible.

"So, who is he?" He tried to sound as if the conversation were inconsequential, but Brooke knew better. His eyes were on fire with jealousy. He was probably already forming visions of her running off with Rebecca's real father. "Who? Have you figured it out?"

"It's not like I have a dozen guys to sort through," she snapped.

"I know that. I'm on your side."

"I'm sorry. I didn't mean to snap at you. This is really difficult."

"I'm not implying anything about your character. I know exactly who you are. You were just a kid." He placed his hand on the tabletop, reaching for her. "But you're not now."

She took in a deep breath.

"I just want to know who he is."

This was not a conversation she wanted to have with him yet. He was insistent, and he would be tenacious until he got an answer.

"Brooke?"

"I know who Rebecca's father is."

"You're acknowledging the fact that it can't be Neal. Good. It'll make everything easier."

She didn't ask what he meant. This was not the time to discuss adoption.

"Who is he?"

"His name is Damon Richmond."

"You're sure?"

"Yes." She had been so sure Neal was Rebecca's father. Or she had fooled herself into believing that untruth. She had only been with three men in her life. There was no doubt Damon was Rebecca's father.

"What's this guy like?"

"He's a good man."

Kurtis rubbed his chin. He was deciding her future again, so she stopped him before he could do too much planning.

"I need time to figure out the right thing to do."

"The right thing to do? Neal is out of the way. I'll adopt Rebecca as planned. This guy—Damon—wherever he is, isn't important. He hasn't been a part of Rebecca's life all this time. There's no need for him to come into her world now. He never even needs to know about her."

Brooke was shocked. "You don't think I should tell him he has a child? Rebecca shouldn't know her father?"

"What would be the point? Neal and I are the only men in her life. Why confuse her? I'll be the father she needs."

"I can't believe how easily you shed your ethics. I can't raise my daughter on a lie. Besides, Neal will tell her the truth, and she'll be curious about her true father. How am I supposed to answer her when she asks me who her real father is?"

"Tell her you don't know where he is."

"What? You want me to lie to Rebecca?"

Kurtis was stunned. "You know where he is?"

She dropped her eyes to her food. "I don't want to discuss this right now. I need to work some things out."

"You keep saying that. We're here now. We'll talk about it now."

There was an implication behind his set jaw she did not like. She started on her food, avoiding his scrutiny.

"Brooke?"

She dropped her fork and looked up at him.

"Do you know where Damon is?"

"Yes."

"Have you been keeping in touch with him?"

"No."

The waitress approached to freshen their drinks, but Kurtis shooed her away. "How do you know where he is?"

"I found him."

He cursed, tossing his napkin on the table. "Tell me you haven't contacted him."

"We had lunch."

"Without discussing it with me first?"

"I don't need your permission, Neal."

"What did you tell him? Does he know about Rebecca?"

"I didn't tell him anything."

"Thank God." He pushed back in his chair.

"I chickened out. He's married with two stepchildren. I couldn't reappear after all this time and tell him he's a father."

"Now you're thinking clearly. There's absolutely no reason to disrupt his life. I love Rebecca. I'll adopt her as soon as we get married. Let Neal tell her what he wants to tell her. I'll be her father. Kids adjust quickly. Everything will work out."

"Just go on as if nothing has changed?" It was the easiest way out. She didn't want to disrupt Rebecca's life. She'd hurt Damon so badly before, she didn't want to hurt him again.

"Exactly," Kurtis went on. "We need to get married as soon as possible. Put everything in motion."

"Okay," she heard herself saying. It would be easier on Rebecca not to cloud the parentage issue. Rebecca cared for Kurtis, and he was good with her. She'd like having him as her dad. They had talked about it when Brooke first accepted his marriage proposal, and Rebecca had been thrilled.

Even as Brooke justified hiding the truth, she knew it was the coward's way out.

"Considering everything, we need to move ahead with setting the date."

"We will, soon," Brooke answered, suddenly coming down with another case of cold feet. Every time she planned a wedding at work, she thought about setting a date with Kurtis. Every time she tried to picture herself standing at the altar with him, her heart raced and her palms started sweating.

"We'll do it this weekend. Neal will have Rebecca so it'll be the perfect time for us to finalize our plans. I'll come by your place after work on Friday, and we'll have dinner with my mother and pick a date."

Brooke lifted her glass to her lips and took a long drink of her soda.

"Settled?" He checked for understanding.

She nodded and reached for the bowl of tortilla chips.

He caught her hand in his and brought it up to his lips. "I can't wait for us to be a real family."

Neal sent Rebecca to the door of Brooke's townhouse alone. He didn't carry Rebecca's overnight bag to her room. Nor did he sit down on the sofa, share their weekend visit with Brooke, and then kiss Rebecca good-bye until the next visitation weekend as he usually did. Instead, he sped off as soon as Brooke opened the door to Rebecca.

"Daddy said he'll call you," Rebecca said, running to her room, her long, brown ponytails flying wildly.

"Come back and give me a kiss."

Rebecca ran to her, throwing her arms around her mother's neck. She didn't look any worse for wear. So Brooke could assume Neal hadn't betrayed his anger to Rebecca during their visit. Rebecca's eyes sparkled with delight as she planted a kiss on her mother's cheek. Whether she was happy, sad, or guilty of childhood mischief, Rebecca's eyes told the story with amazing accuracy. Every emotion was brightly illuminated an open book decipherable by anyone who glanced her way. This was Damon's child. Anyone who could read the clear display of emotions in his eyes, as Brooke could, would know Rebecca belonged to him.

"What's wrong, Mom?"

"Nothing, sweetie. Go play with your toys now."

That night, Brooke evaluated the triangle of men in her life as she measured a perfect part down the center of Rebecca's hair: Kurtis, the man she was officially engaged to, but who could not engage her heart long enough to make her set a wedding date. Neal, the older dominating presence in her life, whose loss of control over Rebecca's parentage had him angry enough to do who knew what. And Damon, sweet, unsuspecting Damon who had no idea he was a father, and in all likelihood would not appreciate the triangular entanglement forced upon him.

As Rebecca chattered on about her weekend adventures, Brooke mindlessly interjected the appropriate "um-huh" or "really" when needed. Her hand froze, suspended above Rebecca's head when she stumbled into the story about "Daddy and Ms. Ella yelling at each other."

"And I heard Daddy tell Ms. Ella he *loves* me!" Rebecca proudly declared.

Brooke let Rebecca ramble on about what had transpired during the weekend visit with her father. "Ms. Ella asked Daddy if was still taking me to the carnival."

Her fingers moved swiftly as she twisted Rebecca's hair into two evenly matched braids. "Did you go to the carnival?"

"No. Daddy said he was too tired." Rebecca twisted her tiny body around to look up at her. "Am I going with Daddy in two weeks?"

"Oh course. You spend every other weekend at Daddy's house. Why?"

"Ms. Ella told me to take my favorite dolls home with me cause I might not come back."

Ms. Ella's position about Neal's lack of paternity was clear. Brooke hid her emotions, pretending nothing was out of the ordinary. "Do you want to see Daddy?"

"Yes."

"Then you'll see Daddy."

Brooke was relieved of her quiet suffering when she tucked Rebecca into bed for the night. It wasn't hard to deduce Neal was torn between his love for Rebecca and his wife's wishes. Obviously, Ella felt it was best to sever Neal's ties to Rebecca, but it wasn't as simple as "honor the results of the paternity test." Neal was the only father Rebecca had ever known. Cutting ties with him would be difficult. Brooke had often complained about Neal's propensity to overpower her wishes in making decisions about Rebecca's life, but she knew he only behaved that way because he loved Rebecca and demanded the absolute best for her.

On the other hand, Rebecca was young and children were resilient. If Brooke allowed Kurtis to step in as her father, he'd replace Neal in Rebecca's life soon enough. Brooke would be saved from telling Damon, and he could continue to live his storybook life with a beauty wife and kids in a perfect suburban neighborhood.

It could all be tidily disposed of if Brooke were only able to swallow the lie, and continue to live in a perfectly planned world that was spinning out of control.

∞

The golden-haired young woman with breasts too perky to be ignored stroked Neal's graying chin hairs. The idea to grow a beard with his mustache was his wife's idea. Ella said the salt and pepper hairs covering his jaw gave him a mature, but sexy appearance. He now represented the type of man who stood around in historic homes sipping brandy and discussing his and his wife's contributions to society with people he did not even like.

Ella had been a part of that world long before he met her. He accepted it in order to have her love. He'd always found ways to make his place in the world of educators without having to be so artifical. He supposed the medical field was different. A beautiful black woman like Ella must have had a hard time being taken seriously as she pursued her studies. But she was determined and unstoppable. It made them a good couple. In areas where he was weak, she was strong. Where she needed support, he was there. They were the perfect couple. Perfect.

Neal liked the way Ella smiled at him from across the room when they went out. She knew the social gatherings were not his favorite thing so she would watch for his signal. If he lifted his brandy glass to her it meant she should start excusing herself and make her way over to him. He'd had enough of the bragging, or was bored with the medical talk. Either way, it was time to leave.

Neal hadn't bothered to draw the sheet up to cover his naked body. He was proud of his fifty-two-year-old body. No love handles for him. They were unsightly. Why someone would equate fat around the middle with a beautiful word like love was beyond him. People always felt the need to label everything, but some things should just remain nameless.

Teaching at the university kept him young and hip to the latest music and fashion. He could compete with the most popular jock on campus for the affection of the head cheerleader. If he lived to be a hundred, he would still be able to get around without the help of a walker or a cane.

"Professor Kirby? Are you okay, sir?" The young woman's hair fell in yellow waves against his face as she leaned over him.

Such formalities when they had just completed the most intimate act two people could commit. He swung his legs over the edge of the mattress, searching for his underwear. "I'm fine, but I must be going now."

The young woman scrambled to the edge of the bed. "My grade this semester? We didn't get to talk about it much."

Next came the dreaded giggle—fingernails on a chalkboard to him.

"I think you'll be satisfied with your grade—" He was going to add her name just to make her feel more assured, but he couldn't remember it. He knew her only as "first seat, row three, with the perky breasts and long blond hair." "I have to go now."

He'd been faithful to his new wife until now, and he suddenly hated the young woman for luring him to her off-campus apartment. Women were so forward these days, accosting him after class, before he had the opportunity to make his move. He'd wanted to be different with Ella—faithful—but his overeager student had enticed him with the skill of a she-devil.

He picked up flowers and an expensive bottle of wine on the way home. They'd been fighting a great deal lately. Ella hounded him over what decision he would make about Rebecca. It wasn't easy for him. Rebecca had been his daughter for five years. He couldn't just stop loving her because a blood test told him he had no right or responsibility to do so. Ella's nagging had helped to drive him right into the grade-needing young coed's bed. For one hour, his mind had been clear, his problems gone.

Before leaving for work that morning, Ella had even suggested Neal had the right to sue Brooke for the money he'd contributed to Rebecca's upbringing. "Let her real father pay child support," she'd said. "It's not your responsibility to support another man's child, Neal." She'd had been rubbing cold cream onto her face in quick circular motions when she said this to him. If she had looked away from the mirror long enough to see his face, she would've seen the hurt she'd inflicted upon him with her words.

Not her real father. It was the argument he used with Brooke whenever Kurtis overstepped his boundaries in Rebecca's life. Now someone would have the right to turn them on him.

It wasn't about the money for Neal. He and Ella had more money between them than they could ever spend. Their careers were a source of prestige—validity from the world that black members of the country had much to offer society. The fact that their jobs supplied them with lucrative compensations was only an extra benefit for doing what they loved. Neither of them was flashy spender, and Rebecca was the only child between them.

"Just walk away," Ella had said. She was childless by choice. She didn't understand the parental bond he felt with Brooke in raising their child. "Walk away before this thing gets more complicated." It had always bothered Ella that his and Brooke's lives would be entangled for life. Brooke shared something with her husband Ella would never be able to share—a child.

"I'm beginning to suspect you're happy the paternity test turned out the way it did," he'd countered.

"I know this is painful for you, so I'll ignore what you just said."

"You're right. This is painful." He wanted her to comfort him. "When I opened the envelope, my world shattered."

Neal had driven to his friend's office and questioned the methods used to come to the conclusion Rebecca was no longer his. His friend had patiently explained the methods used to run the test, and calculated the percentage of error, demonstrating that though the results were painful, they were true. After withstanding Neal's challenges—the technician must have switched the samples, the machine was calibrated incorrectly, on and on—his old friend took a harsh tone and assured him the test results had been double-checked.

Neal had broke down, falling back against the exam table, and for the first time since becoming a man, he cried.

Neal recalled that he had stood behind Ella and watched her in the bathroom mirror, searching for understanding in the smooth lines of her face. "The last thing I want to do is walk away. I love Rebecca."

"I know you do. You're that kind of man." She'd stopped drying her face long enough to catch his reflection next to hers in the mirror. "But what else can you do?"

He'd had no answers.

"It'll be hard at first, but after time passes, Rebecca will forget all about you."

The thought that Rebecca could so easily forget him had almost knocked him to his knees.

Ella had then coldly walked away, leaving him staring blankly in the mirror.

Her lack of affection and support had justified his visit to "first seat, row three." He needed to numb his suffering. The carnal comfort of a stranger had allowed him to escape.

Before he faced Ella, Neal needed to establish an alibi. Saying he was working late in his office wouldn't work. His teaching assistant would never cover for him. She was still upset with him about their playtime together ending once he'd gotten married. He needed to be able to justify being freshly showered. It was a little late to go to the gym, but he would tell Ella he'd gone swimming after his workout. He'd tell her he had needed to clear his mind. He'd give her the flowers and open the wine, and he'd tell her he loved her. His pride wouldn't allow him to tell her he needed her.

CHAPTER 5

Rebecca's hand seemed smaller than usual. Brooke gave it an extra squeeze. "Aw, Mom." She pressed her tiny hand over her mouth and giggled.

Brooke preferred Mommy, but Neal forbade Rebecca to call her that, citing how it would appear when she was older. Brooke kneeled down outside the door of the kindergarten classroom and she brushed the stray hairs of Rebecca's hair into place. The natural curliness of her hair, coupled with the silky fineness, made it a challenge to style in a way which would withstand her hearty play. "Remember, Dad will pick you up after school today. I'll see you on Sunday when he brings you home."

"I remember."

"Okay, you'd better go in before you're late." She gave Rebecca a long hug and sent her into the classroom.

The halls of Cambridge Academy were filled with tiny soldiers bustling about, marching to class. The children reminded Brooke more of college students than small kids. The boys wore stiff black slacks, starched white shirts, and straight black neckties. The girls wore pleated black and red checked skirts and the same starched white shirts. They were all loaded down with book bags sporting the school logo. Even though the halls were full of children, the school was quieter than a church. The instructors at Cambridge Academy tolerated no unnecessary noise. Play was allowed only at the designated times in an environment structured solely for recreational purposes.

Rebecca had never experienced the carefree days of other kids her age, because Neal had been firm in his decision. He had attended Cambridge Academy and so would Rebecca. He was an alumnus and therefore Rebecca was guaranteed admission. They would take advantage of the top-notch education his money could provide. He had mapped out

Rebecca's education all the way through graduation day at Spellman College. "There will be no barriers in Rebecca's education" he'd said, and to argue against his logic somehow felt wrong to Brooke.

Brooke watched Rebecca take her seat, knowing her daughter was much smarter than average. The education Neal was providing was paying off. She wondered if Rebecca was smart enough to forgive her mother for making a mistake that be detrimental to them all.

The teacher frowned as she slowly closed the classroom door, pulling Brooke from her musings. She glanced at her watch, realizing she had just enough time to get across town to work. Cambridge Academy provided bus transportation for its students, but she chose to bring Rebecca to school every morning. She liked to say good-bye and know Rebecca had safely arrived.

Lately, Neal had hinted he would be paying the extra bus transportation fee beginning the next school year. "It will help to develop her independence," he insisted. In other words, he worried Brooke was smothering her.

Brooke had been twenty-two when she met the professor of economics, Dr. Kirby. It was the beginning of her senior year at the university. She had to shuffle her schedule around several times in order to accommodate the hours of his senior economics class. Everyone majoring in business wanted to be in his class. He was known nationwide for his research studies. It was not uncommon to turn to news stations like CNN and find him speaking about the state of the economy. When the price of gas soared, he had been invited to appear on the *Early Show* to debate the underlying causes and offer solutions to the problem. In a word, he was profound.

Brooke would sit in awe absorbing his every word, treating it as if it were gospel. The subject of economics was one of the most uninteresting topics one could discuss—unless it was Professor Kirby giving the lecture. The subdued and somewhat boring older man came alive when delivering his weekly lectures. His intellectual prowess, along with his thickly mustached, handsomely round face, made him the subject of much speculation among the female students at the university. He dressed in fashionable suits and walked with a stride brimming with confidence and bordering on cockiness. The deep timber of his voice when discussing a new economic development captured his female audience and held them mercilessly in his grasp.

During the latter portion of the semester, Professor Kirby required his students to develop a plan for their own non-profit business. It was an elaborate project, but gave his students immeasurable knowledge. Once these projects started, Professor Kirby broke the class up into smaller groups and met off campus at mutually convenient times to discuss the progress of their businesses.

Brooke didn't realize how handsome the professor truly was until she met him for a private conference at the public library. The three other members of her group were absent for various reasons, but Professor Kirby had insisted they meet as scheduled. She finally had the attention of the most impressive professor she'd ever met all to herself. The project discussion turned into a dinner meeting. By the end of the night, she had learned several personal details about her teacher. He was single, never married. He found the dating scene too complicated to attempt to carry on a serious relationship. But yes, he responded to Brooke's question, if the right person and the right opportunity presented itself, he would get married. She grew to respect him on another level, and found herself daydreaming about him during class. Although she knew the crush was silly and one-sided, she couldn't keep herself from looking forward to their weekly meetings.

The end of the senior year came too soon. Professor Kirby was interested in conducting a research study in the changing dynamics of hotel management. Her degree in hotel and restaurant management made her a likely candidate for the summer program. Her non-profit business proposal won her one of the four coveted positions in the professor's summer work-study program for graduates.

After a few weeks of working together, Professor Kirby became "Neal." A few weeks after that, Neal confessed his attraction to her, and they started seeing each other privately. They fed off each other's intelligence until their combined passion spilled over the pages of textbooks and into the bedroom. They ripped off each other's clothing as they rolled across a bed covered with charts, graphs, and reports. They were impulsive, explosive, and foolish. Although she had graduated, Neal feared they would be found out and he would lose everything he had worked for. Neither had any illusions about the encounters. She was attracted to her older, sophisticated mentor. Neal was flattered by the attention of the younger, beautiful student.

Their affair only lasted long enough for two sexual encounters. By the end of the summer, Brooke realized there was a price to passion, and they would pay heavily for those two lapses in judgment. Even today, she could see Neal's shocked expression as the color drained from his dark features when she told him she was pregnant. She was devastated. He was scared. They were angry at each other.

After time apart, they came together and formulated a plan. No one could know Neal was the father of her child, or he could be dismissed from the university. In exchange, he would provide all the financial support the baby would need for its entire life. No court order would limit what he would give to ensure the child's life be the best money could buy. Once Rebecca came along, she stole his heart.

Rebecca ended up being an unexpected blessing for them both. She brought a light into their lives neither had experienced before. They loved her unconditionally, never second-guessing the decision to bring her into the world. Joint parenting had gone reasonably well over the years. Although Neal could be controlling when it came to making decisions about Rebecca, he always had her best interest at heart.

<hr/>

At work, Brooke was distracted. She had tried to break off her lunch with Damon, but he'd been so insistent so looking forward to it, that Brooke began to waver about her decision not to tell him about Rebecca. She was making herself crazy, going back and forth, trying to decide how to do the best by everyone involved. So she had agreed to keep their lunch meeting with the hope that Damon would say something to bring clarity to it all.

Sitting with him brought the memory of how happy she'd been once he entered her life. He and Neal were complete opposites, both attractive in their own ways. Who could blame her for what she'd done in college?

"Did you hear anything I said?" Damon asked, still chuckling about the joke she'd missed.

"I zoned out. I'm sorry."

He rested against the back of his chair, openly appraising her. "I'm so glad you looked me up. This is nice—getting together with an old friend."

She smiled.

"I told my wife about you."

"Really?" She didn't know why this surprised her. Damon would be open and honest with his wife about meeting an ex-girlfriend.

He snapped a breadstick in half and chomped on the end. "I'd like you to meet her." He leaned forward, whispering conspiratorially. "You can tell me what you think of her." He gave her a playful wink.

"More like she'll be checking out the old girlfriend."

His eyes dropped and he lost all traces of his playful nature. "Barbara isn't a jealous woman—when it comes to me."

She did not want to go down this road. Something was bothering him, and he needed to talk. But she didn't want to know about his marital problems. His being married had already severely complicated her telling him he was Rebecca's father. Knowing the intimate details of his marriage would make it worse.

"Jealousy is overrated. It's a sign of insecurity," she offered.

"Hmm." He shook his head, discarding whatever was bothering him. "Listen, I have to get back to work, but we have to keep in touch."

He pulled out his wallet, but she stopped him. "Lunch is on me."

He stood, pushed in his chair, and gripped the back as he stared down at her. "God, it's good to talk to you again." He turned, walking away.

"Damon."

"Yeah?"

"Are you okay?"

He waved it off. "It's nothing. You know me." His smile faded.

"Yes," she said, "I *do* know you."

Something in her words made him tilt his head to the side questioningly. "Are *you* okay?"

"I'm fine."

She watched him walk away, unhappiness visible in his eyes. He stopped several paces away, hesitated, and then turned back to her, rushing up to the table. He gripped the back of the chair, intensely watching for her reaction to his words. "You looked me up after all this time for a reason."

If Brooke had been looking for a sign, a divine intervention, telling her the right thing to do, Damon provided it. He opened the door for her to supply honestly to an already dishonest situation. Her heartbeat raced, making her dizzy. She couldn't tell him here, in the middle of the day without any preparation.

"Brooke?" His voice dropped to a whisper. "Why'd you look me up after all these years?"

She gathered herself, clearing her throat. She knew he would know she was lying before she opened her mouth. "Renewing old friendships."

Those astute hazel-green eyes burred into her, shredding the lie. His fingers loosened around the wood of the chair, and he flexed his hands. "I'll call you to set up another lunch."

She smiled.

He turned slowly, clearly not wanting to leave without the truth.

Brooke's bare feet pushed against the wooden planks, sending the old rocker backward. She enjoyed sitting on Aunt Foster's front porch when the weather was warm and sunny. The next family lived a mile down the dirt road. Brooke had asked her aunt to consider moving closer into the city. She worried about Aunt Foster being in the deserted area alone as she aged. But Aunt Foster had refused with the promise that if she found taking care of herself too much of a task, she would move.

The screen door squeaked when it opened, and slammed when it closed behind Aunt Foster. Age had made her bones brittle. Weight had made her breath short. The combination of age, brittle bones, and excessive weight, made her wobble when she crossed the porch to lean against the banister. The rocker where Brooke sat was her favorite, but her weight made it impossible to fit comfortably into the wicker seat. Now the metal porch swing had become her resting place on warm spring days.

"It's a wonder Rebecca isn't a spoiled brat." Brooke smiled as she watched Rebecca glide down the new backyard slide and run for the swing.

"The mother and father hand out discipline. Auntie Foster is for spoiling." She made a noise between her gritted teeth. "Ssss." She watched Kurtis playing with Rebecca at the swing.

"What is it?"

"He sure is trying hard to make a good impression. Mr. Pompous."

"Auntie." Brooke swatted at her. "Don't call him names. Kurtis cares about Rebecca. They adore each other."

Foster pinched her lips together in disapproval. Brooke ignored the gesture. Her aunt never felt any man was good enough for her. As a teenager, she'd had a severe dating deficiency. Aunt Foster had allowed her to date only one person in high school, Damon Richmond. And that had taken a great deal of convincing on Brooke's part. Aunt Foster had never approved of Neal; he had gotten her pregnant without marring her, he was too old for her, and he tried to control most decisions regarding Rebecca's upbringing. But over the years, he'd proved himself honorable by taking good care of his child and Aunt Foster had grown to respect him for it.

"He tries too hard. Like he's trying to prove something."

"Part of Kurtis's insecurity is because I'm making him wait so long to set the wedding date."

"He may be a good man, but I'm not so sure he's the right man for you. Look how you talk about marrying him. A woman in love is rushing

to set the date so she can snag her *good man* before he changes his mind."
She fanned herself with a magazine. "What about Rebecca's father?"

Brooke pushed the rocker with more vigor.

"Is it—"

"Damon Richmond." She watched Kurtis and Rebecca playing in the
yard, then turned to her aunt. "Did you know?"

"When you told me about the test results, I pretty much figured it
out. You haven't dated much." She paused before going on. "How did he
react?" She threw her head in Kurtis's direction.

"Concerned."

"Not mad?"

Brooke shook her head. "He wants to adopt Rebecca. This helps his
case."

After a few moments of contemplation, Aunt Foster asked, "How did
Damon react?"

"I haven't told him yet. I started to, but things became complicated."
She gave her aunt the details of their lunch meeting. "I never expected him
to be married. I don't know why not. I just didn't."

"Hmmm," Aunt Foster hummed reflectively.

"When I saw him the other day, something was bothering him so I
couldn't tell him then."

"The other day?" Foster pushed her swing through several rotations
before continuing. "You aren't getting involved—"

"No!"

"You're going to tell him, aren't you?"

"I don't see how I can't. It's just…this could ruin a lot of lives." She
stood and moved to the banister. Kurtis carefully set Rebecca on the
ground and she took off running. He was tired, Brooke could see that, but
when Rebecca challenged him to catch her, he hesitated only long enough
to throw Brooke a kiss. She waved back. He wasn't perfect, but he was
good with Rebecca. He loved her, and he loved her daughter. Having second thoughts about marrying him made absolutely no sense.

"This ruins Kurtis's adoption plans." Foster remarked.

"He doesn't want me to tell Damon. He doesn't want anything to interfere with us getting married, or him adopting Rebecca."

"Humph. Of course he doesn't want you to tell Damon because he's using Rebecca to keep you close. And about marrying him—"

"Aunt Foster, you've never trusted Kurtis, and he's never given you a reason to be so hard on him. He does everything to put you at ease. It was his idea to come by today. He wants you to like him."

"The first thing he did was come up in my kitchen talking about setting the wedding date. He thought I would help him pressure you into setting it. Humph. Are you really going to marry him?"

A few weeks ago, she'd been pretty clear on what her future held. Now that Neal had succeeded in upending her world, she didn't know what she wanted. "Everything is so crazy right now, I don't know what to do."

"Humph. If you really wanted to marry Kurtis, nothing could change your mind. Don't rush into anything with him because you're upset about what's going on with Rebecca. Don't make marrying Kurtis be the biggest mistake of your life."

As Brooke watched Rebecca play, the guilt returned. She'd made enough careless, avoidable mistakes in her life.

"What about Damon?" Aunt Foster asked. "He has a right to know."

"Yeah, I know."

"You have to tell him."

She turned to her aunt. "I don't know how. He's married with a family. How can I tell him he has a five-year-old child?"

"You made a mistake. You have to live up to the responsibilities of it."

Brooke returned to the rocker. "Same advice you gave me when I told you I was pregnant with Rebecca."

"And was I right?"

She looked across the yard at Rebecca, running and playing and giggling at Kurtis's antics. "You were right."

"Tell Damon. And don't want too long."

CHAPTER 6

"Hi, Brooke." Damon's eyes lit up when he saw her. Their regular lunch meetings over the past month had become a source of stress relief. They'd renewed their friendship quickly, as if no time had passed between their associations. He likened them to the couple in *When Harry Met Sally*. Their first meeting had been as a romantic couple. Their second meeting was as good friends. He needed a good friend to accept him for who he was without an ulterior motive for being with him. As Barbara's lovemaking was being rationed out more and more at home in direct proportion to the amount of spending money he gave her, he was beginning to realize he was little more than bankroll to her.

Brooke fell into step beside him. "Thank you for meeting me here on such short notice."

"No problem. I missed our lunch yesterday. I haven't been to this park in years. Probably since the last time we were here. What was that, six years ago?"

"Six years." She led him to a vacant bench near the children's play area. "That wasn't such a good night for us—the last time we were here."

He covered his eyes with his sunglasses, preferring not to relive such a painful memory. "We were both immature back then." He couldn't hide the melancholy in his voice. "But we're grown-ups now."

She took in a deep breath and let it out slowly. "Hey, what's wrong? You act like something's on your mind."

"Actually, there is. I need to talk to you about the last time we were together here in this park."

"Okay." He smiled, hoping to brighten her mood. She was proposing they stand on shaky ground, and he wasn't sure if he could contain his anger if it was unleashed. It had taken him a long time to get over her, and he'd only succeeded when he refused to think about her.

"The last time we were here we were arguing." Her voice shook, and he knew something was terribly wrong.

"I remember." He hated to remember. He had chosen to put that night out of his mind a long time ago, instead of dealing with the emotions sure to devastate him if he met them head-on.

"It was completely my fault. I should've never gotten involved with Neal."

He shuddered internally when she mentioned Professor Kirby.

"If I truly wanted to be with him, I should've broken up with you first." She paused. "It seems I make a lot of mistakes when it comes to you."

"Brooke, let me stop you. I don't know where this is going. I don't know where this could go. I'm married. You're engaged."

He wanted her to suggest they go to an uptown hotel and make passionate love until dusk, but he prided himself on being a true and honest man. These thoughts were not the characteristics of an honest man. During their lunches over the past month, he'd succeeded in keeping his thoughts, actions and wishes in the realm of friendship. Today, being at the site of their break-up, he had allowed his mind to wander into dangerous territory. He berated himself, remembering his commitment to Barbara and the kids. No matter what the statistics said, he would not cheat on his wife, no matter how unhappy he was in his marriage.

"We should go." His voice sounded more sure than he actually felt.

"Please, Damon. Let me finish."

He took in her distress and nodded.

"You remember that night?"

He did. She had broken his heart. "I remember every word—every detail like it happened yesterday."

"Do you remember what happened after we stopped fighting?"

He didn't answer. He pushed away raw emotions by concentrating on the kids running across the playground.

"We made love for the last time. We couldn't even wait to get back to my dorm or yours. We did it right in the back seat of your car."

"But we still couldn't work it out," he added angrily. He didn't understand the purpose in reliving the pain—and it was much too late to apologize. "We tried to talk it out, but I was jealous, and you were distant. And then—"

"And then I got pregnant."

"That pretty much ended things for us." He glanced at her, and the pain in her eyes made him want to take her in his arms. If he touched her, he would not be able to stop himself. He would have to acknowledge the inappropriate feelings he'd been trying to fight. During the long silence, they both went back six years and remembered the mistakes they'd made. Brooke was a beautiful woman, his first love. He wanted to hold her in his arms again, and feel the emotions they'd shared again. If nothing else, just to prove to himself he still was capable of loving.

He took a deep breath and spoke quietly, hoping to put her mind at ease. "Listen, Brooke, I wish we could have saved our relationship. We were good together. But we couldn't, and we didn't, and we both have other people in our lives now. Reliving it is pointless. I don't want to associate the constant fighting with you. I want to remember we had something special, and now we're able to be friends."

Brooke blew out a long, deep breath. She arched her back and met his eyes. "I made a horrible mistake six years ago."

He was going to tell her to stop. He was going to tell her he couldn't go to lunch with her anymore because his willpower would eventually break.

Brooke continued. "It isn't about us, directly. I've done a terrible thing. It's why I contacted you after all these years."

"I don't understand." Her distress alarmed him.

A little girl with wild pigtails ran up to her.

Brooke pasted on her best smile. "What is it, Rebecca?"

"Can I go play in the sandbox again?"

"No, it's time to go. Find your shoes. You left them over by the sandbox."

Rebecca ran off to do as she was told.

"So that's Rebecca." He smiled as he watched the little girl stuff her feet into her sandals.

"Yeah, she's my little girl."

"Why didn't you tell me she was here? I'd like to meet her. She's very pretty. Biggest eyes I've ever seen—next to yours."

"Aunt Foster says her eyes are bottomless pits of emotion—just like yours."

Taken aback by her choice of words, his head snapped to attention.

"Rebecca is your daughter."

He opened his mouth to ask her to repeat herself, but no words would come.

She whispered it again. "Rebecca is your daughter, Damon."

He pulled away his sunglasses and stared at the child. He was shocked into anger. "You can't just blurt out something like that."

Rebecca ran toward the bench.

He should say something, but what?

"We have to go." Brooke grabbed Rebecca's hand and ran toward the parking lot, leaving him dumbfounded.

Shocked, stunned, bewildered—all were good words to describe what he was feeling. But none could exactly capture the panic that swept through his body. It was too overwhelming to process. He had a child? By Brooke Foster? All these years... What would happen now? How was he to act? What was he to do? Why had Brooke approached him after all these years? She'd said she'd made a mistake. Keeping knowledge of him having a child from him was more than a mistake—it was criminal.

He sat on the bench until dark, mentally exploring a dark tunnel of confusion, trying to make sense of everything until a policeman on horseback told him the park was closed. He didn't remember walking to his car, turning on the engine, or driving away from the park. He circled the boulevard over and over, not able to go home until he could make sense of what had happened. What would he do with the information he had just learned? Did he want to do anything? Or should he just ignore what Brooke had told him and go on living his life as usual?

It *could not* be true. How could you have a child in the world and not know it? He would have sensed her in some way. Wouldn't he? He flipped on his turn signal, slowed his speed, and turned into his subdivision. His stomach exploded in prickly sensations of panic. He stopped at a corner to compose himself before seeing Barbara.

"Okay." He sucked in a deep breath, causing his chest to swell. He held the breath until the tiny sharp sensations in his stomach went away. "Okay, Damon, think." He stepped outside of himself and viewed the situation as if a best buddy had come to him to confide the story and ask for advice. "The very first thing I have to do is verify the facts. What if I'm the scapegoat in a situation I know nothing about?"

He knew the statement to be untrue the moment he said it. Brooke was not that kind of person. He had to stay rational and handle this with care. Lives could be destroyed by this revelation.

The night Brooke tagged as the date of conception had been stored in the back of his mind, forbidden to ever resurface. Now he voluntarily recalled it. He had been so upset when he walked in on Brooke and Professor Kirby. He was dropping by to surprise her. She was working so many hours on the summer project they hardly saw each other. He had stood in the doorway of the office, shocked when Professor Kirby pushed Brooke's hair back and kissed the side of her face. She turned to him, and he'd wildly consumed her mouth.

He had confronted Brooke in the park, and after several lame attempts at denial, she confessed she had slept with the professor. They had argued fiercely. They shouted and blamed and said words they both wished they could take back later. Emotions were high. They were at the end of their time together. They both knew it. Neither wanted to let go.

Their bodies had gone into emotional overdrive. When they returned to his car, the space was too small and all their emotions mixed together to make a volatile potion. He leaned over to give

Brooke one last kiss—a kiss good-bye. His lips grazed hers as they pulled away from each other forever. Her arms flew around his neck and she held him. There was another kiss, and then all reason left them as their emotions pushed them into sharing their bodies one last time.

He tried to remember if he had used a condom. He couldn't recall with any certainty. It was such a passionate, angry, hurtful night. He had hated her and loved her at the same time. Their intimacy had never been so desperate—and so filling. As he pictured the vision of their bodies tangled together in his back seat, he could still feel the heat of their raw emotions.

"Enough." He shook his head to clear the thoughts away. "I need to know if what Brooke says is true, then I'll decide what I'll do about it."

He mashed the accelerator. His mind was detached from his body, and his eyes didn't see what was in front of him. The signal to his brain telling him to hit the brakes never made it. He plowed into the side of a passing car.

CHAPTER 7

"You did what? You did this on purpose, Brooke. We finally set a wedding date, and you make this situation as complicated as possible. I told you in no uncertain terms *I* was going to adopt Rebecca as soon as we were married. Why couldn't you just leave it at that?"

Brooke locked her fingers together and placed them in her lap. "I had to do the right thing, Kurtis."

"The right thing? The right thing for who? Who do you think is going to benefit by tracing Rebecca's family tree?" He paused for emphasis, still pacing across her living room. "Rebecca is going be confused by all of this. It sure won't help Neal and his 'Father of the Year' cause. And I'm sure Damon is just overjoyed by the disruption of his life with a child he never knew he had. And it's putting some real tension on what we have together." He planted his feet in the carpet, glaring down at her sitting on the sofa. "Now excuse me, but who the hell has benefited by what you did? Besides you?"

"Me?"

"Yes, you, Mother Mary. This was an easy way of ridding yourself of your guilt, but you hurt everyone around you to do it. It was selfish and stupid. I swear, sometimes I think I care more about Rebecca than you do. I would have *never* done anything to hurt her."

Brooke stood, lifting her chin to help her match his height. "You wait just a minute. I love my daughter. My daughter, Kurtis—not yours. I know what's best for her. You might not agree with my decision, but it was my decision to make. I didn't have to clear it with you first. Don't you ever accuse me of using Rebecca to make myself feel better."

"I'm sorry I'm not saying what you want to hear, but it's the truth."

"Get out."

"W-w-what?" he sputtered.

"I need you to leave now before I say something we both regret."

He watched her with narrowing eyes. "You're putting me out?"

"Yes. I'm putting you out."

"I didn't mean—I love Rebecca, too."

She turned her back to him. "Kurtis, leave. Please."

"We don't put each other out." Never had the most severe argument led to Brooke telling him to leave.

"Go, Kurtis."

He ambled to the door. "Everything was falling nicely into place, and now…"

"If I had just kept my mouth shut and let you handle it, you mean."

"I wasn't going to say— ## you've been running around making sure everyone is treated fairly and no one gets hurt. What about me, Brooke? I'm your fiancé. You're not considering my feelings. What happens if Damon wants to spend time with Rebecca?"

"He does have the right."

"Where does that leave me?"

"You're right," she admitted. "I haven't fully considered your feelings for Rebecca, but I have thought about what this means to our relationship." She placed her hand in his as a gesture of apology.

"So you've considered. What did you come up with? How are we going to handle this so it doesn't destroy what we have?"

She inhaled, grasping the opportunity she'd been looking for. "We should call off the wedding until I have a better handle on what's happening."

He pulled his hand away. "What? Call off the wedding? We just set the date." He stomped halfway across the room, turned, and retraced his steps. "I wanted you to consider how I felt about Damon coming into Rebecca's life, not end our relationship."

"I'm not ending our relationship. I want to put the wedding on hold until things quiet down."

"I disagree. We should try to keep things as normal as possible for Rebecca. We'll get married as planned and take Rebecca with us on the honeymoon. I would love to have her come along. It would be a chance for all of us to get away and clear our heads."

Brooke shook her head in disagreement. "Running away isn't the answer." Not facing the truth had put her in the middle of this mess. "I want everything settled before we get married."

His body stiffened. "No other man would put up with all of these delays, and excuses."

"I know. What can I say? I have to straighten out my own life before I can start a new one with you."

He ran a hand across his face, forcing himself to accept her terms. "I don't think I have much choice. We'll hold off on the wedding, but we're not putting off our relationship."

"Fair enough." She hadn't expected him to give in so easily. If she knew Kurtis, he had an ulterior plan he could spring on her later. A small victory, but she would take any win she could get with him.

He came to her and massaged her shoulders. "Postponing the wedding doesn't mean I can't stay with you tonight." He kissed her neck and she restrained herself from recoiling. "Rebecca will be home soon. With everything going on, I want to spend as much time alone with her as possible."

He shoved his fists into his pockets. "I see."

"Goodnight, Kurtis."

He watched her questioningly, but didn't push it. "Goodnight."

She saw him out before dropping down on the sofa, and slinging her arm over her eyes. Had she actually shrugged Kurtis off when he'd kissed her? When had his touch become so undesirable?

He'd offered to stay the night, and she had rejected him—again. The only time she'd felt at ease the entire time he was there was when he agreed to postpone the wedding. She hadn't admitted it to anyone, including herself until now, but she didn't want to marry him. It wasn't about setting the perfect wedding date or what was happening with Rebecca. It wasn't that he had called her a bad mother, and accused her of acting in a self-serving manner, disregarding Rebecca's best interest. She just didn't love Kurtis the way he loved her. Not the way you vowed to spend your entire life with someone.

"I can't marry him," she admitted aloud.

The phone rang. It would be Kurtis calling from his car to apologize, hoping she'd change her mind and invite him to spend the night. Their relationship had more serious problems than a postponed wedding date, and a nonexistent sex life. She had to tell him the truth. She wasn't able to marry a man she didn't love with every fiber of her being.

"Hello?"

"Brooke, it's Damon."

She was speechless. Her heart drummed in the silence.

"I want proof Rebecca is my daughter."

"Okay." She had expected him to demand as much. "You'll have to take a paternity test."

"I know."

She gave him the necessary information. "So, you'll go soon?"

"As soon as I can. It's been six years. Why the rush now?"

"Damon, I'm so sorry. I didn't keep this from you on purpose."

"We'll talk after I receive the test results."

"All right." Silence. "Damon?"

"After the paternity test." He disconnected.

Brooked hugged the phone to her chest a long time before returning it to the cradle. She hadn't thought of the day she'd met Damon in a long time. The best time of her life was also the most painful time of her life.

The first words she'd ever said to him: "That was so *deep.*" And it kept getting deeper and deeper.

——— ∽∞∾ ———

Her freshman English class cleared out of the classroom the second the bell rang. Left behind was a girl with brown eyes made huge by Damon Richmond's performance of the eulogy speech from Shakespeare's "Julius Caesar". She rested her face on her fists and gazed up at Damon as if he were a natural marvel of the world.

"That was so deep.*"*

Her comment rattled Damon. He turned away from his conversation with his former English teacher to see a freshman who wasn't stylishly dressed in the latest fashions like the other girls in school. Her hair was parted down the middle into two long braids that hung to her shoulders.

When his hazel-green eyes turned on her she wished she looked older—more sophisticated. Even if she could afford better than hand-me-downs, Aunt Foster believed fourteen-year-olds were children who should dress like children.

He walked down the row of desks to stand in front of her. His hands were shoved in dark dress pants. A sweater with a vibrant color mixture stretched across his chest. He was sophisticated in a young executive sort of way. "What did you say?"

"The reading you just did, it was deep. I've never heard anyone read like that before."

"Damon was one of my best students, Brooke," the teacher interjected, "that's why I asked him to perform a reading for the class today. I'm hopeful he'll motivate some of you to take Shakespeare's work more seriously." The teacher went on to talk about the lack of enthusiasm the class was showing the first semester of school.

Brooke didn't hear much more of her teacher's sermon. She stared up at one of the most popular senior boys, amazed he had taken the time to say two words to her.

Damon never took his eyes away from the freshmen girl who was in such obvious awe of him. "Can I walk you to your next class?"

Her eyes dropped to the scarred desktop. "I guess so."

The next day, Brooke found Damon standing near her locker, talking to some of his friends from the football team. He offered to walk her to class again. After a week, she expected to see him standing at her locker after fourth period. She didn't expect him to ask her to go to the homecoming football game with him. Soon they were inseparable, stealing time together between classes and after school if Brooke could talk Aunt Foster into letting her stay late for games and dances.

Brooke closed her eyes on the memory of their first kiss at the Valentine's Day dance. She hugged her pillow tight and wondered how she'd ever convince Damon she hadn't known he was Rebecca's father.

⌖

Neal tucked the Barbie doll print sheets underneath the mattress. Rebecca and Ella had selected the same pattern for the curtains and wallpaper. Neal had complained about feeling as if he were inside a giant dollhouse when he entered Rebecca's room, but the women in his life had overruled his opinion and the Barbie decorations remained. Hundreds of stuffed animals filled the corners of the bedroom, and dolls overflowed from the toy box in the closet. A miniature grocery store, complete with cash register and shopping carts, took up much of the bedroom.

"Daddy," Rebecca giggled, "it's too tight."

"No, it can never be too tight." He sat down next to her on the junior bed.

"It is. I can't breath."

"Oh, okay." Neal tugged at the sheets, giving some slack. "Better?"

"Better."

He fussed with her pillow and then her sheets again.

Rebecca tried to keep her eyes open, but her lashes drooped, tired from a long day. "Will you read me a story, Daddy?"

"One more, and then it's lights out." After he read a few pages, Rebecca rolled over and hugged her pillow. He stroked her hair, placing a kiss on her forehead. "Goodnight, sweetie."

"Good night, Daddy."

He watched her succumb to sleep, her entire body becoming relaxed and finding the rhythm that would rock her safely until morning. He wished his mind were free from worry, and he was able to get a good night's sleep. He worried that any day Brooke would call, challenging his right to see Rebecca. As the time grew near for him to pick Rebecca up from school for the weekend, his stomach knotted every time the phone rang. He didn't like the sudden loss of control.

"It would be nice if I could see you every day," he whispered. "Don't you think it would be nice to live here with me?"

Rebecca nodded.

CHAPTER 8

Damon sat stiffly in the recliner in his bedroom. His palms were sweaty, his mouth dry. Barbara sat across from him on the bed with her legs crossed, her foot jumping nervously. He flipped an envelope addressed to him between cold fingers.

"Open it," Barbara barked.

He glanced up at her. The results of the paternity test were inside the envelope. Once he read them, his life would change. His family's life would change. It didn't matter if Rebecca was his daughter or not. Everything between him and Barbara would be different. His renewed acquaintance with Brooke would be different. Rebecca's life would be different. And none of the changes were guaranteed to be good.

He considered not looking at the results. He could walk away from Brooke and leave her to handle the problem on her own. He thought of the adorable little girl in the park and knew he couldn't turn away from his responsibility—if she was his responsibility. More importantly, he wouldn't consider himself a man if he didn't find out if she was his daughter. His hands trembled as he carefully pulled at the perforated edges of the envelope. His eyes scanned the four short sentences on the letter contained inside.

"What does it say?" Barbara edged to the end of the bed.

It says "99.987%."

It says "99.987 % what?"

"Positive—Rebecca is my daughter."

She sprung up and stormed out of the bedroom, slamming the door behind her. He fell back in his chair, closed his eyes, and covered his face with both hands. He had a daughter…with Brooke Foster…his first love. He tried to sort out the feelings bombarding him. Anger, and a strange sence of pride led a parade of emotions, leaving him utterly confused. He needed to discuss what to do with Barbara.

Understandably, she was upset. *Maybe not so understandably.* His relationship with Brooke had ended long before he'd met Barbara, but he had to handle Barbara delicately. She was prone to explosive emotional outbreaks when something impacted her negatively. Before he could figure out what to say and go after her, she stomped back into their bedroom. She shouted, "You had no idea you had a child?" The accusations were clear.

"Not a clue. I would've told you if I did. Why would I hide it? Brooke and I broke up long before I met you."

She paced the room. "I don't understand this. What does she want? Why is she coming to you with this now?"

"I don't know."

"Tell me again every word she said."

"I've told you twice already, Barbara."

"I know the warning signs of a gold-digging woman, and this lady has the markings written all over her. She can just forget it if she thinks I'm sharing anything with her. *I'm* your wife. She needs to find her own man to take care of her."

He let the sting of her words go unchallenged. He hoped she was speaking from anger, not unveiling the truth of why'd she'd married him. "Brooke's not the kind of person to use someone for money."

Barbara planted herself directly in front of him, hands tightly gripping her hips. "Does she want to get back together with you?" Somehow, Barbara didn't sound as upset about the possibility of Brooke wanting him again as she did about Brooke wanting money from him.

"She's engaged."

"That doesn't mean anything."

"I thought you'd be more supportive."

"You come home and casually tell me you have a five-year-old daughter. How did you expect me to react?"

He rose to his feet, making her take a step back. "This isn't about Brooke, or you, or me. Rebecca has never known her father. She's the innocent one here, and she'll probably be hurt more than any of us."

"What are we supposed to do about this kid?"

Damon rubbed his face. "I guess I should meet her."

"Or you could tell that gold digger you want no part of her games. She should've told you five years ago about this child. She didn't, so she can keep doing whatever she was doing up until now."

"I can't walk away from my own child."

"You have responsibilities *here*. Lisa and Roger need you. Another child is one more too many."

"If your kids need me, I'm sure my own needs me as much."

Barbara's eyes were on fire. "I'm not going to let that—"

"Brooke," he corrected her, stopping her from going too far. Brooke was a friend and the mother of his child. He would not let Barbara call her ugly names—angry or not. "Her name is Brooke."

"Whatever her name is, she won't interfere in my marriage."

"Brooke isn't trying to interfere in our marriage."

"Oh, no? She springs this kid on you, and she does it in such a way that you wreck the Lincoln." She took hard strides to the door, turning to him before leaving. "I'm definitely getting my Audi now."

He didn't know what he'd expected from Barbara, but he'd never thought she'd tell him to turn his back on his child. She had been a single mother when he met her. Many nights she'd cried on his shoulder about dealing with a deadbeat dad. He wasn't quite sure how to handle the situation yet, but he wanted a relationship with his daughter. Troubled times were coming with Barbara. Her lack of compassion painted the picture clearly. She would be oppose whatever he chose to do.

He wondered how his life would have turned out if he had known about Rebecca five years ago. Things were so confused then. Neither he nor Brooke had been mature enough to handle the overwhelming power of their feelings for each other. They had made a royal mess of their relationship, and it seemed the repercussions were continuing even today. He dropped back down into the recliner and remembered the pain of being in love with Brooke.

He had almost thrown his future away to hold onto his first love. He had been accepted to the university during the first semester of his senior year in high school. His academic scholarship would pay the bills. A degree in business would determine his future. When he met Brooke Foster, his future didn't seem as important as his *right now*. Every minute of his senior year had been devoted to her. His father had worried they were getting too serious.

"Son," his father told him one evening, "I want to meet this girl and her parents. Invite them over for dinner."

"Why, Daddy?"

"You've been spending a lot of time with her. I want to see who has your nose so wide open."

"I'll ask Brooke tomorrow."

"Good night, son." His father started to leave the living room, but stopped at the archway. "You having sex with this girl?"

"No." It was the embarrassing truth. He would never admit it to any of his jock friends when they talked about their dates, but Brooke was shy and a little scared, and wanted to wait. He respected her wishes. He'd tried to persuade her like any teenage boy would do, at first, before he fell in love. Once he developed strong feelings for her, he understood why it was important to wait until they were both emotionally ready to handle having sex.

"If you were, you would know to protect yourself, her, and your futures, right?" his father bluntly asked.

Damon nodded.

"Good. I don't want to be a grandfather before I'm forty-five."

He remembered the fear those simple words had instilled in him. How ironic he would father a child with Brooke years later and not even know it. His father had guarded his future always, worrying they'd have an "accident." His father had been waiting when he returned from prom night at eight o'clock the morning after.

———— ⊶⊷ ————

"*Where have you been?*"

Damon's eyes fell to the tips of his shoes. His father knew exactly where he'd been. The only way he'd been able to persuade Brooke to stay at the hotel was to let her call her aunt so she wouldn't worry.

His father did not let him cower. "I asked you a question, son."

He lifted his head, straightened his posture, and prepared for himself. This initiation into manhood with Brooke was worth any punishment his parents could impose. He doubted anything could be worse than the tongue-lashing he'd just gotten from Brooke's Aunt Foster. "I spent the night with Brooke—at a hotel."

"What were you thinking? Brooke's aunt called here so upset it was all your mother could do to keep her from calling the police. She wanted to have you arrested for kidnapping. Explain yourself."

"I love Brooke."

His dad rolled his eyes and lifted his hands to the heavens. "You disrespect someone you love like this? Your mother and I taught you better."

"I didn't disrespect her." He was ignorantly defensive.

"If you love Brooke, you should have waited until you were married to sleep with her."

Damon was well aware of his parent's beliefs about premarital sex. It was wrong. Period. They'd tried to be tolerant, and told him if he had to indulge, it should be with someone he loved. He should be monogamous. And they should protect themselves. Still, his parents foolishly hoped he was a virgin.

His father went on. "It was more than disrespectful to take Brooke to a hotel." He realized he was shouting and calmed himself before going on. "Damon, this child is fifteen years old. She doesn't know better, but you do."

"This isn't what you all think it is. We love each other. I'm going to marry her one day."

His father's eyes were locked on him as he listened to his son, seventeen years old, use grown up words like love. His hands went up to heaven again.

"Sure, I took her to a hotel, but it wasn't cheap."

His father grunted.

"What happened between us wasn't cheap. I wanted to be with Brooke before I leave for college. We won't see each other much then." He'd needed to know she loved him, and he'd needed to show her how much he loved her. He hadn't been able to articulate the words then, but as an adult, he now understood his actions better. "Daddy, I know you're going to punish me. I just want you to understand why it was important to me to be with Brooke last night."

He didn't see Brooke for the next two months. There were no late night phone calls. Aunt Foster called the school and demanded the principal keep them separated. All the teachers were put on alert so that he had to stop walking her to class. Whenever he tried to sneak in a few private minutes with her, a teacher would come along and say, "Move it along, Damon," with the utmost compassion in their voice. Aunt Foster did allow Brooke to attend his graduation ceremony—they couldn't sit near each other or speak to each other afterwards, but he could see her watching him.

His parents hoped the imposed separation would lessen their attraction to each other. Two months to the day, Damon was standing in his father's study asking permission to take the car to go see Brooke. His father stalled, saying he needed Aunt Foster's permission. Two months of Brooke's crying persuaded Aunt Foster give in.

When he arrived at Aunt Foster's house, he snatched Brooke up on the front porch and kissed her. He didn't care about Aunt Foster watching them. Afterward, Aunt Foster pulled him into the living room for another scolding. She'd had two months to remember the things she was too angry to say the morning after the prom. He took his scolding in stride. The only thing that mattered was seeing Brooke again.

❦

Damon pushed the warm feelings accompanying his memories of the reunion away, and moved into the bathroom for a shower. He couldn't forget the way his spirit had been broken the day he found Brooke kissing Professor Neal Kirby. After their break up, there had always seemed to be something missing inside him. He channeled all his energy into his career, and saved enough money to start his own employment training agency. Barbara came along soon after, and the rest was history.

Brooke was the first person he had loved.

He was the one to whom she had given her virginity.

She was the first person to value him for his mind instead of his looks.

He had noticed the shy freshman girl and helped her bloom into a confident woman.

They had complemented each other perfectly.

∞∞∞

"Are you sure Daddy asked if you wanted to live with him?" Outwardly she remained calm, but inside, panic swept through Brooke.

Rebecca nodded. She skipped alongside her mother hand-in-hand into the school. Brooke didn't understand the volatile nature of her statement. What could he mean? Did Rebecca want to see him everyday? Of course she wanted to see him everyday. Rebecca adored Neal. Despite the paternity test results, Rebecca's feelings for him would not change. It was a foolish question, and Neal didn't ask foolish, meaningless questions.

Brooke knelt down and hugged her daughter. "Be good. I'll see you after school."

"Bye." Rebecca ran to her desk.

Brooke hurried down the crowded corridor and out of the school. She knew Neal. He would do it...he would try to take Rebecca away. She started her car, but didn't pull out of the parking space. If it could be done, Neal would do it. He would take Rebecca out of fear—for revenge—to teach her a lesson. It didn't really matter what his motives were. Her life would end without Rebecca. The thought made her grip the steering wheel until her fingers ached. She had to calm herself. She pulled out of the parking lot, managing to hold it together long enough to get to work.

She rushed past everyone in the lobby of Vintage Suites to her office. She paced the room, looking at the situation from all angles. Rebecca could have misunderstood something Neal had said. It worried her that she still hadn't held a conversation with him since the day he announced the results of the paternity test. He was understandably angry, but he had cut off all communication. No, Rebecca hadn't been mistaken. Neal was planning to take Rebecca away.

What do I do?

Neal had set this crisis in motion. She wouldn't let him surprise her the way he did when he requested the paternity test again. She had to be proactive. She dialed Neal at the university, and after a brief hassle, the young girl playing gatekeeper called him to the phone. There was a rustling on the line, and she was placed her on hold before Neal answered. "Is something wrong with Rebecca?"

"She's fine."

"You never call me on campus." He was gruff and dismissive, but at least he hadn't refused her call, or hung up on her.

"We need to talk."

"What is it?"

"I don't want to do this over the phone. Can I stop by your office after work?"

Neal held the phone for so long; Brooke thought they had been disconnected. "This evening—around six."

"Six is fine."

"If there's nothing else, I have to get to the lecture hall."

CHAPTER 9

Damon stepped into Brooke's office, adding another dimension to her problems. In an instant, her life had been microscopically reduced to one error. Just as quickly, the error ballooned into a monumental mistake. Damon's demeanor was calm and assertive, but his hazel-green eyes were on fire. She had been dreading her meeting with Neal all day. She knew she'd have to talk to Damon, but she wasn't emotionally prepared to face him this soon—and she was beginning to wonder if not being emotionally prepared had something to do with the way her mind trotted down Memory Lane whenever she looked at him.

"Have a seat." She glanced at the clock.

"Am I keeping you from something?" He was annoyed.

"No—yes." Her eyes slid away from his piercing stare. If she were late, Neal wouldn't wait, and she desperately needed to speak with him. "I'm meeting Neal after work."

He nodded, contemplatively. "About Rebecca."

"About Rebecca."

After a brief pause, he asked, "You had no idea Rebecca was my daughter?"

"None. I wouldn't have kept it from you. I had no reason to."

He turned away. "Unless you were afraid you'd lose Neal." When he looked at her again, the angry implications were clear.

"Are you accusing me of using my child to keep a man?"

"No." His lashes hooded his embarrassment. "No—I didn't mean—I'm angry, and…"

"And?"

"Hurt."

An uneasy silence filled the office.

"I feel betrayed," he added.

Nothing she could say would convey how bad she felt. Her eyes were not reflections of her soul, as were his. She wanted to come around the desk and comfort him. She remembered he was a married man, and she was involved in a serious relationship with Kurtis. It wasn't her place to console Damon. Everything was becoming more muddled, more confused. She couldn't have her feelings for Damon reawakening in the middle of chaos.

"Listen, Damon. I wish I knew how to handle this, but I don't. All I can tell you is I never meant to hurt you in any way. I feel responsible for shaking up your world—not to mention Rebecca, Neal and Kurtis. I'm sorry."

"We have to find a way to make this work."

She nodded, again glancing at the clock. They wouldn't have a chance at normalcy if Neal tried to take Rebecca from her.

"I don't know how to handle this either," Damon said. "We should talk when you have more time. We need to come up with a plan that will work for everyone."

"I agree."

He stood. "I'll give you a call, and we'll make plans."

She stood and offered her hand. It was an awkward gesture. He gave her a quick shake and hurried out of the office. She watched him leave, knowing he hadn't had enough time to process everything. His emotions were still raw, evident in the darkening of his eyes. He wanted to meet to make a plan, which meant he hadn't decided on how involved he wanted to become in Rebecca's life.

She replayed their conversation over and over as she drove to Neal's office. An innocent handshake had ignited warmth she hadn't felt in years. How different her life would have been if she'd known Damon was Rebecca's father. She had no doubt they would have married. But they had been young, and odds were their marriage would not have survived the challenges of a newlywed couple with a child trying to build two careers.

He still looked good, fit. His wife was taking care of him—keeping him happy. Brooke struggled with thoughts that were inappropriate to have about a married man. She pushed them away, promising she wouldn't do anything more to disrupt his home life. If he chose to be an integral part of Rebecca's life, she would respect him and his marriage. She would never ask for more than he was willing to give. She had let him dictate how much, or how little, he wanted to be involved. She wouldn't become the ex-from hell. She owed him at least that much.

When she arrived at Neal's office, he was sitting behind his desk grading papers. Not much had changed from the days when she used to spend her free time there. The walls were lined with heavy oak shelves filled with volumes of books. Pictures of him shaking hands with a variety of television stars and politicians decorated the blue wallpaper in the short hallway to his private restroom. His diplomas were framed in gold on the wall above his head. His numerous awards were arranged chronologically in the trophy case near the window.

"Brooke. Have a seat." This being their first meeting since learning the paternity results, she'd expected him to be more explosive. His politeness escalated her suspicions.

The building was quiet. Most of the professors had gone for the evening, but the maintenance staff milled around. How many times had she visited this same building, late in the evening, when she would not be detected? Young and naive then, she'd found the meetings intoxicatingly clandestine. Having grown older and wiser, she now saw them for what they truly were. The prominent professor had enjoyed her eager young body, but not enough to make her a part of his world.

"Where's Rebecca?" Neal asked, refocusing her attention.

"I let her stay for the after school club."

"She likes the science experiments." A faint smile separated his gray moustache, but quickly disappeared. "You wanted to see me?"

"We should talk about Rebecca."

He neatly stacked the papers he had been grading and pushed them aside.

With his undivided attention, the room shrank, becoming too small. "You know me as well as anybody. You have to understand I didn't do this intentionally. If I'd had known Rebecca wasn't your little girl, I would've told you. I wouldn't have let her, or you, get emotionally attached. I'm asking you to forgive me—and work with me to find a compromise we can all live with."

He searched her face. "You had no idea?"

The way he watched her, searching for a lie, waiting to point an accusing finger, made her squirm. He'd used his power of intimidation to win their arguments about what was in the best interest of Rebecca before, and Brooke still had not become immune to his antics.

"You were never suspicious?" he pressed. "Never had a doubt?"

"Neal…"

He adjusted his expression, made subtle changes Brooke could never quite name, but it was enough to drag the truth from her.

"I never had a doubt, because I never allowed myself to doubt it."

"What does that mean?" He was working hard to contain his anger, probably still stunned at how quickly he'd lost control and put his hands on her when confronting her about the test results.

"You and I were together. I didn't question it," she hesitated, "when I should have."

He steered away from the obvious question, using the time to compose himself. "I was not prepared for this, Brooke. I only wanted the paternity test to keep Kurtis from adopting Rebecca. I didn't want to lose her. I love her more than anything, or anyone. There's no way I can stop being her father because a test says she's not my child. I simply can't do it."

"I would never ask you to. You and Rebecca have a bond that will never be broken regardless of whom her real father is."

He cringed at her use of the word "real," but remained composed. Professor Neal Kirby was always the epitome of a professional. He leaned forward, placing his elbows firmly on his desk. "You know who her father is," he declared, stretching out each word. He didn't say it as a question, because he knew the answer.

She held his gaze.

"The young man you were seeing when we got involved."

"Damon Richmond."

"Does he know?"

She nodded, watching sorrow and confusion overtake his face. "I told him. He was tested."

"Then it's a surety?" A mask fell down over his facial features, shielding his reaction from her.

"He's Rebecca's father."

"His reaction?"

She shrugged one shoulder. "He's trying to come to terms with it."

"How is Kurtis handling all of this?"

"Kurtis is fine."

Neal leaned back in his chair. "I doubt that, but you're not obligated to share your personal life with me."

She wouldn't become derailed by his rivalry with Kurtis. "We're here to talk about Rebecca."

"You were young when we were involved—too young. When I was that age I made a lot of mistakes, too. Even though this has upset me, I'm not angry with you."

A tremendous weight was lifted from Brooke's shoulders. Neal was going to be reasonable, and they would work everything out. Together, they'd find a solution each parent could live with. They would be the model blended family, and Rebecca would benefit from having such strong men in her life—each different, but dynamic in their own way. Some children never knew their fathers, but she would have three men who loved her in her life.

"*But*," Neal added, "this is about the relationship I have with Rebecca. I won't let her go."

"Of course not."

"I'd never stand by and let Kurtis adopt her." His voice grew tighter with every word. He was struggling not to reveal the true depth of his anger. If he truly wasn't mad at her, he was mad at himself for opening this can of worms.

"Don't worry about—"

"I don't know what Damon's intentions are, but Rebecca is still *my* daughter."

Brooke's stomach twisted as all hopes of a happily blended family crumbled. "You can still see her anytime you like—that won't change."

"Of course it'll change. As soon as Damon becomes involved in Rebecca's life, it'll change. If we both have plans with her at the same time, who will be with her? If he wants to take her away for the summer and I want her to go to camp, whose wishes will prevail?"

"I haven't worked through everything, but I'm sure it won't be a problem."

"Well, I *have* thought about all of these things, and I'm not willing to be the one who concedes. Rebecca is as much my daughter—or more—than Damon's. If he can't honor my wishes, there will be a problem."

The look of defiance crossing Neal's face rattled her. The graying beard couldn't cover the unyielding position he was taking. He w going to make this easy. He was going to search for conflict so he w have an excuse to take Rebecca away.

"What if it takes ten years for Damon to decide he wants to be in Rebecca's life? Do I stand in as a substitute father, and get shoved out of the way when he reappears? You hear about it all the time. A parent gives a child up for adoption, but comes back years later and the child turns on the parents who have sacrificed and raised her all her life."

"Damon wouldn't do anything like that. He's not vindictive, or manipulative."

"He has the right to be as involved—or uninvolved—as he wants to be. This has shocked all of us. It might take him years to come to terms with having a daughter."

"The bottom line is that Rebecca is *my* daughter. I'm her mother, and I'll make the final decisions when it comes to her welfare. If there's a dispute over Rebecca, or anything concerning her, I'll decide what happens. I'd never let anyone hurt her. If Damon decides not to be a part of her life, he'll have to accept the long-term consequences of his actions. I'll protect my daughter. I won't be bullied when it comes to what is best for her."

"You choose now to grow a backbone?" The question was venomous, and it opened the floodgates for his anger. "Why didn't you take this stance when Kurtis was trying to adopt my child away from me? None of this would have ever happened." Here was the anger she'd been expecting. "Oh, I see." He laughed bitterly as he stood. "Momma's baby, Papa's maybe."

"Your condescending attitude is uncalled for."

"I'll do anything necessary to stay in my daughter's life."

She hoisted her purse up on her shoulder and prepared to go before things got uglier. "Animosity won't help anyone."

"You're lucky I don't do more than get angry." He pounded his fist on the desktop, startling her. "You're lucky I haven't—"

"What?"

His anger slipped away when he realized he'd almost said too much.

"What, Neal?"

He eased into his chair, pulling the forgotten stack of papers in front of him. "You should go now." He went back to his grading.

"One more thing."

Brooke was headed for the door, but stopped when he called out to her. "What?"

"I want to be there when you tell her."

She searched his face for confirmation he was plotting to take Rebecca away from her.

"I want to be there." His disposition softened. "You owe me as much."

She gripped her purse strap, suddenly wanting to be far away from the memories living in his office. "It's too soon."

"It's five years too late."

"We have a lot to discuss first." She shook her head adamantly. "I need to straighten everything out with Damon find out how involved he plans on being in her life."

"Promise me you won't tell her without me being there."

"I won't."

"We'll have to tell her soon. She's a smart girl. She'll know something's wrong."

"I've always tried to be a good person. I make one mistake, and I destroy everyone's life."

His eyes softened, and for a moment she saw the caring professor she'd been infatuated with years ago. "I do believe it was a mistake." His version of accepting her apology. "But it was a mistake that will be costly to us all. Pray Rebecca comes out of this unscarred." He went back to grading papers.

She left his office, trying to put everything into perspective as she drove to pick Rebecca up from school. There were too many uncertainties. How involved would Damon want to be in Rebecca's life? Was Neal planning to do something drastic, like try to take Rebecca away? What was going to happen between her and Kurtis? The more decisions she made, the more confused things became. She was dealing with three very strong-willed men. She had to pull it together before either of them chose to strike.

One wrong decision and Rebecca might suffer a lifetime. She had to figure out what was best for everyone, but Rebecca's welfare had to come first. She'd made some decisions—she'd told Damon, postponed the wedding, and was trying to compromise with Neal—but it would be a while before she knew if the outcome of her actions would be positive or negative. Contemplating it all gave her a headache that could only be resolved by a large dose of TLC, which was why she didn't turn Kurtis away when she found him parked in front of her townhouse after picking up Rebecca from school.

While they dated, he had formed a relationship with Rebecca, too. Yet another thing she had to consider when deciding what was best for Rebecca.

"Ladies," Kurtis said as he helped Rebecca with her book bag. She grabbed his hand and led him inside, chattering like the old friends they were.

Brooke had been cautious in introducing them, afraid the relationship wouldn't work out and Rebecca would be hurt. When they became serious, she had integrated Kurtis into Rebecca's life and they'd become fast friends. Aunt Foster had warned her it was all an act to win her over, but she didn't believe it.

She was grateful to Kurtis for keeping Rebecca occupied while she cooked dinner. As she pretended everything was normal, he helped Rebecca with her homework, and later—at Rebecca's request—he tucked her into bed. His childhood innocence surfaced when he interacted with Rebecca, becoming carefree and fun loving. Brooke watched him reading Rebecca's favorite story, realizing the rare occasions when Kurtis seemed truly relaxed were connected to his time with her.

"That girl wears me out," he said with a huge smile.

"You have to stop spoiling her, or she's going to be hard to live with."

Kurtis sat at the kitchen table and watched her put dinner away. "I made some phone calls. We should hear something soon about what our legal rights are."

Our legal rights? She hadn't asked him to get involved. She was trying to work everything out amicably with Damon and Neal. She didn't have the energy to argue with Kurtis about adopting Rebecca. Through it all, he still didn't see it was never going to happen. She couldn't make it any clearer, and after an emotionally exhausting day, she didn't have the patience to try again.

"I spoke with Neal today."

"What?" He stiffened. "I told you not to do anything until we had this figured out."

"I know, but I thought if I talked to him we could work it out."

"And what was his reaction?"

"He wants to stay in Rebecca's life. He still considers her his daughter." She joined him at the table "He wants to be here when I tell Rebecca."

"I hope you told him it was out of the question."

She wanted to tell him he had no say in the matter, but she'd had enough emotionally draining discussions for the day. The best thing for him to do was to keep his jealousy in check and remain supportive. She was juggling too many balls, trying to make too many people happy.

"I'm trying to compromise with Neal to make this situation easy on all of us. I don't see anything wrong with him being here. Rebecca will need to know Neal still loves her. She won't stop loving him because he's not her biological father. His support will help her to adjust."

"I'd love to see all the ties between Neal and you severed as soon as possible, but if it helps Rebecca, I'll go along."

Her head snapped up.

"You're surprised?"

"I'm surprised you're not giving me any argument about it."

"You told me you needed me to be supportive. I'm being supportive."

She looked into the handsome face of a successful man who was trying to do his best, and realized it still wasn't enough. She appreciated his effort, but their relationship had changed without her being able to pinpoint the precise moment it had happened. The sparkle had fizzled into nothingness. No matter how hard she tried, she wasn't anxious to see him anymore. In fact, she dreaded their dates, knowing it would end in an argument or power struggle. Planning their wedding hadn't excited her—it'd made her anxious and scared. She wasn't anxious for his touch. Instead made excuse after excuse why she couldn't be intimate with him.

"What's he like?" Kurtis asked, rousing her.

"What?"

"Rebecca's father. What is he like?"

Just the mention of Damon's name made her feel soft and feminine. These were the butterflies she should feel when her fiancé came around. Kurtis waited for her to answer, looking small and timid and unsure. It wasn't his jealousy of Neal bothering him. Damon coming back into her life troubled him. It had been a worry for her too—until she found out he was married with a new family. Knowing he had a family should have halted her renewed attraction, but it hadn't. She had to make a conscious effort not to think about how his soft touches and tender kisses had once made her feel.

"Brooke?"

"He's a nice guy. He's shocked by all of this, but he'll do what's best for Rebecca."

"What happened between you and Damon?"

"What?" she asked, a little worried. Could he read her attraction to Damon?

"When you were dating...what happened between you? Why'd you break up?"

She'd anticipated having this discussion from the moment Kurtis had learned who was Rebecca's father. She would be as honest with him as she would be with Damon and Neal. "I met Damon in high school. We dated into college. Once I became a senior, my interests shifted in another direction and we grew apart."

"And then you met Neal?"

She kept her voice even, answering his questions. She answered in generic terms, not offering any emotional details. There was no need to hurt him with stories from the past. "Neal was my instructor for months before we got involved."

"You were seeing Damon and Neal at the same time?"

"Briefly. I broke it off with Damon soon after I started seeing Neal."

"Damon never suspected you were messing around?"

She felt uneasy going over these details. She knew Kurtis's jealousy of Neal well, and this would only fuel it further.

"He sensed something was wrong between us."

"How'd he find out?"

She turned away from him, moving to clean the countertop. "I'd rather not talk about the details of my relationship with Damon."

Kurits was quiet as he rebuilt the timeline in his head. "But you must have gotten back together since Damon is Rebecca's father."

"We had a lot of feelings invested in each other. We said goodbye the only way we knew how. We never saw each other again after our last night together."

"You broke up after having sex one last time," he clarified. "And you haven't seen each other until now." He digested the information. "A long time has passed. Have you gotten over him?"

"Yes." She avoided looking at him because, she was unsure of her answer.

"Are your feelings for him the reason you postponed our wedding?"

"This isn't the right time to get married. Not until everything with Rebecca has been settled."

"It could take years to come to working compromises with Neal and Damon. I know my jealousy about your relationship with Neal can be unreasonable. I know it, and I try to handle it the best I can, but this is different. This isn't about an older man who used his influence over you to get you in bed a few times. Damon is an old *lover*."

"Are you saying you have a problem with Damon, too?"

"Are your feelings for him going to come back now that he's in your life again?"

"No." She said it with conviction, but inside she knew she had already wandered into dangerous emotional territory with Damon. "You're asking me to predict the future."

He tensed. After a long pause he said, "I don't want to lose you and Rebecca."

"I don't want to hurt you."

"You say you don't, but our entire relationship has always involved another man. Now I have two other men to compete with. I want to be a good stepfather to Rebecca, but now I've been reduced to third string quarterback, and I'm in serious jeopardy of being traded to another team. If you keep postponing our wedding, our marriage will be off altogether."

"Things are changing. I can't stop it."

"And I'm being pushed to the outside, forced to look in."

"Kurtis." Her voice was gentle. "This is a lot to deal with. If you want to back off for a while—"

"No. That's the last thing I want."

"I can't make you any guarantees—not about how my life is going to change, or our future. I have to focus all my energy on Rebecca right now. If you can't handle this—"

"I can handle it," he said, but Brooke wasn't convinced he could.

"What if I can't give you what you want?" She felt smothered by his demands to get married when her life was so unstable. There were so many good things about him, but the bad things were too much for her to tolerate. She hadn't recognized the source of her unhappiness because Neal clouded the issue with his reciprocal bickering. But with their relationships shifting, things were becoming clearer regarding her future with Kurtis.

"What are you saying?"

"Things are changing. When we come out on the other side of this, we might not feel the same about our relationship."

"We? Or you?"

She tried to convey her sorrow through the look in her eyes. She wanted to end it all, taking a huge weight off her chest. But he looked so scared…she couldn't cruelly dismiss him.

"Both of us," she offered as a cop-out. "Both of our needs are changing."

CHAPTER 10

Ella sat up in bed, removing her sleep mask as she answered the telephone. "Rebecca, it's late. Are you okay?"

"Can I talk to my dad?" There were tears in her hushed voice.

"Sure." Ella shook Neal awake. "It's Rebecca. It sounds like she's been crying." She handed him the phone.

"What is it, Rebecca? What's wrong?"

"Mommy and Kurtis are fighting. I want to come to your house. Maybe if I come to your house they'll stop."

"What do you mean fighting? Are they arguing with words?"

Ella clicked on the lamp.

"They're shouting. They're always shouting." Rebecca sniffled. He'd known the tears would come soon when he'd heard Rebecca refer to Brooke as "Mommy."

"What are they shouting about?"

Ella tapped his arm, giving him a scrunched face of disapproval.

"Kurtis wants to go with Mommy, but she says he can't."

"Go where?"

Ella smacked her lips.

"Mommy has to go see a man to talk about me. She says Kurtis can't go, and now he's mad at me. I want to spend the night with you and Ms. Ella."

He tried to piece Rebecca's story together. Before he could, she started crying. "Honey, hang up the phone. I'm going to call back and speak to your mother. It'll be all right. If they stop fighting, will you stop being scared?"

Rebecca sniffled until she could answer clearly. "Yes."

"Dad is going to see you Friday after school, right?"

"Yes." She was so vulnerable.

"I want you to go back to sleep. I'm going to take care of everything. If you get scared again, you call me back. Okay?"

"Okay, Dad."

"I love you."

"I love you." Rebecca disconnected.

"What's going on?" Ella asked.

"I'm not sure," he answered, already dialing Brooke's number. "The best I can tell, Brooke and Kurtis are arguing, and Rebecca's upset by it."

"Who are you calling?"

"Brooke."

"Why? Stay out of it."

"I can't stay out of it. Rebecca's scared. Someone has to tell them to act like grown ups. I swear, if Rebecca calls back, I'm going over there and bring her back here."

When Brooke answered, he bombarded her with questions, catching her off guard. He chastised her for arguing in front of Rebecca and getting her so upset. Once he had Brooke on the defensive, he demanded she explain what Rebecca had told him. With the information he needed, he ended the call and turned to Ella. "She's meeting with Damon about Rebecca."

"Good."

"Good? I won't have them deciding what my relationship with Rebecca will be without my input. We're going."

"You want us to crash their meeting?"

"Absolutely. Rebecca is as much my daughter as his—more so. I want a say in what happens."

"I don't know, Neal. Maybe we should stay out of it."

"It would suit you for me to give Rebecca up for good."

"Rebecca is not your daughter. You have to come to terms with that."

"Why? Why do I have to accept that? I love her. I've cared for her for five years. Why do I have to pretend that she means nothing to me?"

"I know this is hard." She placed a comforting hand on his shoulder, but he jerked away.

"I'm going. You don't have to, but you're my wife and I thought you'd support me." Angry, he turned his back and covered his head with the sheets.

∞∞

"Who the hell does he think he is to call here and reprimand us like we're children?" Kurtis whispered harshly.

"We *shouldn't* have been arguing when Rebecca can hear. I don't want her upset before she even knows what's going on."

"All we do is fight lately. Since you postponed the wedding and insisted on bringing Damon Richmond into our lives."

"I told you weeks ago. If this is too much for you to handle, give me time alone to fix everything. We can pick up where we left off then."

He knew if he left Brooke, she'd never ask him to come back. He had to hang on to what they had with everything in him. "All I have to say is this—if Neal and Ella are going to be there then so am I."

"Kurtis, this dinner meeting was supposed to be for me and Damon to decide the best way to deal with him being Rebecca's father. It's turning into a summit meeting. Damon's wife is coming. Neal is insisting he and Ella be there. And now you."

He pushed his arms into his jacket. "You know the old African proverb—it takes a village to raise a child. Well, you can just call this a town meeting because there's no way I'm going to be excluded."

"I don't want the issues clouded. This is about Rebecca and Damon—nothing else. I won't let your jealousy interfere."

"Everybody at the table will be against you. They all blame you for what has happened. I'm the only one on your side, and you keep trying to push me away."

"I'm not—"

"Are you telling me I can't come?"

"Kurtis—"

"I love Rebecca, too. She's going to be my stepdaughter—I have an interest in what happens. Are you telling me I'm wrong for caring about her?"

"All right. You can come along, but only to support me. One word and you'll have to leave."

"Don't shut me out, Brooke." He didn't like the expressions crossing her face. She was trying to push him away, but he wouldn't allow it. He was losing his family. He would fight to the bitter end to keep Brooke and Rebecca in his life. Neal was steadily losing ground. He would deal with Damon before he became a viable threat. No one would take his family away from him.

———— ∞ ————

Damon straightened his tie. He'd known Brooke for years, yet he was nervous about their dinner. "Why are you so dressed up?"

Barbara moved next to him in the full-length mirror to check herself one last time. She fussed with the collar of her jacket. He didn't remember this suit, which meant she'd been out spending more money they couldn't afford to spend. Her hair was curled and sculptured to frame her face. Her makeup was flawless, highlighting her prominent cheeks. She was as beautiful as the day he'd met her. Why didn't he still get butterflies in his stomach when he looked at her?

"If you think I'm letting you go to dinner with your ex-girlfriend without me you're crazier than I thought."

He sighed loudly. Why couldn't they be a loving couple like his parents? Why must everything he said be met with a derogatory remark? "It's not a date, Barbara. We're going to discuss Rebecca."

"I'm your wife—I should be there. If you insist on bringing this child into our lives, I want to meet her mother." She moved away from him. "I want her to know we have a happy marriage. Any little ideas she has about interfering need to be squashed."

CHAPTER 11

Brooke followed the waiter to a private dining room at Sinbad's restaurant. She'd considered having everyone meet at Vintage Suites, but a neutral place would be best. Everyone on equal footing, so no one could take advantage of the situation. Neal and Kurtis being in the same place at the same time would require a great deal of refereeing. She had no idea what would happen once Damon was thrown into the mix.

Kurtis's hand pressed against the small of her back, guiding her, subtly asserting his place in her life. The waiter watched as they inspected the room, as if they were expecting a presidential council to discuss the latest development in some great reform. The view of the pier was spectacular, and on another occasion, it would have been a perfect romantic setting for two people about to begin a life together. The table situated in the center of the room would comfortably seat three couples for the most uncomfortable conversation of Brooke's life.

"Sit here." Kurtis pulled out her chair. "These seats give us the best vantage point," he added, sliding in next to her.

She clenched her fist underneath the table, hoping she hadn't made a mistake by allowing him to come. At the time of her decision, his support was needed, but if he insisted on being adversarial, things would deteriorate quickly.

"Where are they?" Kurtis bounced his leg next to hers. He was nervous. "It's rude to be late. Especially on an occasion like this." He tapped the crystal water glass with his thumb. "Neal probably wants to make a grand entrance. Like we're his subjects awaiting his arrival."

The more nervous Kurtis became, the more venomous his words grew. Brooke shut him down by changing the subject. "You're wearing a new suit. You got a haircut, too."

"I didn't want to embarrass you."

"Just stay cool. Don't antagonize Neal."

His leg went still for a moment, and then began jumping again.

Brooke was just as anxious about the meeting, but the sooner all the players came together and made the tough decisions, the sooner everyone's lives could go back to normal. It was awkward for her to have the three men—the only three men—she'd ever been intimate with sit down to dinner together. She had been practicing her normalcy all week, anticipating what it would be like to get her first look at the woman Damon had decided to share his life with. The dynamics between Damon and Neal would be awkward. They hadn't seen each other since the day Damon walked in on her kissing her professor. And no matter how much Kurtis claimed his interest was only in supporting her, Brooke knew his curiosity about Damon had driven him to buy a new suit and get a fresh haircut.

"I won't start anything, but I'll finish whatever the Professor starts," Kurtis said just as the waiter came through the door with Damon following closely behind.

Dressed in a dark suit, Damon was so handsome that her response was like a tidal wave that threatened to wash her out the window into the Detroit River. His obvious good looks weren't what overwhelmed her. Although he hadn't changed much since college physically, he had grown into his body, embracing the confidence he found on becoming a man. He'd always been sensitive and considerate, but his mixed heritage had been a sticky point for him, because he'd attend a high school where Caucasians were the minority. He hadn't had the self-assured swagger in his stride then as he did now. He was powerhouse of strength, and she knew him to be a fierce protector with solid moral values. The new self-confidence made him an undefeatable force. His buoyancy put her at ease when he entered the room, knowing he would be her anchor in the storm ahead. She felt connected to him, and as Kurtis tensed beside her, she saw Damon as more of an ally.

When Damon stepped aside to usher his wife into the private dining room, Brooke got her first look at the woman who'd taken her place. The photo in his wallet didn't do her justice. Barbara was startling. She had a perfect face to top a perfectly sculpted body. Her figure showed no signs of having had two children. She was the type of beauty that made men stop and stare, and beside her, Brooke felt Kurtis's posture straighten. The long-legged woman walked into the room with the practiced strut of a professional model. Her dress was very expensive, which meant Damon was taking good care of her. Somehow, for no justifiable reason, Brooke felt she'd been wronged.

Barbara whispered something and Damon nodded his face serious and guarded. She wasn't just refined and graceful—she was protective of her man. She wrapped her arm around Damon's, never breaking eye contact with Brooke.

After awkward introductions, Kurtis bolted out of his seat and shook Damon's hand. Brooke thought Kurtis was asserting his presence, but it quickly became apparent he was trying to beat Damon to pulling out Barbara's chair. As everyone in the room became aware of Kurtis's intent, the gesture became awkward and he clumsily moved back to his seat. Brooke should have been jealous of Kurtis tripping over himself to impress another woman, but she wasn't. She was embarrassed for him. And for herself, when she felt jealousy at seeing Barbara lean over and drink from Damon's glass of wine, leaving her lipstick kiss on the rim.

Barbara caught her watching and didn't like what she saw on Brooke's face. She looped her arm through Damon's and asked, "You were my husband's high school sweetheart?"

"I guess you could say that." The exchange with Barbara was filled with tension. Brooke couldn't miss the suspicious glare in Barbara's eye.

"I guess we could. Or we wouldn't be sitting here right now. Would we?"

Damon settled Barbara with a look.

Neal walked into the room with the broad stride of authority. "I see everyone is here." As was his way, he took control immediately. "Waiter, we'll need some privacy."

The waiter left without a word, closing the doors behind him.

With Ella on his arm, Neal approached Damon with an out-stretched hand. "Damon, we formally meet at last." He was alluding to Damon walking in on them years ago. The unkind remark let Brooke know he had no intention on handling the situation with compassion and dignity. He was ready for a battle, and he'd come out swinging.

"Professor," Damon said. He held his temper, accepting Neal's hand.

"Call me Neal." He glanced at Brooke. "We have so much in common."

Ella didn't appreciate the comment. She whispered something in his ear, and tugged him toward the only vacant chairs. Brooke appreciated Kurtis's wisdom in taking the seats of best advantage.

"Now that that's out of the way," Kurtis said, "can the waiter come back in?"

His comment would set the tone for the evening. Covert insults were passed around the table more frequently than the breadbasket. Brooke looked up, catching Damon's attention several times. She wanted to apologize for not making his transition into Rebecca's life smoother. She didn't want Kurtis or Neal to harass him, making everything harder on everyone. Damon kept his cool during dinner, never letting anyone ruffle him.

Brooke cleared her throat and broached the subject they'd all been carefully avoiding. It had seemed more civil to make uneasy small talk over a meal before delving into what promised to be a heated discussion. Getting through dinner had not been easy, and other than Kurtis, no one ate much. It would've been so much easier for her to meet with Damon alone at the park, or what had become their regular lunching spot. But the other two men in her life, and by extension these women, would not be excluded from the decision-making process.

"Thank you all for coming," Brooke started. "I want to make this easy on everyone, especially Rebecca. We should begin by deciding the best way to tell her about Damon."

Kurtis's leg bounced under the table. "Before we tell Rebecca anything, I think we should know exactly what role Damon plans on playing in her life. If he's not going to be an active father, there's no need for her to know about him."

"For once," Neal said, "we agree on something."

"I think it's the best way to go," Barbara agreed, surprising Brooke. Brooke had assumed Barbara was there to support Damon's decision, but seeing the displeasure in Damon's eyes, knew this was not his stance.

"I'm insulted by the assumption I might be and absentee dad," Damon said. "I have every intention of living up to my responsibilities." He sat forward, challenging anyone to dispute his rights as a parent.

Barbara rolled her eyes.

Ella quickly diffused the situation. "The best way to tell Rebecca is just tell her. Kids are very resilient. If we don't make a big deal over it, neither will Rebecca."

Neal was annoyed by her cavalier attitude. "You're my wife. When are you going to start supporting me?"

Out of embarrassment over the fight brewing between Neal and Ella, Brooke dropped her eyes. Everyone remained silent, waiting for the explosion. The two wives at the table did not agree with what their husbands were doing.

"Telling a child something like this can be detrimental," Neal said to no one in particular. He would save his fight with Ella until they were alone. He looked at Damon to watch for the reaction to his next declaration. "Rebecca has grown up thinking I'm her father. She's very attached to me."

"Another reason I need to get to know her as soon as possible," Damon said. "She should know her real father."

Kurtis didn't want to be forgotten. "This should be handled very carefully. Brooke and I will sit down together and explain what has happened."

Damon and Neal protested, both asserting their right to be present when Rebecca learned the truth.

"Guys," Brooke raised her voice over theirs. "Arguing won't get us anywhere."

Barbara crossed her arms over her chest and muttered something about Brooke enjoying every minute of having three men fight over her.

Ella heard the comment. She watched Neal with suspicious eyes. More fuel had just been added to their impending fight.

Brooke would not be derailed by Barbara's remark. "We came together to discuss what is best for Rebecca. We all agree Rebecca has to know the truth—and soon. You all want to be there when I tell her, but I don't want her to be overwhelmed." Her eyes settled on Neal. "You and I will tell her together."

Kurtis began to protest, but she ended his argument with a heated glare.

Damon nodded. "You know Rebecca better than anyone. I trust you to know the best way to tell her."

"What are you going to say?" Kurtis asked.

"Neal and I will figure it out," Brooke answered, shutting down the discussion before it took them away from the true purpose of the meeting. The details could be worked out later, when there was less chance of a heated debate erupting.

Neal offered some assurance. "We'll be honest."

"But sensitive," Brooke added.

Kurtis jumped in. "When Brooke and I get married, I'm going to be the one she sees everyday. I should be there when she finds out."

"Can something *not* be about you?" Neal asked.

"You'd like me out of the picture, wouldn't you?"

Barbara's eyes widened at the brewing controversy, and a faint smile touched her lips.

"Kurtis, please. We don't need this right now."

"No," Ella said in a stern voice, "I'd like to know what Kurtis means."

Barbara rolled her eyes between Brooke and Neal. "Me, too."

Damon covered her hand with his, trying to silence her. "Don't instigate," he said. "We're all here for Rebecca's sake."

Barbara raised her voice. "Don't try to shush me, Damon. We all have a right to know if something is going on between the teacher and the gold digger."

"Gold digger!" Brooke said. "Are you calling me a gold digger? You don't even know me."

"I know women like you."

Everyone spoke at once.

Damon shook his head, "Barb, please."

Ella said, "I don't like what everyone is insinuating about my husband."

Neal's face went blank. "This is nonsense."

Kurtis raised his voice above them all. "Everything has to be out in the open if this is going to work. I'd like Neal to tell us how he feels about you, Brooke."

A hush fell over the room while they waited for Neal to answer.

"I told you I didn't want to come," Ella said. "You're so passionate when it comes to Rebecca. Anytime I try to discuss her with you, we come to an impasse. You're here fighting to be in the life of a child that isn't even yours. Could this all be about Brooke?"

"Ella, this isn't the time—"

"When is the time, Neal?" Ella's voice rose to an ear-piercing shrillness. "I've been telling you to have Rebecca's paternity tested since the day we married, but you didn't want to upset Brooke. Well, look where we are now. You're more concerned about Brooke's feelings than you are about your wife's."

Brooke listened in horror as accusations concerning her were discussed in open forum. She and Neal had a good working relationship when it came to Rebecca. Nothing more. They'd never been a real couple, and they certainly had never been in love with each other. Kurtis's implications were absurd, and she'd deal with him later. What was more disturbing at the moment was Ella's admission she'd been the one to push Neal into questioning Rebecca's paternity.

"Ella, you told Neal to have a paternity test because you wondered if we were seeing each other behind your back?"

"What goes on between me and my husband isn't your business," Ella sniped.

"You put doubts in his head about being Rebecca's father. That concerns me."

"I was right, wasn't I?" Ella yelled across the table.

"Enough," Damon shouted, quieting them all with his uncharacteristic burst of emotion. He looked around the table. "This is enough bickering. We aren't here to place blame on Brooke. Accusations about ulterior motives aren't helping either. If we can't decide this one simple issue, how are we all going to get along in the future?"

"Future?" Kurtis marveled.

"We're all going through a transitional period, but we're adults and we can get past it."

"What do you mean, transition period?" Neal stroked his beard. "Transition to what?"

"Me taking over as Rebecca's father."

Neal's mouth dropped. "You becoming her father? Taking over?" He tore his eyes away from Damon and locked in on Brooke. "What's going on here? I thought we would decide this together."

"I don't understand," Damon said. His hazel-green eyes clouded with anger. "I'm Rebecca's father. *No one* can decide how involved I am in her life except me. You and Brooke don't have the right, Neal."

"Wait just a minute—" Neal started.

"Yeah," Barbara interjected. "Let's get back to Brooke's ulterior motives."

Brooke ignored her and concentrated on diffusing the argument between Neal and Damon. "Neal wants to remain a part of Rebecca's life, Damon. He's been her father for five years, and Rebecca loves him."

"I'm the only father she's ever known," Neal added.

"Just a minute," Kurtis sputtered.

"Not now," Brooke snapped at him. She had enough on her hands trying to juggle two fathers—she didn't need a third jumping into the mix. "It's a reasonable request, Damon."

"Maybe, but how is he supposed to be Rebecca's father when I'm her father? It'll be too confusing for her." He ignored Barbara's gasp and spoke to Neal. "Of course you should withdraw from her life slowly until she gets to know me, but only one person can be her father, and it's me. I'm not saying break off all communication, but you have to know your rightful place in her life—and it's not as her father."

Neal shouted several curse words at Damon. "I told you, Brooke. I told you he'd come into the picture and try to come between me and my daughter."

"It sounds like he's excluding me, too," Kurtis said.

Neal jumped out of his seat. Ella grabbed his arm, keeping him from going after Damon. "You have never been a part Rebecca's life. For five years, I've been the only father she's ever known—and loved. Do you think you're going to make any decisions about what's best for her?"

"Yes," Damon answered calmly, "it's what a father does."

"Over my dead body!"

The room erupted into a brawl that rivaled a WWF wrestling match. Everyone paired off, and quickly switched partners, and when security arrived, no one had missed the opportunity to argue with anyone. Tempers flared. Jealousy between couples was ignited. Allegations were made, and each couple would continue to argue once they'd returned home. When they were finally separated and escorted to their cars, Brooke realized nothing had really been decided about Rebecca.

CHAPTER 12

"I'm sorry." Kurtis stepped into Brooke's office carrying a dozen red roses.

The diamond engagement ring on her finger caught the light as she reached for the bouquet. Suddenly, everything came clear. As she worked with giddy brides-to-be all day, she had never shared their excitement over her own upcoming marriage. Whenever Kurtis brought up the subject, she cringed.

Everyone always commented on how thoughtful he could be. Successful, intelligent and handsome—they asked where she'd found such a good man.

The local accounting organization where he was a member held their yearly conference at Vintage Suites. It was in July, a little over a year ago, when she met Kurtis at their convention. He was milling around the vendor booths in the lobby when she first noticed him watching her. He hustled down the corridor in her direction, but she was called away by another employee. She didn't think twice about it, until she caught him watching her as she stood in the back of the room during a lecture. By the time a break was called, she was off making sure everything was running smoothly in the kitchen.

She didn't see him again until after the seminar ended. He boldly showed up at her office, unannounced. Swamped with work, she was too hurried in her conversation with him. He'd slowed down the pace by asking her out for a date. She politely refused, giving him an excuse about not dating the guests of the hotel.

She hadn't even given him her name, but he returned that evening. His persistence persuaded her to have dinner with him. Before they finished their meal, Kurtis confessed he wanted to get to know her better.

Before they finished their dessert, he'd convinced her she wanted to know him better, too.

After their first date, he never left her. He called every day. Every weekend was devoted to her. Rebecca took to him right away. He wasn't perfect, but he always tried to do the right thing. Even when he tried to make decisions for her, Brooke felt he was doing it to protect her. After ten months, he asked her to marry him.

"Forgive me?" Kurtis asked, regaining her attention.

She twisted the engagement band around on her finger. Despite his good qualities, she just didn't love him enough to marry him.

"Brooke?" His smile dipped into a worried frown.

"Kurtis."

"What is it?" He rounded the desk and dropped to his knees in front of her. "Did something happen?" He took her hands in his. "Did Neal call?"

"I can't marry you," she blurted out before she lost her nerve.

"What?"

"And I can't see you anymore."

"What? Why? Are you still mad about what I said at the dinner? I'm sorry. I shouldn't have asked Neal if he still wanted you. I didn't—"

"Kurtis, it's not what happened at dinner. You were out of line, true, but this is about *us*." She took a deep breath. "I don't love you enough to marry you." She knew her words were harsh, but she had to make her feelings clear without room for counter arguments. "I don't mean to hurt you." She worked the engagement ring off her finger.

"Wait." He shook his head, clearing his thoughts. "You don't love me?"

"I care about you, but I don't love you enough to spend the rest of my life with you."

He stood and crossed the room, turning his back on her until he questioned her again. "All this time—I thought you kept putting off the wedding because you had the jitters. Not because you didn't love me."

"I don't know what to say, other than I'm sorry. Your love is so overwhelming, I thought it would be enough to make me feel as strongly as you do."

"I don't believe this."

"I have to make the best possible life for Rebecca. I have to work this thing out with Damon and Neal. I don't need to complicate it further by leading you to believe we're going to be a family when my heart tells me it won't happen."

"But, Brooke—"

"No, Kurtis. I've made up my mind. I've been feeling this way a long time, but I didn't want to admit it because I didn't want to hurt you. I'm already hurt you more by not telling you."

He watched her for a long moment, his hurt and anger wrapped into a tight ball, knotting his brow. She expected him to shout and make accusations, but he didn't say a word. He just stood in her office watching her, as if he were waiting for her to change her mind.

She worked the engagement ring from her finger and handed it to him.

He stormed out of her office without taking it, slamming the door.

———— ✇ ————

Neal reached out to stroke the girl's fire-engine red hair. The thing that had attracted him to her now seemed absurd once he got her into bed. She turned toward his touch. The gap between her two front teeth showed when she smiled. "You're good," she complimented him. He was flattered until she added, "I wasn't sure what to expect from a man as old as you, Professor Kirby."

He needed reassurances. He sought her approval, her compliments. "I have a good body." He rubbed his hand across his flat stomach.

"You have a wonderful body." She slithered her hand under the crisp white hotel sheets. She stroked him, encouraging him to harden.

He closed his eyes and relaxed to her rhythm. This affair was justifiable. Things between him and Ella had changed after the dinner at Sinbad's. She'd become distant and cold. He needed her comfort and support right now. He had no energy to pacify her jealousy brought on by a stupid remark Kurtis had made.

There was nothing going on between him and Brooke.

The girl moaned as she watched him grow.

He had thoughts, sure. He wondered how Brooke would receive him if he suggested they revisit the relationship they'd failed to start years ago.

His eyes flickered when he felt the hot wetness of the girl's mouth. The redhead worked her tongue down the length of him. She was good at this. Too bad she couldn't write a decent research paper.

Oh, Brooke. He had to get her in this position—just one time was all he needed. It would put an end to the leftover feelings he had for her. *Yes,* if he could make love to Brooke once more, he could prove to himself his attraction to her was only physical, and easily satisfied.

She was still the beautiful young woman he had swept off her feet years ago. He had been with many women—many coeds—but none could compare to what he'd shared with Brooke. He was sometimes brash with her because he feared what might happen if she knew his true feelings. He was a married man after all. But Brooke was the one who got away. He simply enjoyed being with her. Their age difference never mattered. He should have married her—he *loved* her, but ambition got in the way.

He had never wanted children. He was forty-five when Brooke announced she was pregnant—forty-six when Rebecca was born. He was too old to start a family—especially out of wedlock. An educated man like himself was supposed to know better.

Because of the university's rules against student-teacher relationships, they'd kept his fatherhood a secret. He supported Brooke in every way financially and emotionally, but no one associated with the school could know about their relationship. It would have ruined his reputation, and ended his career. Brooke had been hurt by his request, but soon understood he couldn't support her without a job. When Rebecca was born, and he held her in his arms, he didn't care who knew he was a father. Brooke had reminded him of everything at stake. So, they kept their secret, learning to be parents to their child while remaining friends. The years had flown by, and he had never gotten around to putting his name on Rebecca's birth certificate. He had foolishly believed Brooke's reassurances were enough to establish his parentage.

Rebecca didn't want for anything. He'd paid Brooke weekly support. Rebecca had her own bedroom, toys and clothing at his home. He pulled every string to get her into Cambridge Academy, paying the hefty tuition, and refusing any assistance from Brooke. He'd made sure Rebecca's academic and financial futures were secure.

Most importantly, he loved her more than anyone in the world. She had shown him what true, unconditional love was all about. He was devoted to her.

If he were the type of man who acted on his emotions, he would have married Brooke, and Rebecca would still be his little girl.

"You're going through with this?" Barbara followed Damon through the mudroom to the garage. "Even though you know how I feel about it?"

"Yes, I'm going to be a part of my daughter's life. This isn't something we can negotiate, Barbara. It's my decision, and I've made it."

"Solo?"

"Solo."

"Even though it affects us all?"

Telling Lisa and Roger about Rebecca had been uneventful. They could care less about anything concerning him unless it had something to do with their allowances. Despite Barbara's accusations and protesting, the kids had not brought into it. She had eventually broken out in fake sobs and had run from the room. The kids only asked if they could go back to watching television. Damon wanted to suggest they go comfort their mother, but knew they wouldn't understand what he meant.

"I want to be there when you and Brooke tell Rebecca you're her father," Barbara demanded.

"After what happened at the restaurant? No." He grabbed his car keys. "I'm late for a meeting."

"It's starting already."

"What's starting?"

"You're making them a priority over your real family."

Damon searched for any signs of sincerity or hurt on his wife's face. She poked her lip out as he had seen Lisa do many times before when she wanted her way. He caught a glimpse of the superb acting job that had reeled him into a marriage that was all smoke and mirrors. He didn't like seeing the false expression on his wife's face. And he didn't like the other things he'd begun to question about her sincerity towards him.

"Do you want to spend more time with me?" he asked.

The question took Barbara aback, and she stammered her response. "I-I didn't say that."

"Would you like us to do more things together as a family?"

"Well..."

His voice dropped, revealing the desperation he suddenly felt to try to hold it all together. "If you want those things, all you have to do is tell me. You, me and the kids could go on vacation." When he saw the startled expression on her face, he rushed on, amending his words. "You and I could go away together. A second honeymoon. Alone, we could talk this out." He chanced moving into her body, hoping to find warmth and love there. "Just the two of us."

"You can't go away now. Not while you're still trying to build the business."

"Forget the business. This isn't about money. It's about us."

"We need money to live, Damon," she said as if speaking to a simpleton.

His anger flared. It wasn't the shock of her words that made him mad. It was the realization that his own wife couldn't stand the thought of being alone with him. "Look around, Barbara. Everything I own is in this house. How could I make money more of a priority?"

Barbara followed him into the garage, seeing the damage to his car for the first time. "What happened to your car?"

"I had an accident. I'll put it in the shop next week."

Her tone and demeanor shifted. The whining and soul-wrenching accusations of betrayal disappeared. She seized the perfect opportunity. A sly grin crossed her face. "This would be a good time for me to buy the Audi."

No matter how much he tried to ignore it, or blame himself for allowing it to happen. Barbara wanted him olny for his money. She didn't want to work for the finer things in life. She wanted him to earn them for her. It didn't bother her that he was stretching himself financially to cover the costs of the cars, the clothes, the jewelry and the new house. She didn't care about him being on an emotional roller coaster. His distress over finding out he had been an absentee father five years of his daughter's life didn't matter to her. She didn't care about him at all.

"Damon," she called as he climbed into his Land Rover. "What about the Audi?"

∞

By the time Neal made it home, he had worked himself into a frenzy. Trying to justify his need for Brooke had made him more determined to assert his rights when it came to Rebecca.

"Where have you been?" Ella asked when he walked into their bedroom.

"I had a lot of papers to grade."

"You have a teaching assistant to help you grade papers."

He tugged at his tie, reaching for the phone.

"Who are you calling this late at night?"

"What's with all the questions?" He punched in Brooke's number. When she answered, he blurted, "I want to see Rebecca."

"Okay."

Expecting an argument, he remained cold and business-like. "I'll pick her up after school for the weekend."

"As usual."

There was awkward silence. He wanted her to protest, giving him a good reason to fight with her.

"Neal, I know this is hard for you."

"Goodbye, Brooke." He hung up and met the disapproving stare of his wife.

"What was that all about?"

He began undressing. "I want to see Rebecca this weekend."

"You see her every other weekend."

He tossed his shirt over a chair. "I wanted Brooke to know she can't keep Rebecca from me."

"Where are you going with this, Neal?"

"I can't let her go. I've tried to convince myself to let Damon take over, but I can't." He slipped into his pajama bottoms and climbed into bed. "I wish I had never gotten that paternity test."

Ella took his face inside the warmth of her hands. "It's best to know the truth."

"What is the truth? It doesn't matter what a piece of paper says. Rebecca is *my* daughter. The problem with the truth is that I've lost all my rights as Rebecca's father. I'm not so worried about Brooke, and I'll fight Damon every step of the way if he tries to shut me out. The problem will be with Kurtis. He's been trying to get me out of the picture for months. Now there's little I can do to stop him from adopting Rebecca."

Ella dropped her hands to his waist and listened for the first time to his pain. "It's Damon's fight now."

He continued on, not hearing her. "Rebecca's such a loving child, she'll fall for Kurtis's insincere charm, and I'll be history. I wouldn't be surprised if while we're fighting, Damon comes up and steals her away from us all."

"Why would Damon plot to turn Rebecca against you? You're being paranoid."

"Paranoid? Did you notice the way he was looking at Brooke at Sinbad's?" Something in his wife's face told him he hadn't imagined what he'd seen. When Ella didn't answer, he admitted dejectedly, "He still loves her."

❦

"You're going to pay child support?" Barbara snatched Damon's checkbook and flung it across the living room, picking up the argument where'd they'd left off that morning before he went to work. She'd been going through his desk while he was at work, checking their finances. She never concerned herself with balancing checkbooks or paying bills. She asked for what she wanted, and expected to get it. It was his job to carry the financial burden for their family, and that meant the emotional stress of trying to make ends meet, too.

"Rebecca's my daughter and I'm obligated to support her. If I don't live up to my obligations, how can I ask to see her?"

"She doesn't even know you're her father, and you're going to take money away from your real family to give to Brooke? I thought Neal paid her private school tuition."

"He does."

"And she's engaged to the accountant. Brooke has money rolling in from all directions."

There would be no peace for him tonight. "I've made up my mind. Rebecca's my child and I'm going to support her just like I support your children." Barbara didn't care about him, but the money was enough to get her riled.

"How could you make this decision without discussing it with me first?"

"We've been fighting about Rebecca since I got the test results back. Everything's settled. There's nothing else to talk about. I have to take care of my child. I'm not going to take anything away from you, the kids, or the house. The money I'll give Rebecca will come out of my personal savings."

"I can't believe this!" Barbara shouted.

"Stop before you say something you can't take back."

"What does that mean?"

"It means, I don't like the way you're putting me down for living up to my responsibilities. I'm not throwing away money on alcohol, gambling, or women. I'm doing for my child. You haven't been supportive of me or what I'm going through since this began. Not once have you asked me to tell you about Rebecca. You've never asked to meet her. You didn't suggest Lisa and Roger get to know their stepsister. I wanted you to help me deal with this. All you've done is shoot me down—and complain about the money I want to give to my daughter."

"I'll never accept a bastard child my husband had outside of our marriage."

She had finally crossed the line that would make him stop trying to understand her feelings about the situation.

"What did you say?"

She crossed her arms over her chest and stuck out her hip. "You heard me, Damon."

"I've taken in your children and provided for them like they were my own. As far as I was concerned, if I loved you, I loved them. When I married you, they became my children. I never treated them any differently than I would have treated my own children. How can you stand here and talk about Rebecca that way?"

She didn't have a snappy comeback. Maybe she realized she'd pushed too far.

He asked the question that burned on his mind every night when he came home to her cold reception. "Do you love me, Barbara?"

Her mouth twisted into a frown. "Don't be silly."

"That's not an answer."

"Of course I do."

He saw the truth in her eyes. "Say it."

"Say what?" She turned away.

"Turn around and tell me you love me."

She didn't move.

"Okay. Just tell me you love me."

Her back tensed.

"When did you stop?" It hurt him to ask, but he needed the truth. The truth would help him sort through his own feelings.

"I'm not having this discussion, Damon."

The truth hit him with such force it made him take a step back and away from Barbara. Or maybe he moved away because he didn't trust himself to be this close to her. "Did you ever love me?"

"Don't ask me that."

"You can't look me in the eyes and tell me you love me? I'm your husband. If you can't do that simple thing, why are we together?"

This got a reaction from her. Somewhere deep inside, he held onto the hope that they could rebuild, and find new ways to fall in love again. If only she would tell him she still loved him, or at least she had loved him once, they could try to repair their marriage.

Barbara swung around, and hit him with the last words he would have ever imagined. "You're not leaving me with these bills!"

He stood speechless. It wasn't the shock of learning she didn't love him. He had suspected as much for months. The way she rationed out sex to get what she wanted was a big clue. What made him speechless was the fact he was still living with a woman who thought of him only as her personal checkbook. Without another word, he went to the closet and packed his suitcase.

CHAPTER 13

"Rebecca, why don't you wait in the office while I talk with your father?" Rebecca's teacher was a nun who justified her existence by educating children. She took her work seriously because it was her salvation. She had a reputation for being a little hard on the children, but "kids today lack discipline." Brooke had expressed her reservations about sending Rebecca to a school run by nuns, but Neal reminded her he had been educated there, effectively shutting down her argument.

Neal accompanied the nun to her desk, reliving his own days of mischief at the school. "Is there a problem, Sister Peter?"

"As the leader of the teachers on this team, I have been asked to speak to you about Rebecca's behavior."

"Her behavior?"

"I'm as surprised as you are, Professor Kirby." She swiveled in her chair to face him. "Rebecca has been quite…challenging lately. As you can see by her progress report, her grades are slipping. This has only occurred on a few assignments, but because she's one of my brightest students, I wanted to bring it to your attention immediately."

He listened to Sister Peter rattle on about her distress over the situation as he read the report. Rebecca had failing grades in science and art her two favorite subjects.

"I assure you I'll talk with her mother, and together we'll get her back on track." Neal folded the progress report and placed it inside the breast pocket of his suit.

"Professor Kirby, Rebecca has become quite aggressive on the playground with the other children. She's been denied recess twice this week, once by me. The other teachers on the team have complained about her sassy attitude, and stubborn behavior. It's so uncharacteristic of Rebecca to act this way that we decided a parent conference was in order. "We simply don't tolerate this type of behavior here at the academy," Sister Peter said.

"I don't know what's come over her," Neal apologized. "My daughter is bright and well-mannered. She enjoys school. This just doesn't sound like Rebecca."

"It's my experience," Sister Peter said, "that children act out when there are problems at home. Is there anything going on which might be affecting her negatively?"

He would not confide his personal problems to the nun who controlled his daughter's academic future. He knew the source of Rebecca's acting out, and he would take care of it, but he wouldn't discuss their personal problems with a stranger. "I'm sorry you've had to deal with these problems, Sister Peter. I promise you, you'll notice a significant change in Rebecca's behavior come Monday." He stood, ending the conversation. "Thank you for bringing this to my attention." He fished his card from his wallet. His phone numbers were on file in the office, but he wanted Sister Peter to be able to contact him directly, eliminating the chances of him being cut out of Rebecca's school life. "If you don't see a change, or anything else arises, don't hesitate to call me."

Before going to her office, Brooke stopped in the convention hall to speak with the audio-visual and catering departments. She was successful at smiling while interacting with the staff, when inside she fought the effects of her shattering world. Neal had called yesterday after picking Rebecca up from school for their weekend visit. He blamed Rebecca's declining grades and unruly behavior on Damon's newfound status as her father. She'd listened to him rant and rave about all the hard work he'd put into securing Rebecca's educational future. He used the opportunity to reiterate his point that Rebecca should not be told about Damon. "If she's having this kind of trouble already, just think what will happen when she learns the truth," he had argued.

Brooke had reached the opposite conclusion. Maybe Rebecca was starting to act out because she sensed the tension between the grown-ups in her life. She would be failing Rebecca as a parent if she didn't get this situation under control soon. It was time to tell Rebecca the truth. She'd considered waiting until Rebecca was older, and better able to understand, but with Neal's constant demands, she'd find out soon, and Brooke didn't want it to happen by accident. She wanted her daughter to know the truth, and not have to live her life on a lie. The sooner Rebecca was told, the quicker Damon could get involved as a parent. He'd been patient so far, but he'd made it clear at the dinner he wanted to be a part of her life.

"Brooke, can you deal with this guy?" One of her assistance stood in the doorway of her office, motioning over her shoulder. A stocky man approached, talking to no one in particular, and motioning wildly to encompass the expanse of the hotel. "He's a wedding planner, and he's very annoying."

Brooke welcomed the distraction from her personal troubles. The assistant handed off the clipboard, and after brief introductions, hurried away. They were in the middle of an extremely busy wedding season. Caterers, decorators, and brides-to-be flooded the hotel. She'd learned to handle anxious brides, reluctant grooms and unbearable wedding planners long ago. She'd found nodding and silently agreeing went a long way. She escorted the obnoxious wedding planner back to the chapel where the future bride, maid of honor, and the bride's mother waited.

"They expect you to work wonders", the wedding planner said, sighing loudly before he pushed the bride-to-be down the aisle to practice her entrance. His hips wiggled more than the bride's did. He hurried back up the aisle to Brooke, rolling his eyes dramatically. "Let me give you a piece of advice. Don't skimp, and don't wait until the last minute to plan your wedding."

"I'm not getting married."

He lifted her left hand. "Looks like someone loves you—a lot." He clapped his hands together, gathering the wedding party. "We have much work to do!"

Brooke watched the wedding planner go. Kurtis had refused to take the ring back, and it had been on her hand so long, she'd forgotten it. It just went to show her heart wasn't into her relationship with Kurtis. She regretted hurting him, but she as she watched the giddy bride-to-be laugh with her maid of honor, she didn't regret her decision to call off their relationship. She should have been as happy. And she would be, when she found the right man. Kurtis wasn't that man. She twisted the ring off her finger, admiring the beauty of it, but cringing at the symbol of the mistake she'd almost made.

"Ms. Foster, you have a caller holding in your office."

Brooke almost questioned why the receptionist didn't take a message, or put the caller into her voicemail, but she welcomed the dismissal from the wedding planner's antics. She returned to her office, slipping the ring inside the tiny pocket of her purse. First chance, she would mail it back to Kurtis, cutting all their ties.

"Brooke Foster, can I help you?" she asked, sounding less stressed than she had in weeks.

"Brooke, it's Damon. I thought I might find you there when you didn't answer at home."

Her grip tightened on the phone. She didn't like being caught off guard. She felt as if she were being ambushed. So far she and Damon had managed to remain civil with each other. Neal and Kurtis were angry and confrontational. She didn't want Damon mad at her too.

"I hope I'm not interrupting," Damon said. She had been too quiet, too long.

"No, it's a slow day. What can I do for you?"

"I was hoping I could talk with you. Today. The two of us can sit down together and resolve this without the bickering."

"We were the two most levelheaded people at the dinner."

"That's not saying much."

"You're right. It was a mess."

"We're Rebecca's parents." His words were matter-of-fact, but held an intimate heat in their implication. "Are you busy later?"

"Do you want to meet for a late lunch?"

"I don't want to have this discussion at a restaurant."

No, he wouldn't want that. The last time had proven to be a disaster. "Can you come by my place in a couple of hours?"

He sounded relieved. "Just need directions."

<hr>

"What's wrong now?" Ella jumped out of the way as Rebecca ran by, crying.

"My daughter has turned into quite a hellcat since Damon came into her life."

"Damon isn't in her life yet. Why is she so upset?"

"I'm punishing her for poor grades and a bad attitude." He handed her a note from Rebecca's school. "I've planned her future down to the smallest detail—nothing will ruin it. And if Damon can't get on the train, he better get off the tracks." Neal stormed past her to their bedroom.

"What are you talking about?"

The door shut with a thud.

"Neal?"

Ella read the progress report and understood why Neal was so upset. Education was of paramount importance to him. He hadn't exaggerated when he said he had planned Rebecca's academic future through college. Receiving this progress report must have sent him over the edge. He always indulged Rebecca. His displeasure must have come as a shock.

Ella stood in the middle of her living room, listening to Rebecca sob behind one door, and Neal make slamming noises behind their closed bedroom door. She didn't know who to comfort first. She wasn't mother material. Rebecca was a good child, but Ella had never wanted the burden of caring for someone who needed her to supply them with everything for their survival. She was a practical person, who had selected a practical profession—medicine. And damn them all, her specialty was genetics.

Ella knocked on Rebecca's door before she entered. Several of the grades were low, but the rest weren't bad. The comments about her attitude were concerning, but Ella wasn't sure it merited Neal's severe response. This was about something else.

Ella felt sorry for Rebecca for being placed in the middle of three posturing men, especially since she had been the catalyst for it all. As a geneticist, she couldn't ignore the facts. She had conducted research studies about DNA and genetics for years. Rebecca's eye color alone had raised questions, that unusual mixture of dark greens when the light hit them just right. Any other person wouldn't have noticed, but Ella had because it was her job to pick up such subtleties.

The entire time she was dating Neal, Ella had wanted question him about Rebecca being his daughter, but he loved the child so much she couldn't hurt him. Once they were married and she had to witness the amorous eye contact he made with Brooke, she wanted his paternity established. She needed all the ammunition she could gather to keep her husband. She hadn't waited so long to marry just to end up a statistic. When Kurtis started pushing to adopt Rebecca, she had used Neal's fear of losing his daughter to broach the paternity subject. She had just wanted to strengthen her hold on Neal. She'd had no idea things would turn into total chaos.

Ella was fond of Rebecca, having grown to care for her very much during her visits. If she'd ever wanted children, she would have wanted one as pretty and sweet and intelligent as Rebecca. The problem was, she didn't want children. And she didn't want to raise someone else's child. The harsh reality was that neither she nor Neal was Rebecca's parents, which relieved them of their responsibilities toward the child. It wasn't a financial concern—the emotional toll was too costly.

And getting costlier since Kurtis had so bluntly pointed out Neal still had feelings for Brooke. Neal consciously shielded his emotions when he looked at Brooke, as if he were trying to hide something. Ella had always thought it strange how amicably they got along. Given the history of their brief relationship, and how he had refused to acknowledge Brooke's pregnancy, it didn't make sense—unless Brooke was some kind of saint. Ella wouldn't have ever forgiven him for not being a man and living up to his responsibilities by legally recognizing his daughter. But Brooke had proven herself the better woman by allowing Neal to become involved in Rebecca's life at his own pace.

Ella wondered if Neal was as committed to Rebecca's future as much as he claimed, or if he used her as his connection to Brooke. He'd insisted on putting Rebecca in the best private school in the state and had not let Brooke pay any of the bill. Rebecca had more clothes and shoes in her closet than Mia, the country's top model. He had even helped Brooke purchase a car, justifying it by saying he wanted Rebecca to ride in something safe. There were plenty of reasonable cars with high safety ratings—why did Brooke need a Mercedes? But the car had been purchased before Neal asked Ella to marry him, so she remained quiet.

In addition to all of this, he continued to pay a hefty sum in child support. Brooke had a good job with a good salary, but Neal was adamant about carrying the financial burden for Rebecca. Ella was beginning to see his efforts as a method to control Brooke. He was becoming more fixated on Rebecca, wanting to take a more prominent role in her life. He defended his parental rights while still protecting Brooke. Even in his anger over learning he wasn't Rebecca's father, he defended Brooke's character.

Since all had been revealed, Neal was putting in extra hours at the university. Many nights he didn't come home until Ella was already in bed. It seemed she spent most of her time waiting for him. Waiting for him to come home. Waiting for him to join her at a function. Waiting for him to make love to her again.

She chastised herself for being silly. Neal could be trusted. He wasn't one of those men who cheated on their wives.

But how could she ignore him coming home night after night, freshly showered, and disinterested in making love to her?

She sat on Rebecca's bed, trying to think of reassuring words to quiet her crying. Before she could find the right thing to say, Rebecca shot up and draped her arms around her neck. Her heart melted just a little, and she wondered if she would regret pushing Neal into testing his paternity.

"The cabbage patch dance and brush waves." Damon threw his head back and laughed. He'd always been handsome, but he'd matured into a well-polished adult. His quiet mannerisms were deceiving. He was smart and ambitious, able to ensnare a person with his unexpected magnetism.

"Okay, you've stumped me. How can you remember all the fads from so long ago? I barely remember what classes I took in high school." Brooke's amnesia might have something to do with how much she'd loved him. They'd been inseparable from the first day they'd met. Every memory of her high school experience was attached to Damon.

"I haven't had a good appetite in weeks," Brooke said, refreshing his glass of wine. They sat together on the floor of her townhouse sharing a plate of tacos. After a brief awkwardness, ended by reliving their past, she had thrown together a quick dinner.

"Since dinner at Sinbad's? My stomach has been in knots, too." He stretched his legs out. "And it has nothing to do with the food they served."

Brooke put down her wine. "What are we doing, Damon? This," she motioned between them, "fighting isn't us. In all the years I've known you, I can't remember us having trouble communicating."

"We need to handle this between us. Neal, Barbara and Kurtis are muddying the waters."

"We don't have to worry about Kurtis interfering anymore." She cast her eyes away from him.

"What do you mean?"

"I called off the engagement, and broke off the relationship."

"Because of what's happening?"

"No." She didn't elaborate.

"Are you okay?"

She nodded. "I didn't want to hurt him, but—" Again, she looked away, remembering she had been the one to end their relationship too.

"Do you want to talk about it? What happened?"

She waved away his concern. "I knew it wasn't what I wanted a long time ago. I didn't have the guts to end it—until now. I have to focus on Rebecca."

"Hey." He touched her arm, sending familiar warmth through her body. "I meant what I said at the restaurant. It doesn't help to place blame. Our lives were crazy, and we were young. People make mistakes. You judge a person by how well they handle their mistakes, and you're trying to make it right. It's all any of us can ask from you."

Probably the most wronged, Damon was the only one who wasn't trying to guilt her into making any decisions in his favor.

"How's Kurtis taking it?" He bit the end off a taco, his tongue catching a long string of melted cheese.

It took her a moment to adjust, sidestepping the effects of the gesture. She shrugged a shoulder, not wanting to let Kurtis invade this rare moment of peace.

"He didn't seem like the kind of guy who would just accept your decision without a fight."

"He's persistent, but I think he understands I'm not going to change my mind." At least he had after he'd returned the ring, and she'd mailed it to his mother's address.

"You don't love him. Anyone who knows you can see it."

His declaration startled her. After all this time, he still claimed to know her.

"How come Kurtis couldn't see it?"

"I care about him, but I don't love him the way he loves me. Aunt Foster says he's arrogant, but he's really been there for me and Rebecca."

"You don't want to end up suffering in a marriage you never wanted. You'd hurt him even more." There was a sadness in his words she didn't dare touch.

"I needed him to support me, you know? I wanted him to understand everything in my life isn't about him. I don't think he ever got that."

"Hmm," Damon grunted. He tried to look casual, finishing off his taco and following it with a drink of wine, but Brooke knew those eyes and how every emotion was displayed in them.

"What?"

He watched closely for her reaction. "I left Barbara."

"Damon. I'm sorry." Her eyes burned, and it took her a moment to understand why she felt so bad. She rubbed her temples, fighting a sudden headache. She turned away from him, ashamed her actions had caused this to happen. How could she ever make it up to him? Revealing he had a daughter, taking the blame for the time he'd lost with Rebecca—that could be made up. He could spend time with Rebecca, and build a strong relationship with her. She was young. It wasn't too late. But this was different.

"I never meant to destroy your life."

"What?" His voice was soft, unbelieving.

She turned to him and faced up to her mistake. "It seems it's all I ever do."

He knew what she meant, she could see it in his eyes, but he chose to ignore it. He wouldn't blame or accuse her of ending their relationship too soon because she was curious about another man.

"Sorry, Brooke. I can't let you be the martyr this time." His voice held no malice, just truth. "Like with you with Kurtis, I've known it wasn't going to work out between Barbara and me for a long time. I wanted to be sure I was making the right decision in ending my marriage. I knew once I left, I'd never go back. Never. I had to be sure it was really over."

She nodded, accepting his explanation because he wouldn't lie to her. "I can't help feeling my bringing Rebecca into your life had something to do with the marriage ending now."

"Probably, but it was going to happen. I'm not sure I want to put the blame on you. When Barbara refused to accept me wanting to be in Rebecca's life, I knew I couldn't choose her over my daughter. She should have never asked me to choose. I've been a father to her kids—as much as I could. I wanted her to be a stepmother to mine. She wanted me to walk away. I couldn't do that."

"I don't know what I should say, Damon."

"Nothing. You don't have to say anything."

The silence around them grew thick and warm, and Brooke felt as if they were snuggled together in a protective blanket. Both of their relationships had fallen apart, but they were able to come together and comfort each other as friends. If they could do this for each other, they could raise Rebecca together, always making the best decisions for her together.

"I'm staying in a hotel near my office until things are finalized," Damon announced.

"Finalized?"

"The divorce."

"You're filing for divorce so soon? Aren't you going to try to wait it out? Maybe when things settle down, Barbara will come around. This is hard for everybody. Once we get into a working routine—"

"This is about more than Rebecca." His lashes dropped, hiding something from her. "I don't want to talk about any more than that."

She honored his wishes, because he would do the same for her. "This is such a giant mess."

"I thought so too, at first. Now I see it as a new beginning."

She stared into his smoldering eyes, unable to separate her old feelings from this new reality. She should not feel this way. So comfortable, so safe, so warm with him. How could she not feel like this? He hadn't changed. Only the calendar was different. It was wrong to have a *reaction* to a married man. But how could she deny her feelings? She could pretend. It was the right thing to do. She could pretend her lingering feelings for him did not exist. He had just left his wife. Romance was the furthest thing from his mind—as it should be from hers. For once in her dealings with Damon, she would do the right thing.

"How do we handle this?" she asked.

"We stop analyzing and just do it. We tell Rebecca I'm her father, and I start getting to know her. It'll be hard on her at first. It's our job to help her through it. Neal is an adult and will have to face the truth."

"You don't want me to cut him out of Rebecca's life."

"From what you've told me, they have a good relationship. I don't want to interfere with it. As long as he doesn't interfere with what I'm trying to build with her. If he does, and it becomes a choice between him or me, I'd expect you to choose me."

"He wants to be there when I tell her."

"It would probably be best that I wasn't. Let Rebecca get used to the idea of another man being her father before you spring me on her." He smiled, trying to lighten the mood.

"I want you to be patient with him."

"Neal?"

"Yes."

He dropped his lashes again, shielding his reaction. "I was patient before, and it didn't work out in my favor."

She didn't know how to respond. For weeks, she'd been working hard at pretending she no longer had feelings for him. She was struggling right now. His comment hurled them back to a critical decision that had ended their relationship.

"I blame myself, " Damon said, his voice too soft, cautious. "In the park, six years ago, I should've refused to let you go. I knew Neal wasn't right for you." He took a long swig of his wine. "If I had fought for you, maybe we'd both be in a different place right now."

And it was too dangerous to ask where that place would be.

CHAPTER 14

"Dad is here!" Rebecca shouted. She'd been standing in the window between the drapes, waiting for him to arrive.

Brooke smoothed her hands down her jeans. Nervous energy had caused her to spend hours twisting Rebecca's hair into tiny braids. Today she'd face hurting her daughter. With Neal's obstinate attitude of late, he'd be sure to let Rebecca know everything was Brooke's fault.

Neal came through the door of her townhouse and scooped Rebecca up into his arms. "Hi." He sat on the sofa with her on his lap.

"Hi." Brooke didn't want to waste any time. Too many years had passed without Rebecca knowing the truth. They'd talked beforehand and decided the straightforward approach would be best.

"Am I going to your house today, Dad?"

Neal glanced across the room at Brooke. "No." He turned Rebecca's shoulders so she was facing him. "Mom and I need to talk to you about something."

Brooke moved next to them on the sofa. "It's something very grown up, so I need you to be a big girl for me, okay?"

Rebecca nodded. Her innocent face almost made Brooke back out. What would be the harm in letting Rebecca believe Neal was her father? Couldn't Damon be an uncle? She knew he'd never settle for playing uncle to his daughter. She owed her daughter much more than to make the situation easy on herself.

Neal took over. "You're a very special girl."

"You have a dad that loves you very much," Brooke added.

Rebecca gave Neal a hug.

"And no matter what, I'll always love you." He returned her hug and kissed her cheek.

"Dad is your father because he loves you, and he takes care of you."

"I know." Rebecca grinned at her.

"Some kids are lucky enough to have two dads. One dad because he loves you so much, and one dad because he helped me make you."

"I don't need two dads."

"Think about how much Dad loves you. Wouldn't it be nice to have two people love you that much?" Brooke tried to reason.

"That's what Kurtis is for."

Floundering, Brooke looked to Neal.

He was firm, but gentle. "Rebecca, another man helped your mom make you, and he wants to meet you."

"I don't want to meet him," Rebecca whined.

"This is one of those things you don't want to do, but you have to anyway," Neal told her. "He wants to meet you. He made you, so he can."

"I don't want to meet him," Rebecca repeated, rapidly blinking away the threatening tears. She didn't understand everything they'd said, but the tension between Brooke and Neal told her this wasn't good.

"Your other dad wants a chance to love you, too," Brooke told her.

"I don't want him to love me." She twisted to face Neal. "I don't have to let him love me do I, Dad?"

He challenged Brooke with his eyes.

"You have to meet him," Brooke said.

"Do I, Dad?"

"Yes," he cleared his throat, "you do."

"Are you going away?"

"No. Never."

Rebecca looked between Brooke and Neal, clearly confused about why she was being forced to let another "dad" love her.

"Listen." Neal hugged her close. "This is one of those things you have to do, even though you really don't want to. But I'll tell you something. I love you, and I'm not going away. You'll meet your other dad, and you'll be polite to him but I'll always be your father." He pulled Rebecca into his chest, avoiding Brooke's disapproving glare.

CHAPTER 15

Barbara found the purse she had carried to dinner at Sinbad's restaurant in the top of her closet. She rifled through it, finding what she needed zipped inside the side pocket. She ran her nail over the embossed gold lettering of the elaborately printed business card. She flipped it over; reading the numbers Kurtis had sprawled across the back. Even his business card was a sign of his insecurity. She'd use his diffidence to get her husband back along with the fact he hadn't been able to keep his eyes off her legs during the entire dinner. When the arguing began, he'd immediately taken her side, becoming an ally.

Kurtis had questioned Neal's attraction to Brooke in front of a table of strangers. He wasn't confident about his relationship with her. Barbara would convert his uncertainty into jealousy, which would help her cause. She had no doubt her charms would work on him. She had deliberately brushed his calf with her foot at dinner, and he hadn't moved away. Instead, he had offered her his business card as security escorted them out of the restaurant.

A few hints about Damon spending too much time with Brooke should be enough to get him going. She had to be proactive. Going back to work wasn't an option. She could never maintain her lifestyle on minimum wages, and she hadn't been married to Damon long enough to fight for alimony. She'd like nothing more than to let him go. She'd listened to him preach about the ethics of taking care of a daughter he didn't even know more than enough. This was about finance, not love, and she'd told her friends on many occasions she'd never go back to the life of poverty she'd known before meeting him.

She waited patiently for Kurtis's secretary to put her through. She rehearsed her role as she pictured his surprise at learning she was on the line. The fool would fall all over himself to accept her call. She wondered how long she'd be able to stomach his pompous attitude. No matter how irritating, she had to deal with him until Damon came back.

"Barbara? Sorry for keeping you on hold. This is a surprise. I didn't expect you to call," Kurtis rambled.

She made her voice quiver on cue. "I didn't know who to call… It's Damon. He left me. He's been spending so much time with you and Brooke. I hoped maybe you could encourage him to talk me about what he's doing. Calling you isn't the most appropriate way to handle this, but I'm trying to save my marriage."

"Barbara, please calm down."

She sniffled. "I don't know what to do."

"Don't cry. Please."

She had him. "Can you help me?"

"I'd like to, but—"

"Oh! I'm sorry. I've put you in a bad position."

"No, it's not…" He paused. "Brooke and I aren't seeing each other anymore."

"Not seeing each other?" She hadn't planned for this. "I didn't know."

"How could you have?"

"Did your break up have anything to do with Damon?" She liked being right, but not in this case. Brooke was a gold digger with eyes for her husband, and with Rebecca as bait, she'd play on his righteousness and have him right where she wanted him.

"I didn't know you had separated," Neal said. "When did it happen?"

"A week ago."

"Brooke cancelled our wedding a week ago."

Brooke had moved fast to steal her husband. "Oh, Kurtis. I'm sorry. Here I am calling you with my problems when you have your own."

"No, it's okay." Another pause. "I have a meeting in five minutes, but I'd like to talk to you about this a little more. We should meet for dinner."

CHAPTER 16

"I remember you," Rebecca said, sliding in next to Brooke in the chair across from the sofa. "You're the man from the park with the funny hair."

Damon smiled, running his fingers through his silky dreads. "How are you?" He was nervous, but delighted to meet his daughter. He glanced at Brooke. Her expression reflected worry about how Rebecca would receive him, and how he would handle it.

Brooke tucked Rebecca's braids behind her ears. "I told you about Damon, remember?"

Rebecca looked up at her, clearly confused.

"The dad who helped me make you," Brooke clarified.

He watched the interaction, questioning how much Rebecca really understand. At five, she was still a baby, not able to grasp adult concepts of heritage.

"You'll like Damon once you get to know him. He's a very nice man."

Rebecca turned to him with distrusting eyes. "I want my Dad."

He swallowed hard under her scrutiny. What if she didn't like him, and never came to accept him as her father? Until now, he'd never considered the possibility—he'd been too distracted by Neal and Kurtis's histrionics. He wanted more than a relationship with Rebecca. He wanted to have a connection with her. "Rebecca, I would like it very much if you gave me a chance to be your friend."

She looked at Brooke.

"Damon is going to take us out for lunch. Go get your jacket."

Rebecca climbed down from the chair and ran off to her room.

"It didn't go *too* badly," Brooke offered.

"It could have gone much worse." He lowered his voice. "Do you think she understands what's going on?"

"She's pretty smart."

He should know that about his daughter. A twinge of anger moved through him. He studied Brooke and knew she could not do the things Barbara had alluded to. Brooke wasn't that kind of person. He'd maintained that position from the beginning, and it was more important than ever to keep the thought in mind now that he was stepping into Rebecca's life. "I want this to go smoothly," he said. "I don't want to inflict any emotional scars on her."

"She sensed the tension between Neal and me, Kurtis and me. She was starting to have problems at school. It was time to tell her."

"I didn't know." He thought aloud, "How would I know?" He didn't intend for it to sound as malicious as it did. His stress over the situation was beginning to boil over.

"I didn't mention it because…"

She should have mentioned it. "Let me guess. You handled it with Neal."

The tension and worry marring her face deepened. He'd hit a nerve, causing her pain, and it didn't make him feel as bad as it should have. Sitting in her living room, no more than a casual guest, being introduced to his daughter as a stranger had upset him. He was having a hard time hiding it. He didn't want to hide it. "This isn't right."

"Neal picked her up from school for his weekend. He had the conference with Rebecca's teacher. I didn't find out until he brought her home on Sunday."

"I'm not talking about that." His voice was soft and careful.

"What?"

He glanced toward Rebecca's room.

"If I could spare her the hurt and confusion, Damon, I would."

He turned to her and let his eyes speak volumes.

She looked as if he had struck her. "You want to blame me. Rebecca, your marriage, everything. It is my fault, and I don't know how to make it right. I'm trying to do what's best for everyone."

"It is what it is."

"This is hard for me, too." Overcome with emotion, she hurried from the room.

"Brooke, I didn't mean—"

He sat alone in the emotionally charged room. He hadn't expected Rebecca to run into his arms, welcoming him into her life. It would take a lot of time, and even more patience on his part. As Brooke focused on doing what was best for Rebecca, who was looking out for her needs? If he believed her, she'd been as surprised as them all to learn Rebecca wasn't Neal's child. And everything came down to whether Damon believed Brooke had never had a clue about Rebecca being his child.

He eased off the sofa and found his way through the townhouse to Brooke's bedroom. She stood at her dresser, wiping away her tears.

"You had to find me and tell me I had a daughter. You broke up with Kurtis. You've been working, and taking care of Rebecca." While her world was spinning out of control, she had to pretend everything was normal for Rebecca's sake. "This has been hard on you."

She faced him. "I would never wish this on anyone."

"None of us are innocent—except Rebecca."

"You have the right to be mad."

He watched her, agreeing. He had the right, but it didn't make it right. And it didn't help the situation at all.

"I didn't want you to see me fall apart."

"I've seen worse. I've done worse." He wanted to pull her into his arms and comfort her. The revelation surprised him. Old emotions washed over him with renewed rigor. He stepped closer. His eyes roamed the soft planes of her face, the fullness of her lips. This close, her sadness was palpable.

"Rebecca has with expressions like yours eyes," she said.

"She does?"

"I don't know how I didn't see it before. Or maybe I did and refused to acknowledge it."

He moved closer. "How long are you going to beat yourself up?"

She watched him, waiting.

"Don't stress over what can't be undone." He embraced her with a light touch, placing his hand in the small of her back, tentatively, expecting her to pull away. He moved next to her, watching her expression in the mirror. "We go on from here."

She watched him in the mirror. "How are you holding up?"

"I'm excited about getting to know my daughter."

She leaned into his hand. "It could have gone a lot worse."

"Much worse." His hand wound around her waist, as he watched her face in the mirror. "Someday we'll look back on the dinner at Sinbad's and laugh."

The corner of her mouth moved upward. "That will be a lot of days from now."

"Mom."

They turned together to see Rebecca standing in the doorway. "Mom, I have my jacket."

⣿

Damon leaned over and whispered in Brooke's ear, "Is this really Rebecca's favorite restaurant?"

"Absolutely."

"Japanese-French fusion is her favorite kind of food?" he asked with humorous disbelief.

"Wait until you see her order. She can't read the menu, but Neal taught her how to order what she wants." Brooke smiled at Rebecca, who had insisted on wearing her very best dress to dinner. Rebecca had also wanted her braids threaded with fancy ribbons pink to complement her burgundy dress. Clearly, Neal's influence on her life.

"I'm impressed." He asked Rebecca, "Do you get good grades in school?"

"My dad says I have to get good grades."

Damon didn't let the comment rattle him. "Do you like school?"

Rebecca nodded, sending her braids bouncing. "Yes. I go to Cambridge Academy."

He looked over at Brooke.

"We were lucky to get her in. She scored high on the aptitude test, and Neal is an alumnus."

He reached for a breadstick, fighting to keep all emotion out of his voice. "Neal has a lot of influence in her life."

"He loves her." Brooke wouldn't discount Neal's involvement in Rebecca's life. He'd been a good father to Rebecca and the paternity test would not be enough to sever their ties.

"I have to wonder if I'm doing the right thing."

Rebecca was preoccupied with the aquariums near by.

"You'll be just as influential in her life. You have to find your fit. You have just as much to offer her."

Brooke encouraged Rebecca to make conversation with Damon as they ate dinner. Understandably, she was shy, but always responded to his questions with polite detachment. Brooke considered the dinner a success all things considered. Damon had been formally introduced to his daughter. Rebecca had been reasonably accepting of him coming into her life. She might not understand the dynamics behind it all, and at her young age, Brooke didn't expect her to. She only wanted them to get along well enough to begin to build a trusting relationship. Damon would have to be prepared for the possibility that Rebecca would accept him as her father, but not bond with him as she had with Neal.

"Time for bed," Brooke told Rebecca once they returned to her townhouse.

Rebecca started to leave the living room.

"What do you say to Damon for taking you to dinner at your favorite restaurant?"

"Thank you."

Damon brushed her hand as she walked by. "You're welcome, sweetheart."

She ambled off to her room.

"I'll be in to tuck you in bed," Brooke called after her. She motioned for Damon to sit with her on the sofa. "Are you happy with how it went?"

"I might have been more nervous than she was. What do you think?"

"I think I was worried for no reason. It went smoothly. She doesn't understand everything, but she'll get there."

"I have to be consistent with her. She has to know I'm in her life permanently."

"What do you mean?"

"I'd like to see her again tomorrow."

"So soon?"

"I've missed five years. I don't want to waste anymore time."

Guilt pierced her heart, killing any argument she would make.

"I shouldn't have said…I didn't mean," he stammered, reading her. She waved away his apology.

After a brief pause, he continued. "Do you have plans for her tomorrow?"

"No, but—"

"Too much time between my visits will be like starting over with her every time."

She nervously straightened her skirt over her legs. "It seems too soon."

"She needs to get comfortable with me in order for us to build a relationship. What are you worried about?"

Looking into his wounded eyes, she knew he wanted only the best for Rebecca, and that included a relationship with her father. "Tomorrow is fine."

"I have to work, but I can rent movies and bring pizza after. If you don't mind having me."

"Okay. It'll be fun." Already she was awaiting his return.

"There's one more thing."

She braced herself. *What more could there be?*

"I want to spend some time alone with her tomorrow."

"Alone? She's not ready. She doesn't know you well enough yet."

"She'll never get to know me if the only time she sees me is with you there. She has to have a relationship with me independent of you."

"I don't know," she hedged.

"A little time alone." His push was gentle, but insistent.

He wouldn't hurt Rebecca. This was Damon the first man Brooke had trusted with her heart.

"Let's see how it goes tomorrow. If she doesn't seem comfortable, we'll wait a little longer."

"Fair enough." Damon smiled, and she was relieved he was willing to compromise. Neal had rarely been ready to negotiate about anything concerning Rebecca.

"Thank you for being so reasonable."

He cast his hazel-green, green-hazel eyes on her and she witnessed them change to reflect heated, undeniable emotions.

"One more thing." He dropped his voice to a warm, smoky tone that swirled around her, wrapping her in the tenderness of forgotten memories. "I forgot to tell you how beautiful you look tonight."

"Mom, I'm ready!" Rebecca called from her bedroom.

Damon stood, taking the heat of his eyes away. "I should go."

She nodded, recovering from the private moment. She showed him to the door.

If there was any doubt on her part that she'd misinterpreted his gaze, they fled when he trapped her with his eyes once more. "Tomorrow."

Guilt brought Damon back home. He woke up early the morning after dinner with Rebecca and Brooke and went to visit his wife. He should try to work out his problems with her. Learning he had a daughter had been traumatic for Barbara. Maybe she didn't mean the things she'd said. The passage of time could make everything better. All marriages had hiccups, and finding out your husband had a five year old, was enough to rattle the strongest couple. If Barbara wanted it, he would try to make it right between them.

Damon entered his house through the garage. All was quiet, as usual for Sunday morning. He found Barbara dressing in their bedroom.

"I didn't hear you come in," she said, brushing past him. She tightened her robe and belted it before sitting on the edge of the bed.

"How are you?" he asked, pulling up a chair to face her. "How are the kids?"

"How do you think we are? You left us here with all these bills."

"I've paid the mortgage and car notes. The bills will always be paid. I'd never leave you in a bad position."

"You left us for a daughter you had never even met."

"I was hoping you would be happier to see me."

Her face twisted in surprise.

"Don't you miss *me* at all?"

Her mouth opened, but she couldn't find the right words to say.

"It shouldn't be this hard to tell me how you feel."

She bolted up and crossed the room. "You left us, and now you come in here expecting me to fawn all over you."

"Why are you being so defensive, Barbara? Why can't you tell me how you feel about me? If you love me, you should tell me."

She stomped over to him. "Are you threatening me?"

"Threatening?"

"You can't come back whenever you want, demanding I make a fool of myself." She hovered over him, shouting. "You have to apologize. You need to tell me you've come to your senses about that little girl. There's no reason for you to get involved in the arrangement Brooke and Neal have. The money you make stays in *this* house with *this* family. You shouldn't have come back here without the keys to my Audi."

"What about the fact that I'm Rebecca's father? Isn't that reason enough to be involved in her life?"

"I'm not going to do this with you." She strutted away from him, and for the first time, her long legs didn't have any effect on him.

"Barbara, I came by to talk to you. I was hoping—"

"Hoping what, Damon?"

"I thought if we talked, maybe we could work things out."

She crossed her arms over her chest. "You know what I want to hear."

"That I'm willing to work on saving this marriage?"

"You're trying to be funny."

Funny? Nothing about the situation was funny.

He stood slowly, carefully forming his question. "Are you willing to accept my daughter into our family?" He approached her. "Think carefully before you answer. What you say will decide the future of our marriage."

"Your place is here—taking care of your family."

"Will you accept my daughter?"

She closed her eyes, and when she looked at him, it was not kind.

"Barbara?" One last plea.

"Will *you* put this family first?"

"Haven't I always? *Will you accept my daughter?*"

"You want me to accept an illegitimate child?"

"It's a simple question, Barbara. Can I bring Rebecca here and know she'll be welcomed?"

"I don't see how—"

"You'll hear from my attorney."

Damon left, never looking back. Only briefly did he regret his decision, because truly the decision had been made long ago, and not by him. He couldn't stay in a loveless marriage where the size of his income determined how much his wife could tolerate him. Other than providing the paycheck, he wasn't needed. He had no emotional attachment to this "family." He felt like a tenant in his own home. After experiencing the brief moments of warmth with Brooke and Rebecca, he knew he'd made a mistake marrying Barbara. She couldn't even tell him she loved him. And he couldn't honestly say he loved her.

As he drove away from his house, he felt a fog lifting. He hadn't realized how trapped his emotions had been. The constant stress nagging at him disappeared gradually, as the miles unfolded. His life was changing, and he could decide what direction it would go. This could be a beginning, or it could be the emotional end to him. He still had his business, and he had a new daughter. He would refocus his life, and make the best of both.

He was excited about building a relationship with Rebecca. He shook his head as he thought of her ordering at the restaurant. She was very bright. She'd have a big future. He wondered what she wanted to be when she grew up. He had so much to learn about her.

Working long hours took on a new meaning. Work wasn't an excuse to stay away from home anymore. Building a prosperous business meant leaving a legacy for his child. She would need a car when she graduated. College tuition was astronomical these days. He'd want her to have the wedding of her dreams.

"She's only five and I'm planning her wedding." He scolded himself for moving too quickly. Rebecca had to know him, and accept him, before he could actively participate in her life. It wouldn't be easy, but he was willing to fight to be in his daughter's life.

One of the first calls he made when he reached his office was to his attorney. He should settle things with Barbara as quickly and painlessly as possible. She would go for his financial jugular. He'd do right by her, but he wouldn't be her fool any longer. He'd make a generous settlement offer and hope for the best. If he remained all business, refusing to negotiate with emotions, he had a chance of coming out of the marriage a whole person. He couldn't fight with her about whether or not she ever loved him. He wouldn't allow her to question his decision to be Rebecca's father. It would be best for everyone to end it quickly and move on with their lives.

He began to make plans, staying focused and not wallowing in regret. If he kept moving forward, everything would be all right. Things would fall into place, and his life would go back to normal in no time. He needed to move out of the hotel and find a real home.

He'd start looking right away, and by the time the divorce was finalized, he be ready to remove the last of his things from the house. He'd have to get a place with a backyard for Rebecca to play, and girls needed their own bedrooms.

He was looking forward to seeing Rebecca this evening. He'd always wanted kids, but Barbara didn't want anymore. He'd become complacent, accepting the fact he'd never have his own children. Rebecca had already proved he shouldn't have settled. He shouldn't have settled for a loveless marriage or not having a family.

He worked for a couple of hours, but couldn't concentrate. Letting go of his emotional baggage made him more excited about seeing Brooke—*Rebecca*, he corrected.

It was so easy to be with Brooke. One dinner, and years of absence had been erased, as if they'd never been separated. It didn't help to pretend he wasn't still attracted to her. She was on his mind every second of the day. He kept Rebecca the priority, but his feelings were a spark, lying dormant, waiting to be ignited.

If only he had known she was carrying his child. He would have fought Neal, refusing to let her go. Things would be much different now.

Rebecca would eventually be comfortable with him, and Brooke's presence wouldn't be needed during his visits with his daughter. He imagined a day when he would show up at Brooke's door and she would send Rebecca out carrying her overnight bag. He pictured waving at Brooke from his car, calling out when he'd bring Rebecca home. The vision didn't fit. It didn't feel right. Especially when his mind saw a man appear behind Brooke in the doorway, possessively holding her as she waved goodbye to Rebecca.

"Kurtis, this isn't a good time." Brooke pulled the door partially closed, shielding his view into her place.

"I know this is unexpected, but I thought we should tell Aunt Foster about us breaking up together."

She saw his actions for what they were: an attempt at remaining in her life. Aunt Foster hadn't been fazed by their break-up. Except to say she never believed he was the right man for *her* niece.

"I'm not going to Aunt Foster's for dinner today."

"You have dinner with her every Sunday." He frowned, questioning her with the sideways tilt of his head.

"I know, but I have other plans."

"Can I see Rebecca before I go?"

Damon's hearty laughter floated over her shoulder. Rebecca's giggles followed.

"This isn't a good time," she repeated.

He tried to look over her shoulder, but she hid the scene inside by holding the door tightly against her back. She didn't have to put up with his irrational jealousy anymore. She no longer had to put up with the constant bickering. They weren't a couple anymore. She had hoped they would remain friends—distant friends—but if he insisted on intruding in her life, she'd have to cut him off entirely.

"I can't come in?" Kurtis asked, indignant over being vanquished to the porch.

She studied his face, searching for any sign of an ulterior motive. "I don't think so."

"I hope you aren't falling for Damon again," he snapped.

"Damon is here to see Rebecca—not that I owe you an explanation." She moved to go inside.

"Wait." He grabbed her hand, desperate. "Are you sure you want to do this?"

She untangled her hand from his grip. "It's over, Kurtis. The sooner you get over it, the sooner we can all move on."

"You think he still cares about you. He doesn't. He's using you."

"Using me? For what? He wants to see his daughter nothing more."

"Do you know he left his wife?"

She folded her arms over her chest. "Yes, I do. How do you know?"

He looked sheepish, but recovered his anger quickly. "Barbara called me. She was upset about him leaving."

Brooke lowered her voice, but didn't hide her disdain. "Damon and Barbara's marital problems are none of my business. They certainly aren't any of yours."

He started to speak, but she held up her hand stopping him. "I don't know how or why you've been communicating with Barbara, but I'm telling you to stay out of it. We aren't a couple anymore, Kurtis. My connection with Damon doesn't concern you. I'm trying to remain friends with you, but if you keep interfering, I'll cut you out of my life completely."

"Do you know why he left her?"

"I don't want to hear this from you."

"He—"

"Goodbye, Kurtis."

"I—"

"Goodbye." She pushed the door closed. When she heard his tires screech out of her driveway, she watched him race down the street from her window. He stopped at the end of her block, idling there for a long time. How much trouble would he become? His jealousy hadn't ended with the termination of their relationship. She began to doubt a friendship with him would ever be possible.

"Brooke?" Damon asked. "Is everything okay?"

Kurtis's tires squealed as he sped off.

"Yeah. Everything's fine."

"Are you sure?"

She turned to him. "It's okay."

He watched her for a moment. "I asked Rebecca to go to the park with me."

She refused to let her doubts resurface about pushing his relationship with Rebecca too quickly. Part of embarking on a new life meant giving up bad habits, and her indecision had always been a source of trouble with her.

"Can I take her to the park?" Damon asked.

"You won't be gone long?"

"A hours—tops."

"Take her sweater."

Rebecca dragged her feet in the dirt underneath the swing. She'd been excited about coming to the park with Damon, but understandably, she was shy once they were alone.

"Would you like a push?"

She nodded, but never looked up at him. "All my friends at school have only one dad."

"And you want to know why you have two?"

She kicked out her tiny feet as he pushed her higher into the air.

"Well, we didn't know you had two dads at first, but now we do, and I'm very happy to be your father."

"Do I have two moms?"

He chuckled at her logic. "No, sweetheart. You have only one mother."

She seemed content with his answers.

"Do you know how lucky you are to have so many people care about you?"

"My friends say I'm weird because I have two dads. They only have one."

"Friends don't call you weird."

"That's what Mom said."

"You're mother is very smart."

"How'd it go?" Brooke was sitting on the top step when Damon pulled his Land Rover into her driveway. She tried to hide it, but she was relieved to see them return.

"Good. She's worn out." He scooped Rebecca up into his arms. "She's so tiny."

Brooke held the door open for him, directing him to Rebecca's bedroom. He placed her on the bed, carefully covering her with a blanket. Replicas of the solar system hung from the ceiling. When Brooke shut off the lights, they glowed in the dark, transporting them into calm vastness of the Milky Way.

"She's into astronomy," Damon said, following Brooke to the living room.

"Completely my influence. Her room at Neal's house looks like Barbie's playhouse." She read something in his expression. "Sorry."

"It's strange finding out you have a daughter, but even stranger to hear her refer to another man as her father."

She didn't know what to say. She couldn't apologize any more than she already had.

"Kurtis was angry earlier," Damon said.

"I wasn't expecting him. He won't intrude on your time with Rebecca anymore."

Damon brought his knee up on the sofa, turning his entire body to her. "He's very jealous about you."

She always seemed to be making excuses for Kurtis's behavior. "He'll have to get over it. We're not together anymore."

The last thing she needed was for Damon and Kurtis to be at odds. She wanted things to go as smoothly as possible with Damon and Rebecca. She wouldn't let her ex-boyfriend cause unnecessary problems.

Damon continued, watching her closely. "Someone should tell him to get over you." His voice dropped to a seductive whisper.

"I made it clear today."

His eyes darkened, heated and eager. "I know how he feels."

"Barbara."

"No."

She watched him, and the message was clear.

"Not Barbara."

Someone had to be rational. "Emotions get out of control in this type of situation. After time passes, everyone will come to their senses."

Damon continued as if she hadn't spoken. "I made a huge mistake letting you go once."

"Damon."

Before she could recover and be the rational one, he added, "I wouldn't let it happen again."

"You're speaking in hypotheticals, right?"

He didn't say a word. He didn't have to. His eyes burned with the answer.

"You understand this is all about Rebecca?"

He nodded. "The more time I spend with Rebecca, the more she'll grow to like me."

She laughed nervously. She had misunderstood. She was projecting her salacious thoughts onto him.

"I wonder. The more time I spend with you, will you grow to like me more?"

He'd stunned her into silence. She should stop this in its tracks, but she couldn't because she wanted it to go as far as it could.

"Is your break up with Kurtis temporary?"

"No, but—"

"My lawyer started the paperwork today. For my divorce."

"I shouldn't be involved in your relationship with Barbara."

"Rebecca brought us back together." He reached out and touched a tendril of hair that had escaped her ponytail. He leaned toward her, dropping his voice to a barely audible whisper. "It's up to us to figure out what that means."

CHAPTER 17

Neal had to turn to someone else. Anyone would understand.

He was so stressed over the Rebecca situation. Over the last four months, he'd stood back and watched as his time with Rebecca began to dwindle. His three-day, every-other-weekend visits with her had been reduced to every-other-Saturday, because Damon wanted to spend more time with her.

Brooke had become more distant. She sent him vibes that made him feel his casual visits to see Rebecca during the week were no longer welcomed. She didn't call him on a whim to talk about Rebecca's last achievements. She didn't need his advice about their daughter anymore.

Ella's response had been to tell him to move on with his life. She'd suggested he delve into a research project for the university to get his mind off things. He *got his mind off things* with the young woman lying next to him.

The girl's short blond hair wouldn't look good on many black women, but she carried it off well. It had been the thing to attract him to her. She sat in the back of his Thursday evening class, looking bored, week after week. He'd first noticed her when she pranced into his class late, changing the seating arrangement of the students who had arrived on time so she could sit in the back of the room. She had presented the challenge he needed to *get his mind off things*.

This girl, Carrie, was unlike the others. She was high-spirited, and had put up many obstacles before she let him in to her bed. She didn't need to sleep with him for grades. She was acing the advanced economics class even though her attendance was poor. There was mutual attraction here—enough to make him consider visiting her regularly to assuage his pain. He ran his fingers through the wool-like texture of her short curls.

"I don't like people to touch my hair," she said.

"I have to leave soon."

"Your wife has you on a short leash."

"I'm my own man."

She yawned, not trying to hide her boredom.

He tossed back the sheets and padded across the room. He knelt to pick up his clothing discarded about the room.

"Make sure you get everything," Carrie called. "I don't want my boyfriend to know you were here."

He froze in the bathroom doorway. "You have a boyfriend?"

"Of course. What did you think?"

"But you'll be giving him up since we're seeing each other, right?" Suddenly feeling overexposed, he clutched his clothing against his nakedness. It became urgent to keep her in his life. His intention had been to salve his frazzled nerves, let her down easily, and go back to his wife. He ended every encounter with his students this way. But her lackadaisical attitude about his leaving made him desperate to stay.

"We're not a couple, Neal." She sounded as if she was speaking to a child. "This was about sex. You have a wife, and I have a boyfriend. Now hurry up and get dressed before he gets home."

Ashamed, he secluded himself in the bathroom while he dressed. A robe and boxers hung on the back of the door. He opened the medicine cabinet and found aftershave and a man's razor. Seeing another man's belongings made him feel violated. He briefly wondered if the students he'd slept with in the past felt this way when he discarded them.

He found Carrie sitting on the edge of the bed wrapped in the crumpled sheet, laughing at a program on television.

"You never mentioned your boyfriend," he said, still hoping to salvage the situation.

"You never talk about your wife." She didn't take her eyes off the television.

"I'll call you."

"Whatever."

He bent to kiss her, and she turned her cheek to him. He left quietly, feeling cheap and used. He was her one-night stand. He found himself drawn to her because she was unobtainable. *He* would be the one to end it with Carrie. He was in charge here. Once his self-esteem was restored, and his needs fulfilled, he would let her go.

Brooke had been involved with Damon when he'd met her. It had been a big adrenaline rush to steal her away from him, a man much younger than himself.

When he reached home, he kicked off his shoes at the front door, and tipped lightly across the carpet to his bedroom.

Ella switched on the lamp, lighting the room.

He laughed nervously. "Sorry I woke you."

"I couldn't sleep."

He kissed her cheek and began to peel off his clothes. "I'm going to take a quick shower."

"I smell her on you."

He froze, trying to decide if he should deny his actions.

"Every time you come back from seeing her, I smell her cheap perfume on your clothes." She sat up against the headboard. "The only reason your things aren't packed and on the doorstep is because I'm not ready to end my marriage."

"Ella, I—"

"Your reputation amongst those in academia precedes you, Neal. My friends warned me. I knew your history, but I thought you would settle down once we were married. You just don't seem like the type of man who fools around on his wife. I was wrong. I've been very clear about what I would, and would not, take from you. You agreed to my terms when we stood at the altar and made it official."

"Ella, I'm sorry. I've been so stressed about losing Rebecca."

"I don't care, Neal."

"I can't let her go."

"How does sleeping with another woman and jeopardizing our marriage replace Rebecca in your heart?"

"No one can replace Rebecca."

"I can tell by your actions how important she is to you," Ella added sarcastically.

"I love her."

"And I love you. But if you come home late again, smelling of another woman's perfume, I won't care so much about this marriage." She wriggled her body down in the bed and shut off the light.

Neal had decided *his* child should go to camp for the summer, and Damon wasn't happy about it. Furthermore, Neal was going to pay the exorbitant bill for the upscale camp. Damon didn't care if the camp was sponsored by Cambridge Academy. Rebecca was too young to go away from home for two whole weeks. He had planned to spend more time with her in the summer. He had even considered taking her on a long weekend trip. He had an opinion on the subject, and it bothered him that no one cared. Most of the big decisions in *his* daughter's life had been made by the ever-present, over-controlling Professor Neal Kirby.

Rebecca's enrollment in Cambridge Academy was another thing. The school was full of children who would grow up to have nicknames like Muffy and Tuffy. Rebecca should attend a school which groomed her exceptional intelligence, but also allowed her to be a child.

Damon knew he should just be thankful Rebecca had accepted him without too many bumps. She'd acted out at a little at school, but lately everything had gone back to normal. Brooke had been uneasy when he first asked to take Rebecca out alone, but their mini-outing at the park had put her at ease. It had taken a while for Rebecca to get over her shyness when alone with him, but she seemed to be more comfortable now. It had been rattling for him the first few times out alone, too. Sharing visitation time with Neal limited how often he was able to see Rebecca. He was trying not to start problems, but wasn't he entitled to see his daughter whenever he wanted to?

CHAPTER 18

"Damon, it's Brooke. I'm in the lobby, can I come up?" She hadn't had a private conversation with him since he'd boldly suggested they explore the possibility of rekindling their relationship. After the heated words, he'd left her townhouse, never mentioning it again. When he visited Rebecca, he never alluded to having any feelings for her. After a while, she began to wonder if she'd imagined the moment between them. She had been trying so hard to suppress her attraction to him maybe she had read the wrong meaning into what he'd said.

She stepped on the elevator, her heart racing as she neared his suite. She'd come to console him, but wondered if she subconsciously had an ulterior motive. When the elevator doors opened, Damon was waiting. He was as sexy as ever, dressed in jeans and a button down shirt. The sleeves were rolled up above his elbows, revealing lean, muscular arms.

"This is a surprise." His eyes flashed deep green as he watched her approach. "Rebecca's not with you?"

"She's spending the night with Neal." He wasn't scheduled to have Rebecca until Friday, but Cambridge Academy was having a half-day of school and Neal had volunteered to pick her up a day earlier. With his visitation being cut down so Damon could spend time with her, Brooke had agreed. "I was worried when I heard your message on my answering machine."

"Come inside." He showed her to his suite, snatching up papers and discarded clothing to make a place for her to sit.

"You didn't have to come," Damon said, sitting too closely beside her on the sofa.

"I thought you might want to talk. Divorce is hard."

"I know it was the right thing to do, but no one wants to feel like they failed."

"There's no chance you'll work things out?" She asked the question because it was what a good friend would do. She knew she would crumple if he told her he still loved Barbara. She had been trying hard to be politically correct. Although she tried to be logical, her heart wanted what it wanted—and it wanted Damon Richmond.

"Barbara doesn't love me. You can't work something like that out."

"Do you still love her?" She held her breath, waiting for his answer.

He watched her with soulful hazel-green eyes. "No," he said, "I don't."

"What happens now?"

"What do I *want* to happen?"

"Isn't it the same question?"

He shook his head.

"What do you *want* to happen?"

"We'll save that discussion for another time. I was about to order dinner. Want to join me?"

Damon's quiet nature seduced her over dinner. His creamy skin highlighted the green in his eyes. His dark hair accentuated the planes of his face. They laid out the feast delivered by the hotel in the middle of the floor and were soon reminiscing about their past.

Brooke laughed hard, remembering their exploits. "We would do anything to be together."

"Every second of the day. If we weren't together physically, we were talking on the phone."

"Every second," she repeated. She didn't know if it was emotion or wine that was making her feel woozy, but her head began to spin.

"I think you drank too much." Damon stood and helped her up from the floor.

She weaved. "You may be right. I don't usually drink more than a glass of wine with dinner. I'm going to have an awful hangover at work tomorrow."

"By tomorrow you'll be so sick you won't be able to go to work. Better start thinking vacation day."

"I have to finalize arrangements on several conventions. I should get going. Maybe I can sleep it off."

"I'm not going to let you drive home when you've been drinking, and I'm not in much better shape. You'll have to stay here." He helped her to the bed. He lifted her feet and placed them on the bed, removing her shoes as she protested.

"Really, I didn't drink that much."

"You can't even stand up." He looked amused. "You said yourself you hardly drink more than one glass at dinner. We've finished more than half of the bottle."

She laughed, not really knowing what was funny. "Maybe I did drink a little too much."

He held the bedcovering as she squirmed underneath.

"I can't take your bed."

"I'll sleep on the floor."

"Don't be silly. This is your room. I should sleep on the floor."

"Good night, Brooke." He started walking away. She watched him push their dishes aside and retrieve blankets from the closet to make a pallet on the floor. He was too tall for the sofa. He removed his shirt, tossing it in the corner. The sleeveless tee gave an unobstructed view of the rippling muscles of his back.

"Damon."

He turned to her.

"We're both adults. We'll both sleep on the bed."

"Only if you promise to stay on your side. I'm a newly divorced man. I'm vulnerable."

She laughed at his attempted humor. "The last time we were in a hotel room together was your senior prom."

"Yeah, but we're old people now. We know better."

Damon removed his shoes and slipped into bed beside her.

Fully clothed, it was still too intimate to simply roll over and go to sleep. "Are you tired?" Brooke asked after twenty minutes of lying side-by-side, staring at the ceiling.

"No."

"What are you thinking?"

He turned his head toward her. "I never recovered from our break up."

She turned her head to face him. "You'll be sorry you said that once you sober up."

"It's funny you mentioned the prom. I was thinking about it today."

"Oh, no." She laughed. "You're lucky my aunt didn't have you arrested. You could be serving time right now."

"Our families were livid." He mixed his laughter with hers. In the cool darkness, it became erotic. "I was so scared to go home the next morning." The laughter died, and was replaced with his deep breathing. He searched for her hand, holding it tightly in his. "It was a special night for me. I'll never forget it."

"It was worth every strike of Aunt Foster's belt."

"Ouch." He laughed, relieving the tension between them.

"Damon?" His name hung in the air for a long moment before he answered.

"Yeah?" His voice was soft, hushed.

"Why'd you marry Barbara?"

"The truth?"

"Always the truth."

He propped up on his elbow, looking down at her. The darkness made it impossible to read his eyes, but she knew him well enough to read the sadness in his voice. "I was very lonely."

His admission crumbled the wall of friendship she was trying to maintain.

He continued, "I'm the type of man who needs to be married. I need the stability. It's a flaw, but I can think of worse ones to have." He exhaled, warming her cheek. "Barbara needed someone as badly as I did for her own reasons. I looked up one day and told myself, *Hey, here is this gorgeous woman who loves you and wants to take care of you. What are you waiting for?* I guess you can say I trained myself to love her, but she never loved me. We were doomed from the start."

"Sorry."

"Tell me about you and Kurtis. He doesn't seem like your type."

"Usually people tell me how lucky I am to have snagged a man like Kurtis."

"He definitely was the lucky one."

She told him about how they met, and the way the relationship evolved without much help from her.

"You were going to marry this man?"

"I was."

"Do you realize you never mentioned being in love with him?"

She hadn't.

"Did you love him?"

She hesitated. "I guess I was lonely, too."

Temptation was being dangled in front of her. They had done a good job of focusing on joint parenting. She had foolishly believed they would be the first man and woman in the world able to overlook their attraction and remain friends. Parenting was all she was prepared to share, she told herself. She warned herself to push away her attraction and resume their friendship.

"Brooke?" When she didn't answer, he laid his head next to hers on the pillow. "Brooke?"

"Yes?"

"Can I ask you a question? You have to answer truthfully."

"Yes, and always."

"Would you like me to kiss you?"

Her insides quivered. Her mouth went dry. She was a teenager again, afraid of being caught in a hotel room with her boyfriend.

Damon breathed shallowly. "Brooke?"

"Yes?"

He draped his arm over her midsection. "I want to kiss you." He ran his thumb across her jaw. Her eyes fluttered with the first stroke. He inched his body closer to hers, slowly and carefully. "Answer truthfully."

She wanted it more than she could ever express in words.

"Would you like me to kiss you, Brooke?"

"Yes," she breathed.

His finger traced the outline of her lips. She grasped his arms, holding tightly to the firm muscles beneath her fingers. Her breath came in short puffs of anticipation. He lowered his head, and she closed her eyes. His mouth hovered above hers. She pulled him closer. He put his mouth to hers, barely touching her lips, but she felt ravished. He exhaled at the impact, and pressed his hand to her cheek.

The stark coldness of his wedding band burned its imprint into her cheek. "Damon, stop."

"What's wrong?"

"Neither one of us wants to make another mistake because we're lonely."

"This is what I want."

"Why are you still wearing your wedding band?"

He started twisting the ring off his finger. It sobered her.

She stopped him by placing her hand on his chest. "Good night, Damon."

He laid his head next to hers, sharing her pillow. "Good night, Brooke."

Damon couldn't sleep. How could he with the object of his desire pressed snuggly against him? He'd removed his wedding band as soon as Brooke drifted off to sleep. Forgetting to remove it had been an oversight not a hidden desire to rekindle his relationship with Barbara. The only rekindling he wanted to do was with Brooke.

The bright sunlight slashed across Brooke's pecan skin. She still slept wildly. His arm was caught beneath her upper body. Her head was on his chest, and her arm around his waist. He glanced at the clock. It was early. His scratched his stomach, and— He hadn't been this aroused since he was seventeen. He lifted her arm, shifted her weight, and eased out of the bed. He couldn't let her find him this way.

Brooke was standing at the window when he returned from his cold shower. She averted her eyes when he emerged wearing only a towel tied around his waist.

"Hangover?" he asked, gathering his clothes.

"Not too bad. You?"

"A little. Do you have time for breakfast before you go?"

"I have to go home and change before work. I didn't want to leave without saying good-bye."

"Let me get dressed and I'll walk you down to your car."

"No, it's not necessary." She moved to the door, avoiding looking in his direction.

"Brooke? Did I complicate things between us last night?"

She turned, resting her back against the door.

"You're rushing out. You can't even look at me."

She rubbed her temples. "Aren't things complicated enough without us involving our feelings for each other?"

"How can we pretend we don't care about each other?" He stepped up to her. "Let me take you to breakfast."

"I have to change for work."

Crushed, he worried he had alienated her. He had waited a respectful amount of time after leaving Barbara to start a relationship with Brooke. He had avoided her for months, picking Rebecca up at the door and never staying longer than it took to make arrangements for his next visit. He ignored the urge to call her during the day. Maybe the wine had loosened him up too much, erroneously making him think she was ready to see him as more than a piece of her past.

"I can whip up a quick breakfast at my place," Brooke offered.

"Do you have time?"

"If you help while I shower, yes."

"It's a deal."

"Meet you at my place."

He dressed in a hurry, reaching Brooke's townhouse shortly after she had arrived. She put him to work in the kitchen while she showered and dressed for work. He was concentrating on flipping omelets without them falling apart when Brooke joined him.

"Looks good," she complimented. She placed four slices of bread in the toaster.

"My treat next time."

She helped him put the omelets onto their plates before adding the toast. He poured their juice and they sat down together.

"I can't remember the last time I sat down like this to have breakfast," he said. "It's nice."

"Rebecca and I start our day together, but it's too hectic to sit down to breakfast. But we always have dinner at the table together. Aunt Foster instilled the importance of family eating together."

"Aunt Foster." He smiled, filled with warm memories of the feisty woman who raised Brooke. "I've thought about her over the years. How's she doing?"

"I'm a little worried about her weight. It's making it hard for her to get around."

"Have you talked to her about it?"

"You know my aunt. She does what she wants to do."

"I'd like to see her."

She tasted her eggs. "Good job." After a few more bites she asked, "Would you like to go to dinner at Aunt Foster's next weekend? Rebecca and I have dinner with her every-other Sunday. She'd love to see you again."

"I'd like that."

They were finishing up when Damon asked, "Can I still pick Rebecca up Saturday?"

She grabbed her juice, taking a long drink. "Neal made plans."

"*I* made plans, Brooke."

"You didn't tell me—"

"You said it would be okay to take her for the day."

"Neal really hasn't been able to see her as much as usual, and he brought tickets to *Muppets Live*."

He pushed his eggs around, seeking calm before he spoke again. "You're trying to make this work so we can both be a part of Rebecca's life, but I don't see how it's going to. I'm her father, and as harsh as it may seem, I should be able to see Rebecca whenever I want."

"Things are going smoothly."

"They are all things considered," he admitted. "But there are things Neal finds important I don't agree with. We're bound to disagree, and I should have more say in Rebecca's life."

"What don't you agree with?"

"This whole Cambridge Academy thing for one. Those children aren't allowed to be kids. They're little robots. She should be at a normal school where she can run and play and make friends. Especially since she's an only child."

"Cambridge Academy is one of the best schools in the country. We're lucky Rebecca was accepted. She has friends here, and at Neal's house she plays all the time."

"Neal has her entire future planned. He wants her to do exactly what he says like a pre-programmed robot a little clone of him. She should have a chance to discover what she wants to do with her life."

Brooke pushed her plate away. "Rebecca is a well-adjusted little girl, Damon."

"I agree she's well-adjusted. You've done an amazing job with her." His appetite was gone. He knew he shouldn't push the issue, especially since they'd had such a good time together last night, but these things had been on his mind. "I can't imagine Cambridge Academy was your first choice of a school for her."

"Neal did choose Cambridge, but it's a prestigious school. She wouldn't have been invited to enroll if it wasn't for Neal's alumnus status and his connections. I wouldn't have been able to afford it without his help. It's an excellent opportunity for her."

"I see *your* beautiful face sitting across from me, but I heard Neal's voice coming from your lips."

"I don't always agree with Neal's suggestions either, but he was right about Cambridge."

"Maybe for his child, but not mine."

"Are you saying I don't know what's best for Rebecca?"

"I want what's best for her, too, and I'm not sure it's Cambridge Academy."

"Why? Because it was Neal's idea?" She began clearing the table. "Neal has done right by her for five years. It's hard to make the absolute right decision about your child each and every time. Don't minimize what it takes to raise a child."

He rose, trying to contain his anger. "If I had known, I would have been here for her—and for you."

"But you didn't know, and you weren't there. Neal was. It's not his fault any more than it's your fault. It's not fair to second-guess how we've chosen to raise Rebecca."

"I'm not trying to be fair, Brooke. I'm trying to be Rebecca's father."

"Do you want me to pull her out of Cambridge?" Her frustration was obvious.

"I don't want to uproot her in the middle of first grade."

"What do you want, Damon? Neal has done so much for Rebecca. They love each other. Excluding him from her life would hurt her as much as it would hurt him."

"I don't want her to go to camp this summer—at least not at Cambridge. She should be able to have fun, and I want to spend time with her. I'll find a day camp for her to attend."

"Fine. You find a camp, and we'll talk about it."

He helped her rinse the dishes. "I don't want to be difficult."

"But you are."

"Would it be better if I didn't care? Don't you want me to take an interest in my daughter? You wouldn't have found me if you didn't."

Her eyes were shooting daggers, but a slight smile was touching her lips.

"You know we can't stay mad at each other," he told her. He pushed her with his hip.

"Don't think you won this argument."

"I don't," he smiled innocently. "You put me right in my place."

"I most definitely did." She tried to hide her smile from him.

"We're not too bad at this parenting thing after all."

CHAPTER 19

"Your son is here," Damon announced as stepped inside the home he had grown up in. His mother wrapped him in a bear hug. "Hi, Mom."

"It's been too long since we had you for dinner." She cupped his face in her palms. His mother's long golden hair had been sacrificed to age. Once it turned white, she chopped it off and styled it to frame her face. She had always been thin. The love emanating from her had always seemed too powerful to come from such a tiny woman. Her forehead had wrinkled, and there were tiny lines around her eyes. It always surprised him how much she had changed when he returned after a long time away from home. In his heart, she would always be young and vibrant. "How are you holding up?"

"I'm fine, Mom."

"Barbara and the kids? How are they handling the divorce?"

"I don't talk to Barbara much. As long as I pay the mortgage, she's happy."

"How long are you going to keep that up?" Her hands fell away, and she pulled him into the living room.

"I told her I'd pay the mortgage for a year. We returned the Lincoln. I have the Land Rover. Barbara has the Mercedes. I'm going to pay the note on it for six months. After that, she's on her own. She'll have to find a job."

"Or another man to support her." His mother's comment didn't surprise him. She had warned him to reconsider marrying her the first time she'd met Lisa and Roger. She'd been somewhat relieved when he announced his divorce.

"You and Daddy doing okay?"

"We're fine."

"You don't need anything? I'll take care of the yard today."

"Your father will tell you he can do it, but he needs to take it easy. He doesn't want to accept we're getting older and can't do everything we used to do."

"Don't worry. I'll take care of it. Where is he?"

"Where is he always?"

Damon found his father in the study watching football. "Your son is here."

"Son." He rose from the sofa to greet Damon.

"Hey, Daddy." He noticed the wrinkles tugging at his father's face and scorned himself for visiting so infrequently. His father usually wore dark turtlenecks and tweed slacks. Relaxing in his favorite room on a Sunday, he watched the game in a dark suit. Appearance and propriety were very important, which was why Damon's relationship with Brooke had been so trying for him. He hoped his father had mellowed over the years, because he had a lot to talk to him about today.

"Sit and watch the game with me until your mother finishes dinner. How's the business doing?"

They discussed his plans to expand Employment Network Unlimited. His father asked about his divorce and his plans for the future. "Your mother explained to me why divorcing Barbara was best, but I—## There wasn't any way to work out your problems?"

"She never loved me. I don't think you can work that out, Daddy. I didn't want to end my marriage either, but I didn't want to be trapped in a loveless marriage, either."

"I see your point." It would be his best offer of acceptance.

Dealing with being a product of a mixed marriage had been traumatic for Damon when he was young. Some still didn't accept racially mixed couples—twenty years ago, it had been much worse. He'd never had many friends, and no matter where they lived, they'd never seemed to be welcomed. It had taken him a long time to realize he couldn't internalize others' intolerance. He had shunned his father's African-American heritage when they lived in the suburbs. He had resented the Caucasian features he inherited from his mother when they settled in urban areas. He often scolded his father for choosing to marry outside his own race. And he rebuked his mother's inability to understand that race did matter. As he looked at his own child through hazel-green eyes, he adored his heritage.

It had taken Brooke's love to show him what was in his heart was the only thing that mattered. She had been a shy kid, rejected by the in-crowd because she couldn't afford the latest fashions. At a time when teenagers were rebelling, Brooke adored her aunt, making her more of an outcast amongst their classmates. Quoting Shakespeare—the lamest thing for a high school senior to do—was what had drawn Brooke to him. He was straddling the fence, trying to hang with the jocks, but maintain good grades so he could get into college. Brooke had allowed him to be his own person. She'd never expected him to be one way or the other. She'd asked him only to be what made him happy.

"Damon has some news," his mother announced over dinner.

"What is it, son?"

He didn't hesitate, learning long ago it was always better to give his father the unpadded truth. "I have a daughter."

His parents looked at each other. They silently exchanged all the questions he knew they would ask.

"We didn't know Barbara was pregnant," his mother said.

"Barbara's not her mother."

"Don't tell me you had an affair." Already his father was becoming angered.

"Rebecca is five years old."

"You better explain, son."

"Brooke Foster called me a few months ago and told me I had a daughter."

"Brooke Foster?" his mother clarified. "Your high school girl-friend?"

He gave them the details they needed to fully understand the situation. "I've been spending time with Rebecca, trying to establish a relationship with her. It's difficult coming into her life so late."

"Your mother and I raised you to be morally responsible."

"I know, Daddy."

"I have a granddaughter?" His mother smiled, trying to contain her happiness until she had a read on his father.

He dug Rebecca's school photo from his wallet and passed it to his mother.

"She's so pretty. And she looks so grown-up."

"She's very smart, and a sweetheart."

His father studied the picture of Rebecca. "If I have a grandbaby, I want to meet her." He handed Damon the photo. "She is a pretty little thing."

⸺⸺ ᪥ ⸺⸺

Aunt Foster joined Brooke on the front porch. She was watching Damon and Rebecca play. Rebecca giggled as Daman chased her around the yard.

"Damon can put together the doll house I bought for Rebecca. It'll help him win some points with her."

"You have to stop spoiling her, Aunt Foster."

"She's a good girl. She can be spoiled a little bit. It's getting cold. She needs something she can play with inside."

"You never spoiled me."

"You were a handful."

Brooke hugged her aunt.

"Let's go inside. Let them have some time alone."

"You're being good about this. I didn't think you liked Damon."

She put her stubby arm around Brooke's waist and led her inside. "You can't protect your children forever. It's the hardest lesson a mother has to learn." Aunt Foster was the only mother figure she'd known.

"You thought you had to protect me from Damon?"

"Of course I did. He was a teenage boy, and you were still a kid."

She took one last peek out the window before joining her aunt in the living room. "They get along well."

"Seems so. Is Neal still coming around?"

"More than ever. He's afraid Damon will steal Rebecca from him."

"Kids have a lot of room in their hearts. She can love both of them."

"You're okay with Neal now?"

She twisted her mouth disapprovingly. "He's always done right by Rebecca. I respect him for it."

Rebecca ran inside, jumping into Aunt Foster's lap.

"Stop running," Brooke corrected her.

"She's fine," Aunt Foster hugged Rebecca tightly.

Damon entered the living room, his face flushed from the chilly temperature. "Thanks for having me for dinner."

"Your welcome. It was good to see you again. I'm glad you're doing well for yourself."

"We should be going," Brooke said. "It's getting late."

"Do we have to?" Rebecca whined, burying her face in Aunt Foster's bosom.

"Let's get all your stuff together." Damon reached out for her. She climbed down from Aunt Foster's lap, and they left to gather her things. Brooke said good-bye and met them at the Land Rover.

Damon steered the SUV off the dirt road, onto the main highway. "It's nice you still have a close relationship with your aunt. Rebecca adores her."

"My aunt spoils her." She turned to check on Rebecca in the backseat. She was asleep. Damon had purchased a booster seat for his SUV and she was securely strapped in, covered with a blanket.

He chuckled. "Remember the time she chased me off the porch with a broom because she caught us kissing?"

"Get the story straight." She laughed with him. "She saw you put your hand up my shirt."

"You're right. I was so clumsy. I wasn't as experienced as you thought I was."

She wondered how making love to him now would be different from the awkward days in the dorm. They would be able to take their time without worrying about roommates or curfews. He wouldn't get over excited. She wouldn't be timid. Silence settled in the SUV. She reached for his hand.

"We were both so young," Damon reflected.

"We thought we knew it all."

"We didn't know anything. Look how we screwed up things between us."

"You always knew what you wanted, and you went out and got it. Look at you. You own your own business just like you said you would. I'm proud of you for living your dream. Rebecca is fortunate to have you for a father."

"I wanted you, but I let you get away."

"Did I?"

"What do you mean?"

"Are you sure I ever really got away from you?"

Damon glanced at her, but didn't answer.

"There has always been a part of my heart that has stayed with you," she admitted.

"I've never gotten over you, Brooke."

They rode in reflective silence the rest of the drive. He pulled the Land Rover into her driveway. "Things are getting better." He hitched his thumb back at Rebecca.

"How'd your parents take the news?"

"They want to meet her. I promised I'd bring her over when I felt she was completely comfortable with me." He stretched his long arm over the backseat, resting his palm against Rebecca's cheek.

"She's a hard sleeper."

"Just like her mother."

CHAPTER 20

"Why'd you ask me to meet you here?" Brooke asked after parking her car next to his in the parking lot of a subdivision still under construction.

"This place serves great breakfasts and I owe you breakfast." He took her hand and started up the sidewalk. "How's Rebecca?"

"Good. Neal picked you up yesterday after school. It's cold, Damon. How far do we have to walk?"

"You're wearing a big sweater and boots. How can you be cold?" He laughed at her.

"How far, Damon?"

"Still afraid of exercise?"

She swatted at him.

"Relax, we're here." He greeted the man admitting them into the clubhouse of the exclusive gated community of Briarcliff Woods. "Are you starving?"

"I am. How did you get invited to breakfast at the Briarcliff Club? I've been hearing about how good the weekend buffets are here. Everyone in town is clamoring to get in here. Membership in the yacht club is almost impossible unless you're wealthy, connected, or—"

"I live here." He pointed out the window to his new house. "I'll show you my place after we eat."

"You've found your own place?"

"I did. It was time. The bill at the hotel was astronomical. Besides, I have to get on with my life."

"Do you like living here?"

"Hard to picture me living in such a haughty place, huh? I actually like it here. It's quiet. The neighborhood is good." He stood and pulled out her chair. "Ready to try the buffet?"

They filled their plates with the delicacies offered at the breakfast buffet. Chefs with tall white hats served them, pronouncing names Damon would never remember. Brooke seemed impressed, holding conversations with each chef she encountered. She asked questions only a person who worked in the hotel industry would want to know. It reminded him of how he had fallen so deeply in love with her so quickly. He enjoyed her inquisitive nature, and the way small things excited her. She liked luxury, but didn't dwell on acquiring it.

"I enjoyed dinner with Aunt Foster," Damon said, alternating bites of eggs and strawberries.

"She told me you sent her flowers and a thank you card. She was impressed. Me too."

"She was the perfect hostess."

"I worry about her a little. She's getting older and slowing down a bit. I've been trying to convince her to move in with me. I have a spare room Rebecca uses as a playroom."

"Your aunt is too independent to move in with you."

"Exactly." She added salt to her hash browns. "I've told her she would be a big help if she was living with me. I can always use help with Rebecca."

"If you need anything, I'm more than happy to take Rebecca. She liked hanging out at my office."

"She did."

He dipped a battered shrimp into sauce.

"How can you eat like this?" Brooke motioned to the wide variety of food he'd chosen from the buffet.

"What do you mean?"

"You have eggs, bagels, shrimp, hot cereal, bacon, and salmon on your plate. How can you eat all those different foods and not get sick?"

"Don't forget the strawberries." He popped one in his mouth. "They're good." He lifted the bowl and offered her one.

"Sweet—and juicy."

His eyes cascaded down her body, agreeing.

"Aunt Foster has to realize she can't keeping living alone. She's isolated from her nearest neighbor by the highway. I tried to get her to move when they first put the road in, but she wouldn't even consider it. If something happened....# The biggest hurdle is getting her to sell the house. Her husband brought the house soon after they were married. It's the last piece of him she has to hold on to. She doesn't want to let it go."

"She'll come around."

"I know. I have to remind myself not to push her. If I do, she'll fight harder."

He sampled more of his food. "Have any plans for the day?"

"No."

"Let's make some."

"I've had a long week at work. A quiet outing works best for me."

"What do you have in mind?"

She smiled. "I'd like to see your new place."

No convenience had been overlooked in the designing of Briarcliff Woods. Across the highway from the gated community was a strip mall with a vast array of services. They stopped at the grocery store for junk food, picked up a bottle of white wine and champagne, and grabbed a few videos.

"This is a nice house," Brooke called from the living room. "It has a lot of potential."

"I need help decorating." His place was a typical bachelor's home. The furnishings were sparse. One bedroom was completely empty, and a huge desk scattered with papers filled the third. The master bedroom and living room were furnished with large screen televisions, and other necessities. Recliners were angled directly in front of both televisions. A black leather sofa and two love seats accented with glass tables to completed the living room. He admitted it took little imagination.

"It looks like you left everything where the deliverymen put it," Brooke said, standing in the middle of the living room.

"Pretty much."

She pulled open the drapes. "You have a view of the marina."

"I should get a boat. Rebecca would like sailing."

She wandered into the master bedroom.

"You have to excuse me. I'm not the best housekeeper." He hurried after her, gathering up the clothing haphazardly discarded from the floor.

"True. I remember your dorm room." She laughed. "I've seen worse." She stood in the bathroom door and watched him shove his dirty clothes in to the hamper. "You're right. You need help decorating."

"Maybe you'll take pity on me and help me out. Did you notice the empty bedroom?"

"I did."

"I'm going to fix it up for Rebecca. I'd like to keep her overnight sometime."

"She'd like that." She stood next to his four-poster bed, testing the mattress by bouncing it with her hand. "You have a fireplace in here." She moved to the mantel, running her hand across the smooth marble. She lifted a framed picture of Rebecca and looked back at him before replacing it.

"I should get a maid to come in a couple of times a week."

"Or you could learn to pick up after yourself."

They grinned at each other.

"I've wanted to do something since I first walked in here." She unzipped her ankle boots and kicked them into a corner.

"What are you up to?"

"The same thing Rebecca would do if she was here."

Before he could ask what, she jumped up on the bed. She squealed, bouncing up in the air. She stood in the middle of the bed, giving him an unobstructed view of every curve. "I knew this would be a good bed to jump on." She started off slowly, winding her arms like a windmill. She giggled like a child, freely enjoying herself.

"Stop jumping on my bed!" He playfully scolded her while gathering up the blankets falling on the floor. "Brooke! Stop it!"

She giggled uncontrollably as she watched him scurry around, cleaning up her mess. "Stop acting like an old man, and have a little fun. Get up here."

"Did you just call me an old man?" He was not amused.

"You're the best looking old man I've ever seen." She jumped higher, wiggly as she squealed with laughter. Her innocence touched him, reminding him of a better time in his life. He watched her, envious of her ability to let go. She noticed him watching her. "Why are you looking at me like that?"

"You're beautiful."

She turned her back on him, teasing him with her generous backside. She spun around, jumping higher and higher.

He became intoxicated with her laughter. "Time to come down," he told her.

"You join me, old man. You need to learn how to laugh. You've always been too serious."

"I'm a thinking man."

"You think too much. Sometimes you have to do what feels good."

Taking her cue, he grabbed her waist, snatching her down into his lap. He brought his face to hers, inhaling the flowery scent of her perfume. She was flawless. Smooth pecan skin, big brown eyes, and full lips made to cushion his thin ones. He smoothed her hair, tucking tendrils behind her ears. "How do you see me now?"

"What do you mean?" Her laughter stopped.

"Am I the same man you met in high school?"

"You are."

He held her tight around the waist, resting his chin on her shoulder. Being near her soothed him.

"I didn't mean anything by the old man crack. I was trying to get you to loosen up."

He liked holding her. She fit well in his lap, her curves molding around the muscles in his thighs. He could keep her in his arms forever.

"Can I jump some more?" She gave him a mischievous grin.

"No, silly."

"C'mon."

"I like the sound of you pleading with me."

"Pleading?" She squirmed out of his lap. "Let's move some boxes around so we can watch the movies."

He watched her walk away, her hips swinging enticingly. He followed, because it was all he could do.

After two movies—they talked more than watched—Brooke decided to help him decorate.

"You're supposed to be having a quiet day. Don't you want me to help?" he asked as she pushed him out of the living room.

"I'll call you if there's heavy lifting. Don't you have work to do?"

Being in the way, he started on dinner. It was nice knowing she was in the other room, touching his things, arranging them in a way she believed he would like. She knew him well. She remembered his likes and dislikes. He pulled two steaks from the refrigerator along with two potatoes and the ingredients for a salad. Steak, baked potatoes, and omelets he could cook. When he got tired of steak, he switched to takeout. He seasoned the steaks, taking special care with the meal. The reversal of roles was refreshing. Brooke would be a true partner in a relationship. They both brought strengths and would support the other's weaknesses.

"Can I help?"

"Everything's finished but the salad."

She washed her hands and searched the refrigerator for tomatoes. She moved next to him at the sink and started on the salad. She dumped the cherry tomatoes in the sink, rinsing them under cold water before popping one into her mouth. "Good," she hummed. "Taste." She held a tomato up to his lips. Her fingertips grazed his lips. Instinctively, he grabbed her hand and held it against his mouth until he had devoured the tomato. He released her, but her hand lingered in mid-air, watching him.

"Yeah," he said, not taking his eyes off her, "it is good."

She turned back to the sink as if the air weren't so warm it was hard to breathe. If not for her trembling hands, he wouldn't have known she felt the heat too.

He broke the silence. "Are you finished in the living room already? It took me all day to arrange the living room."

"Arrange?" She elbowed him. "You put a recliner in front of the television."

"Can I take a look?"

With a few well-placed knickknacks, Brooke had transformed his living room into a comfortably modern room. He wasn't inept, but he lived as most single men did. There was very little food in the refrigerator. His place was furnished with the bare necessitates. Decorating and cooking were out of his league. He planned on having Rebecca regularly, so he had to do better. His refrigerator would have to be stocked with healthy snacks and decent food for making complete meals. She was such a little lady she'd never tolerate her bedroom being unfurnished and bare.

"You need window treatments," Brooke roused him.

"What?"

She grinned. "Curtains, drapes."

"Oh." He turned to her. "Why was it so hard for me to do this?"

She shrugged. "You can't be good at everything— it would make you perfect."

"I'm far from perfect."

"Really?" He couldn't interpret her expression. "Not from where I'm standing."

He let his gaze wander the length of her body. "Are you flirting with me, Brooke?"

"I'm hungry. Let's finish dinner." She walked away, leaving him standing in a cloud of questions. He couldn't get a read on her. Did she plan on having the same kind of relationship with him she had with Neal? Amicable co-parenting? Or did she feel the vibe thumping between them whenever they were in a room together? He followed her into the kitchen, determined to get answers.

Damon licked his lips, and Brooke felt as if he were caressing her most sensitive places. She sat across from him, eager for his touch, but cautious. If he kissed her, she would remember how natural it had been to love him, and all her self-control would disappear. She glanced at him as he carefully spaced the potatoes on a serving dish. As adults, they could walk into his bedroom, lie across his bed, and make love. They didn't have to sneak around behind their parents' backs. They didn't have to balance classes, or schedule meeting time around their dormitory roommates. There were no roadblocks. Not one reason to hide their feelings. He stood too close. She could reach out and touch him. She *should* reach out and touch him. Her heart thumped erratically. This one thing she could do for herself. She wanted him. No matter how hard she tried to deny it, she still had feelings for Damon and no amount of time apart could ever erase them.

"The steaks," he remembered. "I hope I didn't overcook them." He hastily pulled the steaks from the oven, burning his hand on the heated rack.

"Are you okay?"

"Can you get me the butter?"

"Butter to heal a burn is an old wives' tale. Butter is an insulator—it'll only make it worse."

He raised an eyebrow.

"Mothers know these things. You have to place it under cold water." She took his hand and gingerly held it under the water. "I didn't mean to give you a science lesson when you're in pain." She was nervous, rambling on about home remedies. She kept her back to him, concentrating on treating his burn. "It doesn't look too bad. Does it feel better?"

He placed his mouth near her ear. "Much better," he whispered.

The cold water—not his body so close to hers—made her hand icy. "Okay, that should do it." She released his hand, shut off the water.

He grasped the ridge of the sink on either sides of her body. She didn't dare move. If he touched her, she wouldn't be able to continue the façade of friendship any longer. All her desires would spill over for him to see. Each time he exhaled, his warm breath tickled the back of her neck. She didn't dare flinch. He leaned his body against hers from behind, molding the muscles of his chest around her. His hands slid closer together, trapping her between his body and the sink. He blew a puff of air into her ear. "Turn around." His voice was husky with unful-filled desire.

"No," she whimpered. She had to hold it together. She couldn't let emotion overwhelm her until she melted in tears.

"Why not?"

"I'm afraid to."

"Afraid of what? Me?" He nestled his nose in her hair.

"Afraid."

"Afraid of what?"

"What might happen."

"*Might* happen?" His lips touched the space behind her ear.

"Yes."

"It's *definitely* going to happen."

"What?"

"You're going to fall in love with me again."

Her legs buckled.

He pressed his body closer to steady her. "Brooke, don't be afraid."

"I am."

"Why?"

"Just am."

"Maybe you *should* be scared." He licked her earlobe.

"Why?"

"Because I love you too much."

"Impossible."

His fingers wrapped around her jaw. He wiped a tear away with his thumb. "Are you crying?"

"Yes."

"Why?"

"It's scary knowing someone has loved you this much for such a long time."

"It's not like you to be afraid of anything. Don't cry anymore."

She lifted her hand and wiped away the tears.

He held her captive in his arms, pressing her between his body and the sink. "Turn around, Brooke."

"Back up."

"Turn around and look at me."

"No."

"Turn around."

"I can't."

"Turn around and accept me."

"I'm afraid."

"Me too. Turn around and let me make love to you."

"Damon—"

"Turn around, look into my eyes and know I'm real. I promise you everything will be all right."

She twisted her body around in the confined space.

"This is good. This is right. Don't cry anymore." His hands cupped her face, his thumbs wiping away the tears.

"It's been so long."

"Too long."

"I feel the same way I did when I first saw you."

He grinned. "Reciting Shakespeare. You stole my heart that day."

Without warning, his lips consumed hers. She drifted into a clouded haze as he wrapped his arms around her, bringing her securely into his body. He was hard and soft at the same time. His scent reminded her of safe, warm places. As his tongue gently probed her mouth, he took her back to a simpler, better time. He nibbled at her mouth, allowing her time to be comfortable with him again. She released all inhibitions and hugged him close.

He placed a firm grip on her hips, guiding her through the house to his bed. His lips never left hers as they undressed. Every piece of their clothing was removed with the same precision he used to guide her through the house, but never once did his lips leave hers. He moved slowly, patiently, careful not to overwhelm her. He folded back the bed-covering and laid her down in his bed.

"You're shaking," he said, coming to bed with her.

"It's prom night all over again." She was transported back to the hotel where he was about to take her virginity. This time he would not teach her the pleasures locked inside her body. He would teach her the joy of the love hidden in her heart.

He moved over her, caressing her body and kissing her lips. "I want to make love to you—here, now."

She ran her fingers across the softness of his skin, over the hard planes of his back, the smooth dip of his hips. "Damon?"

"Yes?"

"Make love to me."

He loved her unselfishly. She gave to him freely. The joining of their souls undid her, and she cried again. Making love to Damon was powerful. They moaned with pleasure as he moved inside of her. They made the mellow music of reunited lovers. Emotions distorted her face, obscured by the darkness, as he commanded her body to rupture with pleasure. Afraid he would disappear from her life again, she fought the sensations tightening her body. But their love was too powerful to keep locked away. He plunged into her and she lost control, calling his name on the tide of her explosion.

Damon's desire grew, peaking in intensity. His release came without encumbrance.

She held him close, not allowing him to move away.

He kissed her temple. "This is what destroys kingdoms and starts wars."

CHAPTER 21

Damon was still nude when he strutted across the carpet and added a log to the fire. The fireplace across from his bed made the room glow, punctuating the romantic setting. Completely satisfied, Brooke lay on her stomach; legs sprawled on his side of the bed, breathing deeply in her sleep. He smiled, not from arrogance but delight at having pleased her. It felt good to know she enjoyed being with him, and received as much pleasure as she gave. He leaned over her, pushing the stray hairs away from her cheek so he could kiss her there.

She stirred, smiling.

"Would you like something to sleep in?" he whispered.

She rolled over onto her back. "No."

He stroked her hair, enjoying having her with him.

"What do we do now, Damon?"

"Do you want to make love again?" He grinned.

"What do we do about us?"

"Nothing to do."

She caught his hand in hers.

"Sorry."

"What do we do now?" she asked again.

"I'm hungry. Do you want to eat the steaks?"

"It's one in the morning."

"So? We can do whatever we want to do." He was referring to more than eating dinner at one in the morning.

"Maybe I can eat the salad. It's lighter."

"And if the lettuce is wilted?" He was asking about more than the salad they had left on the counter while they made love.

"It's enough for me."

"What if salad isn't enough? What if you're still hungry after all the salad is gone?"

"I'll get full on the salad."

"How do you know?"

"I've had it before, and it filled me up so full that much later, it was still all I needed."

"But you said, *maybe I can eat the salad.* It doesn't sound like you're sure it's what you really want."

"When you're standing in front of a buffet, it's hard to know what *one* thing you truly want until you sample everything there is."

"Better be careful doing that, Brooke. There's a lot to taste. You might get full and walk away before you get to the best part of the buffet."

"You'd never let me walk away without tasting everything."

"Exactly. I'll take care of you. You don't have to ask me to define our relationship. Or ask me what comes next. I'm in this until the end. I won't let you go this time, Brooke."

Damon sat on the floor in front of the fireplace, nude except for his specs. He sat between Brooke's legs as they dangled down from the bed. After they finished the steaks, she had gathered enough energy to shower with him before slipping into one of his t-shirts. He held her tight throughout the night. She hardly believed they had found their way back to each other.

Damon tilted his head up to see her face. "Scratch right there."

She pushed his head back down before putting the wide-tooth comb to his scalp. He purred at her touch. She sectioned his hair in small patches, applying oil to his scalp.

"You're good at this," he said, draping his arms over her thighs.

"It's getting cold."

He pushed himself up from the floor and placed a log on the fire. The muscles in his back flexed as he walked. The high haunches of his behind contracted with each long stride, exciting her. He gathered the logs and then stood his full height, exposing the well-defined muscles in his legs. He turned to her. The smoothness of his creamy light skin was interrupted by the patch of wiry hair framing his erection.

"Are you going to get dressed today?"

"You don't enjoy having me at your advantage?" He held his arms out from his body, giving her a full frontal view. His body was perfection, his silky dreads and hazel-green eyes his finest features.

"How is your being naked my advantage?"

"If you don't know the answer, I need to school you some more Ms. Foster." He moved to his dresser and pulled on a pair of pajama bottoms. "Will this help you control yourself?" he teased. He stoked the fire one last time before returning to his place between her legs.

"I'm glad you're here." He laid his head against her thigh.

"Me too." She continued to massage his scalp in silence. They could be together this way. No television, no music, no conversation. Together. After every section was parted and oiled, she massaged his scalp with the tips of her fingers. She tapped his shoulder, signaling she was finished.

He closed his eyes, letting his head fall back into her lap. "I would give up all my material things for a lifetime of weekends like this," he murmured, wrapped in contentment. He climbed onto the bed, bringing her down underneath him.

"I miss Rebecca."

"Neal brings her home tomorrow?"

She nodded.

"He's been taking her for weekends. Why do you miss her so much?"

She shrugged. "I don't know. It seems different this time."

"She should be here with us. Then we'd be a whole, complete family."

"Everything is happening so fast for you. You find out you're a father, your marriage ends, you buy this *fabulous* house—how are you coping with it all?"

"Don't forget I fell in love with you again."

She pulled him into her arms. "It feels so good to hear those words." She loosened her embrace to see him clearly. "How can you be sure this isn't a rebound relationship for you?"

"Or you."

"How can you be so confident about your feelings after getting out of a bad relationship?"

"I know myself. I know you. And I know how I've always felt about you." He tangled his fingers in her hair. "The key was admitting I never stopped loving you. Once I did, I knew exactly what I wanted."

"I keep bracing myself for something to happen to keep us apart."

He rolled over, taking her with him. He held her tightly against his side. "Have you ever gone to the movies alone to avoid being lonely? It takes your mind off your problems for a short while, even if the flick isn't any good. When the movie ends, the same feelings are haunting you—and you've squandered away valuable time in your life." He kissed the tip of her nose. "What I had with Barbara wasn't real. It solved my problem for a little while, but it was doomed for failure. I really thought I loved her when I married her, but it didn't take long for me to start to question my decision. When you came back into my life, I knew what I wanted. There's never been a question in my mind. Not when we were kids, not now."

They climbed underneath the comforter, and lay in each other's arms watching the fireplace glow.

"How are you doing after breaking up with Kurtis?" Damon asked her.

"It's strange. I miss him sometimes, although I know we weren't right for each other.""These times when you miss him, is it because you still have feelings for him?"

"No. I'm not sure I ever loved him. I think I was having my 'going to the movies alone' moment."

Damon untangled himself from her arms and coaxed her onto her back. He reached for the heated oil she had used on his scalp and began to knead it into the curves of her back. She relaxed as he manipulated her muscles, removing all her tension. She closed her eyes and enjoyed his touch.

"Brooke?"

"Yes?"

"Why did you leave me for Neal?"

She stiffened under the motion of his fingertips. He responded by working her muscles deeper.

"That was so long ago, Damon."

"I should have asked then. I should have found out what was wrong with our relationship and fought for you. If I had, I could have spared us many regrets." His fingers moved to her lower back. "Why did you choose Neal over me?" he asked again.

She was instantly transported back in time to her days at the University.

"Brooke?" He rolled over next to her and stared up at the ceiling.

"Damon, I can't explain why I did what I did. I was young and inexperienced. Things weren't clear. It's hard to explain, even in hindsight. I can't remember the specific thing that made me make the decisions I made. I do know losing you was painful. I spent a lot of years regretting my decision while trying to put you out of my mind. I made a tremendous mistake. I'm sorry."

"Can we start fresh if we don't know what mistakes we made the first time?"

"We're both different people now."

He captured her with troubled eyes. "I know you, Brooke. You remember that time as if it was yesterday. Don't try to shield me from the truth. Be honest with me."

She turned away from his piercing hazel-gone-green eyes. The crackling of the fireplace was a welcomed distraction. When Damon stroked her chin, she knew he would not let the conversation end without an answer.

"It wasn't any one thing. Neal was a distinguished, older, intelligent, local celebrity. Having a man like that lavish you with attention is flattering. Before I knew it, I was involved in something I couldn't handle."

"When you found out you were pregnant, did you think I might be the father?"

"No." She leaned over him, placing her hand on his chest. "I didn't find out until three months after we ended it. If I had, I would have contacted you right away."

Damon held her tight, looking into the fire as he reflected on the past. He planted tiny kisses on her neck.

"Why didn't you come after me?"

His head shot up, meeting her pain head-on. He embraced her face in his palms. "You hurt me so badly when you ended us. I didn't know how to handle it. I didn't know what to do. I tried to save face, keep my ego intact, so I walked away and pretended it didn't matter."

"If you could do it all again?"

"I would have been in your face everyday, convincing you how much you loved me." He pressed his lips to hers, conveying the truth of his words in his kiss. "I never stopped loving you, Brooke."

"I love you, Damon."

He ravished her with his kisses, but his touch remained gentle and loving. He pulled away, resting his head on her breast. "Brooke?"

"Yes?"

"If you could do it all again?"

"In the park…I would have begged you to forgive me."

CHAPTER 22

"Relax, Brooke," Damon said, trying to hold her.

She pulled away, pacing her living room. "Neal is never late returning Rebecca. If he wanted to keep her longer, he would have called. He knows I would worry—he's not answering at home, or his cell."

"Check your answering machine again. He could have called while you were at my place."

"I've checked—twice. There is no message." The phone rang. She ran across the room, snatching it off the cradle. "Hello? Neal?" She looked over at Damon who appeared as relieved as she was. "I've been calling for hours. Rebecca should've been home a long time ago."

"I'm aware of what time Rebecca is to come home," Neal answered, using the pompous tone she remembered. Since his paternity had been questioned, he had been a little more cooperative, but things were going back to normal.

"When will you be here?"

There was an uneasy pause.

"Neal, what's going on? Where's Rebecca?" Her voice was too loud. Something wasn't right. She didn't like Neal's sudden change in demeanor. He was a stickler for order and rules. Not bringing Rebecca home on time without calling meant more than it appeared on the surface. Damon felt her fear and moved next to her.

"I'm not bringing Rebecca home, Brooke."

"What do you mean you're *not bringing her home*?" Her voice trembled.

"I've filed for custody of Rebecca."

"You mean visitation?"

Damon watched her, his eyes changing from hazel to an angry shade of green.

"Custody, Brooke full custody."

"What are you talking about?" she shouted.

"I'd advise you to have a lawyer look over the papers when you receive them." He hung up.

"Hello? Neal?" She redialed his number, furiously punching the digits. "He hung up on me," she told Damon.

"What did he say? He's not bringing Rebecca home?"

Ella answered.

"Put Neal on the phone!" Brooke shouted.

"Our lawyer told him not to have any contact with you. He shouldn't talk with you on the phone. Please don't call here again."

"He can't get away with this!" She couldn't control her anger. "I want to talk to Rebecca."

"Rebecca's sleeping. I'll have her call you. Good-bye, Brooke." Ella hung up.

She dialed back immediately, but no one picked up. She hurled the phone across the room.

"What?" Damon was there, feeding off her hysteria. "What's going on? Where's Rebecca?"

Brooke ranted, giving Damon the details of her brief conversation.

"They won't get away with this," Damon said, pulling on his jacket. "They can't just keep her."

"Where are you going?" She followed him out onto the front porch.

"I'm going to bring my daughter home."

"Wait, I'm coming with you."

He was already climbing into his SUV. "Stay here."

"Let me get my coat. I want to come along."

"I'll handle it." He crawled the engine, backing out the driveway.

"Don't make it worse, Damon," she called after him.

"Open the damn door!" Damon banged on Neal's door with his fist. He no longer cared if he disturbed the entire upper eastside neighborhood. Embarrassment would pain Neal enough to comply. "Neal Kirby, open the door!"

Neal snatched the door open. After shattering Brooke's world, he'd been comfortable enough to go to sleep. He tucked the edges of his robe together, tightening the belt around his waist. "If you don't leave immediately, I'm calling the police."

"Please do. I can press kidnapping charges against you."

"Take it up with my lawyer." He moved to close the door, but Damon's hand shot out, stopping him.

"If you don't let me in to get Rebecca, I'll take it up with you tonight and you can call your lawyer in the morning to bail you out."

"Empty threats."

"Try me." He barged through the door, startling Ella. "Where is my daughter?"

"The court will decide who is Rebecca's rightful father. Now get out."

"I'm calling the police," Ella said.

"Wait!" Neal said, stopping her.

Damon advanced on Neal. "Rebecca is *my* daughter. Brooke has been trying to accommodate you, but I won't spare your feelings. You're twisted. You've been using Rebecca to hold on to Brooke. Rebecca cares about you, so I haven't interfered with her seeing you, but now you've gone too far. Get out of our lives. Start your own family."

Neal gathered his courage. "Who do you think you are? You show up five years too late and think you're going to run things? I won't have it."

"You don't have a choice." Damon turned to Ella, who was frozen with the phone pressed to her ear. "Get my daughter, please."

She looked between them.

"You know Brooke loves Rebecca more than anything. Can you imagine what shape she was in when I left her?" he asked Ella. "Your husband is doing the wrong thing, the wrong way. Don't be a part of this."

After a moment, she turned and disappeared down a dark hallway.

Damon turned back to Neal. "If she isn't back in five minutes with Rebecca, I'm calling the cops."

Brooke was standing in the door when he pulled the Land Rover into her driveway. He carried a sleeping Rebecca inside and handed her over to Brooke. She smothered Rebecca in kisses before putting her to bed.

"Neal called." She joined him on the sofa. "He said you kicked down his door and made a huge scene in front of the neighbors."

"He's exaggerating, but if I'd had to do those things to get Rebecca back, I would have."

She draped herself around him, burying her head in his chest. "Thank you."

"He was bullying you."

"Do you think he really is going to try to get custody of Rebecca?"

"I wouldn't put it past him. Neal doesn't treat everyone the way he treats you and Rebecca. I watch him interact with you two and see him being kind and concerned. He's an opportunist. If he feels he has a point to prove, he'll try to take Rebecca."

"This can't be happening. I've tried to do right by him, even though he's not her father."

"I know." He held her close, wanting to protect her and Rebecca with his life. "Neal is not going to take my daughter away. No matter what we have to do, we'll fight him."

Entering the tower of Sunkrest Accounting made Kurtis's chest swell with pride. A wide grin uncovered his dentist-made-perfect teeth. He crossed the white marble flooring of the lobby, pushing past his subordinates without returning their greetings. Two more people had to retire before he would park on the private level reserved for the partners at the firm. His brisk step was interrupted when he heard a distinctively feminine voice call his name. When he turned around, he saw long, shapely, brown legs moving with haste in his direction.

"Barbara, what are you doing here?"

She looked distressed. I thought I could trust you."

"What are you accusing me of?" And when had they become such trusted friends?

"It's Damon. It's bad enough he divorced me for Brooke, but now he's trying to leave me penniless!" Her voice escalated, and she drew the attention of the crowded lobby.

"Keep your voice down." He took her arm, pulling her into a corner.

"I thought you were going to do something about her." Barbara began to sniffle.

"Damon may have divorced you, but it wasn't to be with Brooke." He couldn't fathom the thought of Brooke leaving him for another man. She had told him the time wasn't right—Rebecca's well being had to come first. As soon as things went back to normal, they'd be together again.

"What happened between me and Damon is directly related to Brooke. They've never gotten over each other. Rebecca was the perfect excuse for them to get back together." Barbara pulled a tissue from her purse and dabbed at her eyes, although he saw no tears.

"Brooke isn't with Damon."

"You don't see it, Kurtis? You better open your eyes to what's going on around you."

"What do you know?"

"I know he's been spending every free moment with *Rebecca*—or so he says. Whenever I call him, he's on the way to Brooke's place. If he's only visiting Rebecca, why doesn't he take her to his house?"

He found himself making excuses, refusing to believe Damon was making moves on the woman he planned to spend his future with. "Brooke may not be comfortable with them being alone."

"He's taken Rebecca plenty of times."

His chest tightened. Brooke had never let him take Rebecca on an outing alone.

"He took Rebecca to meet his parents last weekend. Why did Brooke need to go along? They're becoming the perfect little family."

He'd been so busy at work he had let Damon get under his radar.

"Face it. You and I are out—unless we do something about it. What are we going to do?"

"I don't know," he said, stunned. He was in danger of losing Brooke for good.

"You'll help me?" Sniffles disappeared.

He'd help himself. "I'll look into it." With that reassurance, he escorted Barbara back to her car.

"You'll call me as soon as you know something?" She angled into her car, bringing her long legs in last.

Her supermodel looks were hypnotic. He forgot the true objective, and imagined what it would be like to come home to Barbara every night.

"Kurtis?" She looked up at him from the driver's side window. "You'll call me?"

"I'll call." He watched her drive away. Getting Barbara would be like taming a wild cougar. She'd enjoy the finer things, never nagging him about spending too much time at work. Having her on his arm at the corporate dinners could only help him advance up the ladder. Why would Damon divorce her? If Barbara was right, Damon still had feelings for Brooke. But Brooke belonged to him. Didn't she? He hadn't spoken to her since their last disagreement—and Damon had been there to witness it. He had to convince her they still belonged together.

CHAPTER 23

Knowing that her legs were too stubby to make it to the front door before the caller left the front porch, Aunt Foster sent Rebecca to peek out the living room window. "It's Damon, Auntie." She bounced from foot to foot, anxious to return to the cake bowl in the kitchen.

Aunt Foster shooed her away from the window. She bent at her ample waist to Rebecca's level. "What's this 'Damon' nonsense? You don't know better than to call an adult by their first name?"

"What should I call him?" Rebecca laced her fingers together behind her back and stared at her feet.

"What about Dad?"

"I already have a dad." She looked up into her aunt's round face. "Dad is my dad because he loves me. Damon is my dad because he helped Mom make me."

"Kids these days are too smart, and too smart-mouthed," she mumbled. "Call him 'sir' then, smarty." She patted Rebecca's behind and nudged her in the direction of the kitchen. By the time she reached the front door she was winded. The doctor had been after her for years to lose weight. Simply walking from the kitchen to the front door wore her out. And it was getting harder to get around—her knees ached and her legs were weak. She might have to give the doctor's suggestion some consideration.

Damon was looking out into the front yard when the screen door squeaked open. "There are a lot of memories for me here," he said, stepping inside.

"How many days did you spend on this very porch waiting for me to decide if I was going to let you see Brooke?"

"Too many to count."

"Glad you could come. Sorry it took me so long to get to the door. I don't allow Rebecca to open the door to anyone."

"I understand." He sniffed the air. "Are you baking one of your famous cakes?"

"Rebecca's helping." She motioned for him to follow her into the kitchen. "I need to check on dinner."

Rebecca was on her knees in a chair at the kitchen table, leaning over the mixing bowl. She dipped her fingers into the cake batter, licking her little fingers.

Damon scooped her up in a hug. "How are you, sweetheart?"

Aunt Foster watched the interaction with vested interest. She was moved by the way Damon brightened up, smiling when he saw Rebecca. He held her close, lovingly. He returned her to her place in the chair. "What do you have there?" He swiped his finger around the edge of the bowl.

"Hey!" Rebecca giggled.

"Lemon." He tugged at one of her braids before pulling a chair up beside her and sitting down. "Have you been good at school?"

"Yes, sir."

"Sir? What's this *sir* business about?"

"Auntie said."

Aunt Foster was at the stove, stirring a bubbling pot. She turned and Damon averted his eyes. He leaned into Rebecca's ear and whispered, "We better stick to it."

They shared a smile.

"Can I go play, Auntie?"

"Yes, child, but don't wake up your mother."

Rebecca handed her the mixing bowl before running out of the kitchen.

"Rebecca is a regular kid when she's with you," Damon said. Sentimentality was in his voice.

She knew exactly what he meant. Neal had turned her into the proper young lady, focusing on her future at the tender age of five. She agreed someone had to be mindful of Rebecca's future, but that didn't mean she had to sacrifice her childhood. She offered her support. "The camp you chose will be good for her."

"It's hard to make parenting decisions when you're coming into the game at half-time."

She wiped her hands on her apron and sat down at the kitchen table. "I invited you to dinner this Sunday because I'm worried about Brooke."

"What's the problem?"

It wasn't like her to be hesitant, or worry about anyone else's opinion, but she knew Brooke would balk at her talking to Damon without her permission. She had lived her life speaking her mind. If others couldn't get behind it, shame on them. She had raised Brooke, always doing the right thing for her. Just because Brooke was grown with a daughter didn't mean she could stop mothering her.

"What is it, Aunt Foster? You know I'll help Brooke any way I can."

Removing a napkin from the holder in the middle of the table she and wiped away a bead of sweat. "Brooke received the papers about Neal wanting custody of Rebecca." She ignored the Damon's disbelief and told him everything she knew.

"I know he's been threatening court action... Why didn't Brooke tell me about this?"

"She didn't believe he'd go through with it. She's taking it hard." She nodded toward the hallway. "She hired a lawyer and he made her more upset. Neal might have a shot at taking Rebecca."

"I'm not going to sit by and let Neal take Rebecca away from Brooke—or me."

This is what she was hoping to hear. "I can't get around as well as I used to. I want you to help my girls."

Damon squeezed her hand. "Can I check on Brooke?"

She nodded, feeling some relief.

He stood, but turned to her before leaving the kitchen. His brow knit together in determination. "Rebecca is special, and she's my daughter. I'm not going to let anyone take her away from me when I just found her."

———❧———

"This was bound to be rough no matter how adult everyone tried to be at the onset," Ella said.

Neal understood how difficult sharing Rebecca would be. It angered him that when tempers started flaring, Brooke hadn't run to him for her peace of mind.

"Don't think Brooke is going to lie down and let you take Rebecca without a fight," Ella went on while rubbing cream into her arms.

He climbed into bed. "You would have me turn Rebecca over to Damon?"

"She is his daughter, Neal. He seems to care for her."

"*I* love her," he defended too loudly.

"I'm just saying—"

"I know what you're saying, Ella. You've been saying it since we got married."

She placed the cream on the nightstand and turned to him. "Are you accusing me of something?"

"You were the one who pushed the paternity test."

"And I was right—Rebecca isn't your daughter."

"But she was my daughter," he shouted, "until you interfered. Brooke and I were raising Rebecca together. Now I can't even see her without prior permission. I have to schedule visits with her like I'm insignificant in her life. Meanwhile, a stranger can see her whenever he wants."

"You're blaming me?"

"This isn't about you."

Her anger rose. "You're wrong, Neal. This has everything to do with me, and with our marriage. If you win, Rebecca comes to live with both of *us*. You don't live here alone. Having her here means I become a full time mother. I've made the conscious choice not to have any kids, but I'll be raising a five-year-old baby. Don't tell me this doesn't affect me as much as it affects you." She snatched up her robe and stomped from the bedroom.

⟨∞⟩

The squeal of the door hinges made Brooke open her eyes. Damon stepped inside without ceremony, sitting on the edge of the bed. He pulled the pink comforter up to her chin. "Aunt Foster would kill me if she knew how many times I've been in this room."

"What are you doing here?" she asked, still groggy from sleep.

"Aunt Foster invited me to dinner."

"Really? You're friends now?"

"It's taken a lot of years, but I think she trusts me now." He fingered the edge of the comforter. "She's worried about you."

She watched him cross the room.

"I have so many memories about us in this room," he said. He bent to look at the pictures framed on her old dresser.

"Our future is in our past."

He turned to her, his green eyes fading to warm honey. "Our future is in our hearts."

"Still poetic." She reached out to him. "Come here." He took off his shoes and climbed beneath the covers with her. The twin-sized bed was still too short to accommodate his long legs. The mattress had become too narrow, giving them barely enough room to lie side-by-side.

He nuzzled his nose against the back of her neck. "What did the attorney say?"

"He's investigating. I have an appointment with him later in the week. We're going to come up with a strategy to shut Neal down."

"I want to be there."

She lifted his hand, pressing his palm to her face.

"Did you hear me? I want to be there when you speak to the lawyer."

"I heard you." She closed her eyes, feeling safe again.

He slipped his arms around her waist, holding her tightly. He didn't speak. He kissed her face, neck and shoulders until she slipped into a warm, comfortable place somewhere between being awake and being asleep.

"I want you there, Damon."

His fingers ran through her hair. "Why didn't you call me?"

She turned to face him, pressing their bodies together. "I wanted to come home. I needed to think without you—or anyone—influencing my decisions."

"Are you upset with Aunt Foster for calling me?"

"No."

"What decisions did you have to make?"

"I've made them."

He watched her, eager for her to continue. His arms tightened around her waist, bringing her solidly against his chest. "What decisions?"

"I've decided to fight Neal with everything I have—money, possessions, spirit—all I own will be pitted against him until he drops this stupid custody case."

He kissed her forehead, offering his support with a smile.

"There's something else."

"What?"

"I've decided to fight for you. I'm happiest when I'm with you. Rebecca and I need you in our lives. I won't let you go again."

"I'm not going anywhere. You and Rebecca are stuck with me—forever."

She placed her palms to his cheeks, bringing his mouth to hers. She devoured him, leaving him weak and dazed.

CHAPTER 24

"How long has this been going on?" Kurtis stood in Brooke's living room, steaming, and demanding answers.

"I gave you a straight answer. You and I are over. You have to accept it and move on."

"I didn't think you were *serious*. I thought you were mad at me for interfering with Damon's time with Rebecca."

She remained firm, but gentle. "I am serious. I couldn't be more serious."

His eyebrows came together. "Did he leave his wife for you?"

"What are you saying?" He wouldn't know Damon and Barbara had gotten divorced unless he had spoken to one of them.

"Have you slept with him?"

"That's none of your business. How do you know Damon left his wife?"

He hesitated, avoiding her glare. "Barbara came to see me at work."

Brooke moved to the door, ready to throw him out. "I don't want to know how you two became friends."

"She's desperate. She was so upset—"

"I don't care what you talked about, or when you saw her." She pulled the door open. "I don't have time for this." She couldn't have Kurtis and Barbara interfering and causing more havoc while she fought to keep her daughter. "You have to go, Kurtis."

"Let me explain. It's been so crazy lately—"

"You have to leave and never come back."

"What?" His face froze in shock.

"I've tried to be friends with you, but it's not going to work. I have a lot going on in my life. I can't pacify you anymore, Kurtis. We have to make a clean break."

"But I love you. We were going to be married. We can still save this."

She toned down her annoyance and tried to let him down easily. "I care about you, too, but I don't love you. You have to find someone who can give you what you want. It isn't me."

"It's Damon."

"It's not Damon. It's us. We don't *fit*."

A low rumble moved to his throat. "This is a joke, right? You're breaking off everything. I can't believe this!" He kicked the sofa. "Do you know how much I put up with to be with you? I've been holding on for months while you gave me excuse after excuse about setting the wedding date. You wouldn't even make love to me anymore. Barbara was right. Damon ended his marriage, and now you're ending our relationship. All this time. Right under my nose." He kicked the sofa again.

"Kurtis, it's time for you to leave."

"You've made a fool of me."

"Please, go. You're going to wake up Rebecca."

The ridged planes of his face softened at the mention of Rebecca. No matter how angry he was at her, he still cared about Rebecca.

"I'm not going to let Damon have you and Rebecca without a fight."

"This isn't about Damon. This is about what I need to make me happy. If you love me and Rebecca, you'll let us be happy."

"I love you and Rebecca. Tell me what's wrong and I'll fix it."

"Kurtis—"

"We can work through this."

"Kurtis," she was firm, "it's not going to happen between us."

He looked into her eyes, searching for a reflection of hope. She offered none.

"I won't beg." He raised his head and sauntered out the door.

———

"Can I help you?" The twenty-something woman with dark flowing hair ran after Brooke as she barged into Neal's office. He sat at his desk, typing fiercely on his laptop computer. His head snapped to attention when the heavy oak door to his office swung open, hitting the wall.

"I tried to stop her, Professor Kirby." The girl tossed her hair over her shoulder.

"It's okay." Neal stood up. "Leave us alone, please."

The girl stared at Brooke as she backed out the door.

"You're teaching assistant?" Brooke asked sarcastically. She recognized the possessive mannerism of an enamored student—she had been one. She wondered if Ella had learned the signs of Neal's infidelity. He was a master at the game, always on the lookout for a newer, younger companion. Brooke had assumed he'd toned down his appetite since getting married, but the teaching assistant made her doubt it.

"Why did you storm into my office?" He scratched his beard, remaining cool and hardly sparing her a glance.

"Why are you trying to take Rebecca away from me?" She dropped her purse in the chair and placed her hands on her hips ready to do battle.

"We shouldn't talk without our lawyers present." He pushed his chair away from the desk.

"Are you listening to yourself? 'Our lawyers.' Since when are we not able to talk to each other directly when it comes to Rebecca?"

"Since you sent that thug to my doorstep in the middle of the night."

"Damon is not a thug, and if you hadn't kidnapped his daughter, he never would have come."

"Is that what you told him? You accused me of kidnapping my own daughter? Oh, I forgot, Rebecca's no longer my daughter—if you have your way about things." He looked his age today. The fine lines around his eyes and across his forehead were prominent. He had the attitude of a stubborn old man set in his ways, unwilling to listen to anyone else's opinion.

Feeling empowered by her resolution to fight for Rebecca, she did-n't hesitate to challenge him. The old Brooke would have deferred to his wishes, as she had done whenever they couldn't agree about raising Rebecca. Not anymore. In all the recent turmoil, Rebecca had always been sure Brooke was her mother. As her mother, she had to protect her daughter. She took menacing steps up to Neal's desk. "I should have my way when it comes to parenting Rebecca. When you wanted to keep my pregnancy a secret so you wouldn't lose your job, I went along. You've made every major decision in Rebecca's life, and I've always gone along. You wanted to stay active in Rebecca's life after you found out you weren't her biological father, and I agreed. I've always had Rebecca's best interest at heart. Do you?"

"Always."

"Taking her away from her mother is in her best interest? You can't believe that, Neal."

"Brooke, you and I both know it's only a matter of time before Damon phases me out of Rebecca's life. She's my daughter more than she'll ever be his daughter. I can provide a better life for her than you or he ever could, and I plan to do just that."

"You're so wrong. Rebecca needs all of us in her life. It doesn't have to be this way, but if you want a fight, you'll get a fight. I'm not going to let you push me around anymore."

"You have to leave." He pulled his laptop towards him and started keying.

Her anger rose at his dismissal. She grabbed her purse from the chair. "What did I ever see in you?" she mumbled.

Neal stood and rounded the desk. His intimidation didn't work. She butted out her chin, standing her ground as he moved within inch-es of her. "You used to be able to get me to do whatever you wanted with a little intimidation. And you did get what you wanted—me in your bed. But things went wrong. I became pregnant. And you got what you wanted again. You talked me into going along with your scheme to save your job. When it turns out you're not her father, you're upset. The only thing bothering you is that it wasn't *your* decision to deny Rebecca this time. So what do you do? You forget about what this custody fight will to do Rebecca and try to hurt me. Why do you want to hurt me so badly that it doesn't matter if Rebecca gets hurt too?"

Neal's mouth dropped open, shocked at her rebellion. She had always been easy to control. He made the decisions about Rebecca, and she never questioned him. Her defiance had always been thwarted by his well-constructed words, twisted into persuasive dialogue. He didn't know how to handle this side of her.

He spoke through clenched teeth. "You make me sound like a monster. I love Rebecca. I want what's best for her—end of story."

"This has nothing to do with Rebecca. You know I'm a good mother. How can you tell all of these strangers I'm not?" Her voice threatened to crack, but she held her composure. "What *is* this all about, Neal?"

He stumbled over his words as he tried to argue his position. "I want Rebecca with me. I love her. I live for her."

She pushed him. "Is this about getting revenge on me?"

"Don't be ridiculous." He turned his eyes away.

"You're trying to hurt me, and I don't understand why. I've been nothing but accommodating to you when it comes to Rebecca. Why would you want to destroy me this way?"

"I can't leave Ella to be with you," Neal blurted out. "Together, we're one of the most powerful couples in the city, one of the most respected in the state."

Her eyes grew wide with the revelation.

"What?" He asked, fear crossing his features.

She stared at him in disbelief. All these months she'd considered Kurtis's complaints jealous ramblings. She remembered the explosive dinner when Kurtis had challenged Neal to disclose his true feelings for her.

"What are you thinking?" he asked.

"You said too much—and you've proved Kurtis right."

He stepped back, tugging nervously at his tie. "I don't know what you're talking about. Kurtis doesn't know anything about me."

She didn't let up. "Is it true?"

"I don't know what you're talking about." He retreated to the safety of his desk.

"Kurtis has been right all this time." She planted her palms on his desktop and leaned over in his face. "Answer me, Neal! Are you doing all of this because you still have feelings for me?"

Neal's emotions gushed out uncontrollably. "Yes, I love you. I have always loved you." He bolted out of his chair, visibly relieved to have confessed. "Don't you understand I can't let Damon take you and Rebecca away from me? I love you both too much."

"You can't *love* me. Our relationship was so short, and we never loved each other."

"I loved you, yes I did. You've always been the one that got away. You challenge me. You tantalize me whenever you're near. I think about you all the time."

"But you just married Ella a year ago—"

"Because it was the smart thing to do for my career." His words shocked him. He sank down in his seat. "I love Ella in a certain way. She's done so much for my career." He raised his eyes to hers. "I wish I could leave Ella for you like Damon left Barbara. Ella would never allow it."

"I don't—"

"Speechless?" His smile was venomous. "Too much to process? You shouldn't have pushed." He stood slowly. "Now that you know how I feel about you, what will you do?"

"Are you doing this to get me back?"

"I can't leave Ella—I've made that clear. I want things like they were."

"Married to Ella, but running my household?" She had been his mistress without knowing it. Ella was his wife, serving at political functions to further his career. She had been the other woman, keeping house with his daughter.

"You have to admit, things were good. Until Kurtis stepped in questioning everything—and then Damon showing up claiming Rebecca."

"I came here about the custody case."

"And you discovered my feelings for you."

"You can't be serious about going through with this. Not now."

"*Not now?*" He shook his head. "My Brooke, never able to handle life's little curves. Nothing has changed. I want things the way they were. Are you prepared to give me what I want?"

"Don't be ridiculous."

"You let me know if you come to your senses."

She backed out of his office, never taking her eyes off him.

"Say the word, Brooke. I'll make the call and everything will go back to normal."

Brooke hiked her purse strap up on her shoulder, running across the lobby with Rebecca in tow. Her heels clacked, calling more attention to her tardiness. She smiled apologetically at the secretary. "May I leave her here?"

"Sure." The woman smiled, rounding the desk. "How about we get something from the vending machines?"

"Great." Brooke was frazzled. She dug through her purse for change, spilling most of the contents onto the floor. "Sorry." Her hands were shaking as she scooped up her things.

"Don't worry about it," the secretary told her. "I have the keys to the machine." She stooped to Rebecca's level. "You can have whatever you want." She had comforted the children of distraught parents before.

Rebecca looked up at her with anxious eyes. "Can I, Mom?"

Brooke kissed the top of her head. "I'll be back in a little while."

The secretary took Rebecca's hand and led her down the corridor. "You can go in, Ms. Foster. Mr. Richmond is already inside."

She straightened her suit and tried to settle her nerves. She hated being late. She hadn't been able to get away from the hotel—there seemed to be one crisis after another no one else could handle. The nuns didn't have Rebecca ready for early dismissal as she had requested. Brooke wondered if they were on Neal's side in all this. She was sure they saw him as the more stable parent. He attended each and every conference, whereas her work schedule sometimes kept her away. He sat in the front row of all school productions. He participated in every fundraiser—candy, Christmas wrapping paper, candles, whatever. Yearly, it was his big, fat check that topped the parent donation list. After enduring the nun's disapproving glare, road construction had thwarted her final effort to make up time on the drive to the lawyer's office.

Damon was sitting with the attorney, calmly discussing the latest sporting event. He wore a dark suit and multi-colored tie. He removed the briefcase from his lap so he could stand and greet her.

"Sorry I'm late."

"It's fine," he assured her. His voice was smooth and low. He could feel her nervousness and sought to comfort her. "We were waiting for you before we got started."

After shaking Mr. Cavalier's hand, she took her seat next to Damon.

The man ran his fingers through his balding bronze hair. "Mr. Kirby is suing for custody of Rebecca on the basis of you being an unfit mother."

"He can't do that, can he?" Damon asked. "I'm Rebecca's biological father."

"He can do whatever he wants to do. This is America. Whether or not he'll win is another story. I've read the motion in great detail. He makes a logical argument. He also wants visitation until the case has been decided."

"He's already taken Rebecca once," Damon said.

"Damon had to make him give her back," Brooke added. "I don't want to chance him taking Rebecca and running."

Mr. Cavalier perused the file. "I don't know if we'll win on this issue. He's been acting as her father for five years. He has a stable job and permanent home. His reputation in the community is spotless. It might be considered detrimental to Rebecca to keep them separated when he's the only father she's ever known."

Brooke shared a look with Damon.

"The judge will look on you giving Professor Kirby visitation as a sign of good faith."

Damon nodded in agreement.

"But what about my daughter? What if he refuses to bring her back home again?"

Mr. Cavalier reached across his desk and lifted the phone. "We'll put safeguards in place with his attorney right now. He'd be foolish to try something. It would jeopardize his whole case."

Damon leaned over, taking her hand from her lap. "Are you okay? You don't look okay."

"I need to use the ladies' room." Brooke excused herself while Mr. Cavalier debated visitation scheduling with Neal's attorney. Rebecca was with the secretary, munching on a bag of chips while they played tic-tac-toe. She placed her purse on the bathroom counter. Damon was right. She looked awful. Her eyes were red and puffy from lack of sleep. Neal's proposition had made her toss and turn for too many nights. Her hair was pulled back in a hasty ponytail. Stray hairs hung near her temple and down the back of her neck. She refused to let Neal win. No way he'd take Rebecca from her, but she couldn't let his attempts rattle her. She adjusted her suit, held her head high and returned to Mr. Cavalier's office.

"They've agreed to continue every-other-weekend visitation as before. I added the stipulation that there a third party present—to keep him from trying to take the child."

"Aunt Foster," Brooke and Damon said together. Their like-mindedness got a smile from her.

Mr. Cavalier pulled papers from his printer. "It'll only be temporary, until he proves he's not a flight risk. The attorney will push it through. I need you to sign the agreement."

She looked over at Damon. "He's going to be upset."

Damon took her hand again. "Where do I fit in all of this?" he asked Mr. Cavalier.

"You're Rebecca's father. Keep being her father. How's your relationship?" He gestured between them. "Do you get along?"

Damon squeezed her hand. "Very well."

"Good. Keep it that way. You're united in this fight?"

"Yes," Damon answered without hesitation.

Mr. Cavalier turned to her.

"Yes. Since Neal is legally establishing visitation, should Damon?"

"Good point," Damon said.

"It can't hurt to have a paper trail of your involvement in Rebecca's life."

She'd rather avoid a lengthy, expensive court battle over her daughter. "I feel like my every move is being watched under a microscope."

"It is," Mr. Cavalier answered. He gave her a devilish grin. "Let's see if we can turn the microscope on Professor Kirby and his wife."

Damon moved to the edge of his chair. "What do you mean?"

"I don't want to take the chance of getting some judge who's trying to make his name in family court so he can advance up the ladder at your expense. From what I've seen thus far, Kirby's case is weak, but it has some merit. It's in our best interest if we can settle this without going in front of a judge. I'll try to negotiate permanent visitation and see if he'll drop the custody fight." He shook his head. "His attorney says he's adamant." He slid paperwork across the desk for her to sign. "Maybe we can put the professor under a microscope and find leverage to keep this thing from going any further."

"I don't want to fight dirty." She wouldn't stoop to Neal's level of deception, threats and bargains with the devil. She'd have her daughter without giving in to his skewed demands.

"But," Damon interrupted, "we'll do whatever we need to do to keep Rebecca." His hazel-green eyes asked confirmation.

"I won't give up my daughter."

Mr. Cavalier smiled. "That's what I want to hear. This might get a lot dirtier before it gets any better. I need to know you're going to hang in there with me."

"We're in," Brooke answered. Her hands shook as she signed the documents.

"Are you sure you're okay?" Damon lowered his voice. "Your hands are shaking."

"I need dinner. I need respite. I need you."

His eyes darkened to a deep, seductive green. "I can help you with all those things."

❈

"Enough talking." Neal had had a long, exhausting day and when he arrived home there was a message from his attorney. Brooke had agreed to restore his scheduled visitation with Rebecca. Next week, he'd pick her up after school on Friday and have her for the weekend. Or so he thought, until he called to confirm with his attorney. Oh, he could see Rebecca, but only at Aunt Foster's house for two hours each day. The attorney had tried to soothe his anger by suggesting this was some sort of start—a compromise would look good as the fight went on. Finally, he blamed the lack of room to negotiate on Neal's threat to keep Rebecca during their last visit. He'd given the attorney an earful, slamming down the phone to punctuate his meaning. Ella's disapproving glare had set off another round of arguments between them. He'd stormed out of the house, directly to his office. Then this beautiful young woman had appeared on his threshold requesting tutoring.

He'd given Brooke a clear ultimatum. He should have done it years ago, when she was inexperienced and easy to control. There was a way he could have it all. He was Teflon—nothing ever penetrated his armor.

Brooke had won the visitation battle, but it was only one small battle that would make him push harder. She hadn't accepted his offer yet, but he was sure the threat of losing Rebecca would be enough to change her mind. She'd come around once she realized her finances couldn't sustain a long custody battle. Once losing was inevitable, she'd beg to accept his terms.

"Professor?" The girl questioned, wide-eyed.

He helped her put away her books. "How about we continue this over cocktails?"

"Cocktails?" She was young, and inexperienced. Pretty with a firm body. The ideal girl to substitute for Brooke.

"I know the perfect place. There's a bar in the hotel right off campus..."

CHAPTER 25

The warming jazzy ambience of the Sweet Georgia Brown restaurant in Greektown provided the nourishment Brooke needed to fill her belly and rest her weary body. Having the sexiest man in the city sitting next to her filled her heart. They started with a bottle of Far Niente chardonnay while they shared escargot. The imported escargot was sautéed with roasted garlic and sweet plum tomatoes, olive oil and lemon. Served over angel hair pasta it was garnished with asiago cheese. Starving, Brooke ordered maple barbeque glazed shrimp on lobster with grilled corn hash and fresh asparagus. Damon started with smoked turkey *farfalle*. The dish was made of asparagus, artichoke hearts, roma tomatoes and mushrooms in sage cream with marinara, garlic and fresh herbs. With his appetite, it didn't surprise Brooke when he added fried lobster as his second entrée. Sweet Georgia Brown's signature lobster dish was dipped in tempura, served with drawn butter, spicy *remoulade* and crab fried rice *timbale*. After being escorted to the ladies' room by the wait staff, Brooke was pleasantly surprised with peach cobbler served 'a la mode with peach ice cream.

"Thank you for coming today."

"You don't have to thank me for doing the right thing, Brooke." He reached for her hand across the table. The piano player provided background music for their quiet conversation. "I don't want to talk about Neal or the custody fight. Rebecca is safe and sound with Aunt Foster. Let this night be about us."

"Sounds good."

"I've filled your belly," Damon said. "Now I want to offer you respite."

"And how do you plan to do that, Mr. Richmond?"

"I want to entice you to spend the night at my place."

"Why not my place?" She openly flirted, enjoying the attention of the most handsome man she'd ever met.

"I can't properly pamper you at your place."

"Really? I wonder what you have in mind."

He waved for the bill. "I can't wait to show you."

The pampering began the moment they stepped inside his house. He ushered her through the master bedroom into the bath where he helped her sink into a steamy hot tub packed with bubbles. He oiled her body as they lay nude across his bed watching a *Sex in the City* marathon on his big screen television. He tangled his legs with hers when she laughed at the casts' adventures in dating. When the hero didn't respond the way Brooke thought he should, Damon covered her body with his, kissing the back of her neck. He never complained about the sitcom being too *girlie*. He enjoyed her enjoying the show.

On the break, he pushed her onto her back, pressing his nakedness against hers. He was aroused, but didn't acknowledge his need. Instead, he fished an ice cube out of her water glass and melted it in the hidden curves of her body. He followed the cold trail with the heat of his breath, touching all her intimate spots. They rolled across his four-poster bed, her relishing in the silky softness of his skin. Just as he heated her to feverish arousal, he pulled away.

"Not yet."

"Now is perfect," she said, reaching for him.

"I promised you respite."

"And you did a good job of delivering."

He left the bed to stoke the fireplace. Having a fireplace in the bedroom allowed them to be naked in the middle of the winter. The muscles of his long legs flexed, and she wished they were wrapped around her waist. The muscles of his back rippled as he threw a log in the fire, and she imagined touching each one on the tip of her tongue. He stretched his arms above his head, and the gesture pushed her over the edge.

"Damon, come back to bed."

"Control yourself." He glanced back, grinning.

"Don't tease."

"Teasing is half the fun." They made eye contact and he smiled, taking a deep breath. "I can smell your perfume from here."

"I'm not wearing any perfume."

His head fell back; he closed his eyes and inhaled deeply. He looked at her with blazing green eyes. "Then it must be *you*." When he said *you*, a shiver moved through her body. Damon was the master of seduction, and she was beyond ready to be captured and forced into submission. His ran his fingers through his dreads. "Do you still like poetry?"

She nodded her mouth too dry to speak. He did unnatural things to her body. Took her so far beyond arousal she couldn't think straight. She watched his lips as he quoted Shakespeare, hanging on his every word. He stood across the room, tantalizing her with the full view of his nudity. His legs were apart, spreading their strength. He placed his hands on his narrow hips as he puffed out his chest with masculine possession.

"You want to be my teacher."

His face reddened slightly. "Is that a question?" He stepped closer, but was still out of reach.

"An observation."

He asked. "Don't forget your dating etiquette."

Etiquette? He had her peaked, almost feverish, and he was discussing dating rules.

"Damon, this is killing me. Give me a kiss."

"One."

"Torture."

"You'll live." He sauntered to the bed, climbing up one knee at a time. He crawled forward, wiping away her personal space. He touched her shoulder. The touch went through her like raw electricity. His fingers drifted down her arm to her hand. He intertwined their fingers. "Come and get your kiss, Brooke."

She had never, ever—not in a million years—forget that kiss. He nuzzled her neck, tugging at the tender skin and leaving his calling card. His lips met hers, igniting the urge to ravish his perfectly molded body. He held her face in his palms, steadying her as he pressed his lips to her eyebrows, nose and eyelids. He placed his lips next to hers, whispering erotic promises. He whispered what he would do to her, how and where he wanted her to kiss him, and every position he wanted to try before morning. Her body screamed for his dominance. He changed his rhythm, moaning as he entered her mouth. He tasted her with maddening patience, pulling back when she became too aggressive. He caressed her face and neck, his hands resting in her hair as he pulled her into his web of seduction. His tongue touched hers, moving to the corner of her mouth. He suckled her top lip, and then the bottom. He pulled away, ending the kiss with a quick taste of her lips. He promised so many things with one kiss. He told her he loved and cherished her. He told her there were many more nights like this ahead. He gave her…respite from her troubles.

He tickled her nose with his. "Time for a little sexploration."

"Sexploration," she repeated, breathless.

"Lie back on the pillows." He helped her get comfortable before retrieving a mirror from the bathroom. "Before the night is over, I want to know every inch of your body." He started with her scalp, massaging firmly. Then he moved across the planes of her face, his lips following his touch. He mapped each of her erogenous zones. His tongue licked at her sternum as he manipulated her breasts. His tongue guided him on a tour across the planes of her belly. He lingered at her navel, making her giggle with the tip of his tongue. He moved to her feet, using his fingertips to caress her instep, and aggressively taking each of her pedicured toes inside his mouth.

She was clawing at the bed when he ordered her to roll onto her stomach. He placed her arms above her head as he stroked the back of her neck. He kissed her shoulders. His tongue danced down her spine. He lie next to her and tasted her fingers. His kiss moved upward, over her elbow, to her shoulder, igniting the nerves in her armpit with tingling licks of his tongue. When she couldn't stand any more, he pressed his front to her back and did devious things with his fingers to her bottom. He made her beg for release.

"No more," she whimpered.

He offered her a brief reprieve, helping her onto her back while he arranged her legs just so, positioning himself at angles to allow her to see the flicker of his tongue and the intimate folds of her body. His eyes went hazy as he watched her. "Watch what I do to you in the mirror."

Damon licked his finger and painted a figure eight around her folds. He moved inward, repeating the gesture until her legs flailed. He calmed her by pulling away. He moved in quickly, spreading her open as his forefinger and middle finger hovered over her pleasure spot. His touch became a circular cyclone, varying the size of the circles. She twisted on the bed, losing control. He took a victory roll, making a V and placing it firmly around the center of her erogenous zone, entrapping the erect bud firmly between his fingers. He stretched her wide. She watched in the mirror as his head descended. His tongue tapped against the bud. She dropped the mirror. She cried out. He locked her thighs against the bed, sucking her between his lips as his fingers entered her. She screamed, pleading for mercy but he gave her none, pushing and pushing until her body exploded and melted around him.

Somewhere in the distance, she heard Damon's cross the carpet and open the fireplace screen. She slowed her breathing, inhaling the woodsy smell of a cozy fire. The water in the bathroom was running. The bed dipped. Damon's hand bent her knee outward. A warm cloth moved between her folds. He kissed her cheek, but she was too exhausted to open her eyes. He moved across the carpet again. Water. Damon's footsteps. He covered her with the comforter. The mattress dipped and he wrapped his arms around her waist, resting his head on her shoulder. "I gave you dinner," he whispered. "I gave you respite. Next, you'll have me."

Brooke awoke to find Damon watching her with soft hazel-green eyes. He touched her face, running his finger across her lips. He kneeled over her, holding her waist as he entered her, moving at different angles, searching for the perfect direction of penetration. His eyes warmed to emerald green as he gently pulled her hips into his thrusts. His momentum increased, but his strokes were too shallow.

He pushed her knees up to her chest, resting her feet on his shoulders. She held onto his hips for support. His hands grasped her bottom, pulling her up into his energy surge. She moaned, his penetration too deep. He placed her legs to the right, and massaged her internally with the tip of his arousal. He pressed his hand to her belly and his face contorted with wondrous pleasure. He guided her hand there, watching for her reaction with brazen green eyes. He thrust against her palm, allowing her to feel him inside and out. He watched himself sliding in and out. His strokes quickened. He pushed too deeply, sending a powerful wave through her belly.

He exploded, collapsing in a heap. He rested only long enough to catch his breath. They didn't speak while he cleaned them both, rubbing cream into the overworked muscles of her thighs. It smelled of sandalwood, like his cologne, and it aroused her again. No words were needed as he fed her strawberries and had her drink fresh orange juice. Silence engulfed the room when he wrapped his body around hers from behind and held her until they fell asleep.

Brooke awoke hours later and waited patiently for Damon to open his hazel-green eyes. His lids rose lazily. He was satisfied.

He pushed his hand through her hair. "Are you feeling better?"

"Much."

"The sun's coming up." He glanced at the window above their heads.

"And the fire's gone out."

"I can fix that." He moved to leave the bed, but she stopped him with her touch.

"I'm warm." She was always warm when he held her in his arms.

"You were pretty frazzled yesterday." He pulled her close, rubbing their noses together. "What's going on?"

"Work, Kurtis, the custody case, Neal."

"Kurtis still won't let go?"

"I think he got the message." She placed her hands on his narrow hips.

"I could talk to him."

"It's fine." She stroked him, enjoying the velvety sensation of his skin. "Did you know he and Barbara have been seeing each other?"

He pulled back to see her face clearly. "What do you mean 'seeing each other'?"

"She told him you left her to be with me."

"No." He paused. "I didn't know they were in contact."

"Could this be trouble?"

"Could it be anything else? I'll talk to her."

She let him caress her, hating the fact their time together was coming to an end. Soon they'd have to get dressed for work.

"Brooke?"

"Yes?"

"Neal and the custody case are two different things?"

"What?"

"When I asked you what was wrong, you listed Neal and the custody case separately." He was too observant. It was the poet in him. Always searching for meaning beneath the surface.

"Why?" He lifted her chin. "Tell me."

"Let me tell you the entire story before you react." She gave him the details of her conversation with Neal, sparing no details. She didn't want any secrets between them that might jeopardize their efforts to keep Rebecca in their lives.

"He admitted he's still in love with you?"

"Don't overreact."

"Overreact? He's in love with you and wants you to agree to—to— some sort of *arrangement*, or he'll continue this custody fight." He tossed back the covers, ending their time in their private cocoon.

"Damon, wait." She scurried from the bed, following him into the bathroom. "Where are you going?"

"I want to have a talk with Professor Kirby." Although his voice was as low and calm as it always was, she could see the anger in the angry green color of his eyes.

"Thats what he wants."

"No. He wants you."

"He wants to win. If you go over there when you're angry, it could cause me to lose Rebecca. The judge won't see you as a fit parent, and since we're together, he might question my judgment."

"So what am I supposed to do? You want me to be quiet? Do nothing? He's trying to take *you* and Rebecca from me."

"It's all part of his strategy. He's playing a sick game."

"I won't lose you to Neal again."

She moved carefully, wrapping him in her arms. "After what we shared last night, do you think there's any chance you'll lose me?"

He pulled her close, palming the back of her neck. "You're right."

"You gave me dinner. You gave me respite. You gave me you. Why would I ever want to leave?"

He kissed her neck and pressed his lips against the shell of her ear. "I love you."

"I love you, Damon."

CHAPTER 26

Barbara slipped into the tightest red dress in her closet. She hoisted her breasts and held her breath until the material lay smooth against her generous curves. The hem stopped just above her knees, exposing her greatest asset—her legs. How dare Damon come storming in her house telling her who she could and couldn't be friends with. He had chosen to end their marriage because of an illegitimate child. He couldn't be the moral police for her life.

As soon as her sister arrived to sit with Lisa and Roger, she would meet Sam Markowitz for drinks. If not for her friends, she never would have found this man. A little spying, an Internet search, hanging out on the university campus and, *ta da,* they had located Sam. Barbara smiled. They were a sneaky bunch. Her girls would never leave her. They'd been scorned by cheating men before—and hell hath no fury…

She wasn't above fighting dirty. She had had a difficult life, her ex having deserted her and the kids. She wasn't about to go back to being a waitress, living in a cramped apartment with two kids. Not everyone had three men fighting over raising their child like Brooke. She used her pinky to stab at her lipstick. Damon *owed* her the life she deserved. The divorce settlement had been *adequate*, but she had a whole life to live. Who would pay the mortgage and car note a year from now?

———— ∞∞∞ ————

Kurtis eased off the gas pedal as his Stealth approached Brooke's townhouse. Her car was in the driveway. The house was still, but glowed with lights in the living room. He cruised by her place, and when he was sure the roar of his engine couldn't be heard, he pressed the accelerator. He paused at the corner and considered rounding the block once more, but worried a neighbor might spot him.

He so badly wanted to take back everything he had said. He wished he could make things right between him and Brooke. He had been wounded by her mistreatment of his feelings. Like an old toy a child tosses away when the new version comes out, Brooke had thrown him aside for Damon. He glanced in his rearview mirror. If she should step outside, maybe to retrieve the evening paper, he could at least see her. When everything blew over, it might be possible she would let him explain.

His cell phone pulled his attention away from Brooke's house.

"Kurtis? It's Barbara." He'd know her sultry voice without her announcing her name.

"Hi, Barbara."

"Can you meet me for dinner? There's someone I'd like you to meet."

"I'm not really up to meeting anyone tonight." A quiet evening with her would be something different. She had long, voluptuous legs that she used like weapons against his common sense.

"It'll give me an excuse to see you again," she continued. "Please," she said, liquefying his will.

"Where should I meet you?"

Damon walked across the length of the room, collecting the workshop participants' résumés. He paper-clipped the stack together and tossed them in his briefcase. "Someone tell me why you're here."

"I need a job," a young man called from the back of the room.

"What is a job?" He loved interacting with the participants at his workshops, so he didn't mind picking up a class if one of his employees was absent.

"Something you do to make money so you can live," answered an older gentleman recently laid off from his job of twenty-plus years.

"Live or survive?" Damon challenged.

"Survive," the majority of the class agreed.

A bright woman in the front clarified. "Surviving is about paying the bills. Living is about going on vacations and driving a phat car."

"Okay, I'll accept your answer. Work, job, career—are they all the same?" He wrote the words on the dry erase board and waited. "What's the definition of work?"

A young women chewing gum raised her hand. Damon grabbed the trashcan and went over to her. "This is a seminar on interviewing techniques."

She spit out the gum before answering. "Work is a service you perform for pay."

Damon perched himself on the corner of his desk. "Good answer. A job is also a service you perform for a salary. Meeting our basic needs is usually the driving force behind work or a job. A career, your life's work, is the ability to use your interests, talents and skills to earn a salary. Doing what you want to do in life to meet your basic needs and beyond. When you're at work, you love what you're doing, and you don't want to leave. You can't wait to get there each day. It challenges you. It stimulates you." He met the eager eyes of all the participants. "That's what I want for each of you. I want you to make a comfortable living while pursuing your career. I know this course is a requirement for many of you to continue receiving government assistance of one form or another, but I want you to really get something out of this. There won't be a test. You'll be judged by the standards you set for yourselves." He surveyed the class. He still had their attention. "Do you all understand what I'm trying to make you see?"

Silent nods confirmed their comprehension.

"Great. Let's get to work."

Mrs. Freidman met Damon in the hallway after the seminar. He felt energized after teaching. It was truly his calling. "You look very nice today, Mrs. Friedman. What's different?" He snapped his fingers. "Your hair is blonder. Curlier."

"Can't you stop at the compliment? Do you have to analyze everything to death?"

"Fine. You look gorgeous." They passed one of the maintenance staff. "Did you see the way he looked at you?" Damon teased.

She fought back a smile. "This is hardly appropriate talk for the workplace."

Damon handed her the stack of papers he was carrying in exchange for the stack of messages she was holding. He leafed through them as she updated him on the events he had missed while instructing the class.

"Can you take care of these?" He handed her several messages after reading through them. "I'll take care of the others in the morning." He checked his watch. "I have to be going."

"Before five? When was the last time you left the office before the cleaning staff?"

"My calendar is cleared."

"Yes, but…" Mrs. Friedman was at a loss. "Should I call you if something comes up?"

"You can, but my cell phone will be off." He smiled, deliberately being coy. "See you Monday."

"Monday?" She almost sounded panicked. "You're not coming in over the weekend?"

"Not anymore." He had living to do. Rebecca had helped him realize the future was too important to waste time shuffling papers behind a desk. He had good people working for him. He no longer needed an excuse to stay away from home. There was no reason to hide at the office. Brooke had helped him realize he'd missed out on too much. These days, he looked forward to the end of the workday.

"I like the new you," she called after him.

"Me too." He pushed the metal-trimmed glass door open and headed out into the world.

CHAPTER 27

Brooke was waiting for Damon in the lobby of Mr. Cavalier's office. She wore a form-fitting tan skirt with a red silk blouse. Long boots with tall heels accentuated her calves. She stood immediately upon seeing him. He rushed to her. "What is it?"

"I don't know." She grasped his hand, dragging him to the elevator. "Mr. Cavalier called my office and said get here." Once they were inside the elevator, she pushed the button several times.

"Hey." He pulled her into his arms. "Calm down. Whatever it is, we don't give up."

She exhaled. "Right. It could be good news."

"Exactly."

The secretary asked them to be seated while Mr. Cavalier finished up a phone call.

"Sorry, but that won't be possible." He gestured toward Brooke who couldn't stop shifting from foot to foot. "Mr. Cavalier asked us to come right away. Ms. Foster is very anxious to know why. He needs to see us immediately."

The secretary nodded, and excused herself to Mr. Cavalier's office.

"I hate what Neal is putting you through. This is outrageous. You're a good mother and don't deserve to have your loyalty to Rebecca questioned because he can't get over you."

She wrapped herself around his arm. "Thank you. I needed to hear you say that."

He kissed her forehead. "Where's Rebecca?"

"After school program."

The secretary returned, showing them into Mr. Cavalier's office.

"Mr. Cavalier, what did you find out?" Brooke asked.

"Has something happened?" Damon tried to remain calm, but the custody threat was getting to him too.

"Please, call me Tom." Mr. Cavalier ran his hand through his wild bronze hair. "Let me pull up your file." He punched the computer keyboard. "Professor Kirby has fired his previous attorney and hired Sam Markowitz. He's one of the best family law attorneys in this state." He punched more keys on the computer. "Neal is putting his ducks in a row. He's emphasizing the fact he's in a stable marriage. He and his wife are outstanding members of the community. They both have high six figure incomes. Between the two of them, they know every influential person in Michigan from the governor down to the biggest bully collecting the university's garbage."

Brooke sank down in her chair, defeated. "While I'm a single mother with a five figure income. I live in a townhouse where the upper level is so crammed with junk we don't even use it. And the only influential person I know is the crazy man who lives out of a shopping cart in the alley behind Vintage Suites who tells everyone he's the president of the United States."

"Oh, honey." Damon wrapped his arms around her shoulders. "Has Brooke told you about the extenuating circumstances here?"

"Yes, she's told me everything." Tom looked away from the computer screen and focused on Damon. "Professor Kirby is alleging that Brooke is an unfit mother. He has hired top private investigators and a child psychologist. He has several witnesses who have given sworn testimony about Brooke's unsavory character."

"They're lying," Brooke shouted

Tom handed her copies of the statements.

"I don't know any of these people."

"They claim to know you." His gaze turned back on Damon. "Your wife—"

"Ex-wife," he corrected.

"Your ex-wife is very verbal about accusing Brooke of breaking up your marriage—

alienation of affection."

Damon's anger began to grow.

"She's twisting the facts."

"Then we'll be able to straighten them out."

"Or there more?" Brooke asked at Mr. Cavalier's conspicuous pause.

"The psychologists are saying Brooke is the cause of Rebecca's PAS."

Damon leaned forward. "What is PAS?"

"Parental Alienation Syndrome. Psychologists believe that systemic denigration by one parent with the intent of alienating the child against the other parent is sometimes used to gain custody. In this case, Professor Kirby is saying Brooke's constant ridiculing of him has turned Rebecca against him. It is a very effective legal device for getting custody."

"I have never said anything bad about Neal in front of Rebecca. I wouldn't do that. She loves him."

Damen helped defend her. "Brooke has done nothing but consider his feelings. Why would the psychologists say something like this?"

"I can't believe Neal would go this far," Brooke added.

"Everything you've told us is negative. Are you saying Brooke is going to lose Rebecca?"

"I'm sorry if I have given you the impression the case is hopeless, it isn't. I wanted to present everything to you so you'd know exactly what you're dealing with. Brooke is the child's biological mother. You're her biological father. You're united in her fight to keep Rebecca. I can poke some holes in the witnesses' testimonies once I have the opportunity to question them. We still have a good chance."

Damon reached over and squeezed Brooke's hand.

"I have to be honest," Mr. Cavalier said. "Professor Kirby has unlimited resources both financially and with influential contacts. Under the law this shouldn't matter, but we have to be realistic. He has enough money to tie this case up for years in court. If I know Sam Markowitz, he'll advise his client to do just that. They'll try to bankrupt Brooke, and then say she doesn't have the financial means to care for her daughter."

"I make a decent living," Damon said.

Brooke turned to him. "What are you saying?"

"I'm helping you finance this fight."

"I can't let you do this."

"You don't have a choice. I'm sure Mr. Cavalier doesn't care who signs the check; he'll cash it."

Mr. Cavalier scratched at the bald spot on top of his head. "Don't make me sound so money-grubbing."

"Sorry," Damon apologized.

"I don't have unlimited finances. What can I do?" Brooke asked.

"Two ideas. I can contact Markowitz and suggest mediation between you and Professor Kirby. The decision is legal and binding and usually fair to both parties."

"The downside?" Damon asked.

"Professor Kirby's influence spreads far and wide. I don't know who owes him favors or how far he'd go to win."

Damon glanced at Brooke. Neal would do anything to have her. He'd already tried to blackmail. It was all about winning her back. "What's the other idea?"

Tom sat back in his chair and locked his fingers together behind his head. "You could take custody of Rebecca. On paper, you look like the more stable parent. You'll win the judge's sympathy when we tell him you divorced your wife because she didn't support your relationship with your child. After custody is established, you can make a liberal visitation schedule with Brooke."

He felt Brooke's eyes burning into him. He rubbed his hands up and down his thighs while Tom continued.

"The good of the child is the goal here. Courts like to honor the biological parents' rights. If I can show I have two biological parents who love their child, and are willing to work together for her best interest, well, Markowitz couldn't touch it. I'll discredit the accusations about Brooke being an unfit mother, but meanwhile Rebecca will be living with her biological father."

"We need to discuss this in private."

"No," Brooke shouted. "No, we don't need to discuss this at all, Damon."

"Brooke—"

"No, Damon."

"Brooke," Tom interrupted. "Mediation would be the best approach, but I believe in staying a step ahead of the game. Professor Kirby is fighting. You have to put away your emotions and fight harder." He spoke to Damon. "Get back to me by the end of the week. Meanwhile, I'll have my investigator take a look into Professor Kirby's life. If you want to find the dirt, follow the money trail. It's been my experience the rich have too much time on their hands, and they often use that time nurturing self-destructive behaviors."

<hr>

Damon took extra long strides to keep up with Brooke as she headed across the parking lot. "Brooke, wait," he called as she got into her car.

"I have to pick up Rebecca."

"I'll meet you at your place so we can talk."

"No. I don't want Rebecca to overhear us." She started the engine.

"We should at least consider Mr. Cavalier's suggestion."

"I won't let *you* take Rebecca from me either." She threw the car into drive and sped away.

Damon watched Brooke's car until the taillights disappeared. Cavalier's suggestion wasn't all that radical. Sure, they were both single parents and he hadn't been in Rebecca's life for the first five years of it, but with Neal's argument, he did look like the more stable parent. Once he found out he was a father, he'd immediately met his financial obligations. No time had passed between his finding out and his forging a relationship with Rebecca. He had chosen her over his wife and marriage. He lived in an upscale community in a nice neighborhood where the schools were top-notch. The ailing local economy had resulted in increased business for Employment Network Unlimited, which meant his finances were looking very, very good.

Brooke was so emotional these days, understandably so with Neal threatening to take her child. Maybe once she had time to think about it, she'd reconsider Cavalier's strategy. Or she would feel further threatened by the thought of losing Rebecca to Damon. He couldn't have her pushing him away. After rekindling their relationship, he couldn't accept becoming distant friends. He couldn't let their relationship deteriorate into joint parenting only. And he had to remember Neal was standing in the shadows trying to force Brooke into a sick, onesided relationship with him. She was too smart to fall for it, but who knew what a mother would do to keep her child?

He couldn't lose Brooke and he wouldn't jeopardize his relationship with Rebecca. They had come to be too important in his life. Because of them he'd found new focus for his life. He was happier than he had been in a very long time. He wanted them to become closer, not be torn apart because he had entered their lives. He walked to the Land Rover, searching for an amicable solution. There had to be an answer Brooke would be pleased with. There had to be a way to pacify Neal—although he still had lingering doubts about whether Neal truly wanted to preserve his relationship with Rebecca. Brooke assured him Neal really loved Rebecca, and he knew Rebecca loved Neal, so he'd have to accept the validity of it for now.

He didn't want Brooke to be alone. She had been distraught at Cavalier's office. He didn't want her to think of him as her enemy. She should know she wasn't fighting this battle alone. He grabbed Chinese and headed to Brooke's place. He was sitting in the lobby, waiting for his order when the solution to their problems popped into his head. He laughed aloud, turning several heads in his direction. It was the simplest, most logical conclusion. Why he hadn't thought of it right away, he didn't know. He snatched up his order and raced to Brooke's, anxious to share his idea.

⸎

The house was unusually quiet. Roger and Lisa were in the living room playing video games. They had been fighting over who had played longest, and whose turn it was to choose the next game. The screaming had become unbearable right before they came to blows, rolling around on the carpet and knocking over Barbara's favorite lamp. They'd quieted down when she told them to shut up, or she was sending them to live with their father. Since no one had any idea where the man was, the kids were scared witless. The threat had worked, because now they were playing quietly together.

Maybe her children were a little unruly; it still wasn't a good reason for Damon to leave. It was a great reason not to have any more. When Damon suggested she should be a happy stepmother to his illegitimate child, the thought had made her weak. The burden on their finances was enough to make her reject the idea. Not that things had gotten better when he'd left her. Soon, according to the terms of their divorce, his financial obligation to her would end. Her mortgage and car note were to be paid by Damon for another four months. She had a nice amount left in the checking and savings accounts he'd set up for her when they were married. Damon had also set up college accounts for Roger and Lisa she could tap into if need be. The way she calculated it, she had six months tops to bring Damon home or find a replacement. If she couldn't replace him by then, she'd have to get a job. She shivered. "The hell with that." She regretted not marrying him—or divorcing him—in California, a state where fifty percent was the law.

She moved around the bedroom, already dressed for bed although it was still early in the evening. The leopard print nightgown trailed behind her as she stomped around the room gathering the incidentals Damon had left in their bedroom. He had been in such a hurry to get to Brooke he hadn't even packed all his things. What was it about this girl that had men falling all over themselves for her?

Barbara smiled. Maybe not every man was fighting as hard for Brooke as he pretended to be. Kurtis was definitely on her radar. She'd noticed right away, at the Sinbad dinner, that he couldn't stop sneaking peeks at her legs. When she called, he came. She liked that quality in a man. "I've still got it." She observed her long, shapely legs in the full-length mirror. Her legs had always been her greatest attribute. She was a good looking woman, she knew, and was not embarrassed to say it aloud, but her legs were what first got a man's attention. Once she snagged a man with her legs, his eyes would gradually move upward past her round behind, spot her well defined waistline, peep at her curvaceous breasts, and be captivated by the flawless complexion of her perfect face. "There isn't a man out there who wouldn't be proud to have me wrapped around his arm every night." She wasn't done with her efforts to turn Damon around, bring him back, and salvage her lifestyle. But if things fell through, Kurtis wasn't so bad a second option.

She shouldn't have married Damon in the first place. Her friends had tried to warn her. Damon was too intellectual. He was struggling to make his fortune. She needed someone from old money, already established—like Kurtis. Damon was the type of man who had strong work ethics and placed more value on family than money. "Your mistake." She wagged a finger at the mirror. "But you can fix it."

She needed the kindly man who'd gone to prep school, drove fast cars and lived off his family's money. This man would have to get married because "Mummy" told him it was time to or he'd lose his inheritance. This man would not care if she could cook, or clean. She only needed to be beautiful and able to satisfy him in bed. He would send her kids away to boarding school and drape her in the finest luxuries. He might even live his own life while she lived hers. They would look like the perfect, happily married couple at all of Mummy's functions. She closed the suitcase packed with Damon's things and searched for something provocative to wear. Yeah, that was where she'd gone wrong.

She should never have chosen a blue collar, hometown boy thinking she could train him to meet her needs. But she was in too deep now, and it was easier to get Damon back than to find a replacement, so she would do what she had to do.

"I'm going out," she called as she passed the living room. She lugged the suitcase to the garage. She still didn't have her Audi. You'd think, after all she'd gone through, Damon would have thrown her that little bone. She jumped into the Mercedes and started the engine. "One last attempt." She fixed her lipstick in the rearview mirror. "Damon, this is your last chance."

She was rehearsing her seduction when she finally found Damon's house. The new community was a little too low class for her tastes, but she could see why Damon would be happy there. The house was dark, but she rang the doorbell anyway. She checked her watch. Growing angrier every minute she stood on the porch in the dark, cold night, she punched the bell over and over. Cursing, she kicked the door. "I wonder where in the world you can be?" She asked with a sneer. "Gloves off." She returned to her car and retrieved her cell phone. She had worked up enough tears to get Kurtis's sympathy by the time he picked up the phone.

———◦≈◦———

"Neal, I'm just saying there has to be a better way." Ella was horrified when she added up the running costs of the custody fight. "This lawsuit is putting a strain on our budget."

"I don't care about our budget. We're talking about my daughter here." He pushed the checkbook at her and left the table.

"We're not finished," she called after him. They always managed their finances together. His sudden lack of concern with the running of their household was another warning sign she wouldn't overlook.

Neal begrudgingly returned to the table. "I can't put a price on how important Rebecca is to me."

"Can you put a price on your sanity? Every time you have to visit her at Brooke's aunt's house you come home angry and full of venom and then you take it out on me."

He looked sheepish.

"This battle is tearing our family apart."

His eyes snapped up, undoubtedly wondering if she would accuse him of having an affair again. The signs were there—she wasn't a stupid woman. She'd given him her ultimatum. If she ever found proof of his infidelity, she'd leave him.

"You haven't supported me from the beginning," Neal accused.

"You're right. I've been less than enthusiastic about you fighting for custody of a child who isn't yours." She reached across the table and rested her hand atop his. "I see how much you love Rebecca. I'll stand by you if this is what you want to do. I'm just wondering if there isn't a better way. Can't you speak to Markowitz about some kind of formal visitation rights?"

He pulled his hand away.

"What about mediation? Brooke's attorney suggested it. Maybe she's ready to make a fair compromise."

"There is no compromising when it comes to my daughter. Besides, what do you think she's going to offer? Regular visitation at Aunt Foster's *farm*? I want my daughter here, with me."

"Won't you even consider sitting down with her?"

"No. You say you want to support me—then don't push this." He left the table.

"You have to find a solution before this gets any messier," she called after him.

CHAPTER 28

"Why do I have to put my pajamas on now?" Rebecca whined.

Brooke knelt to her level. "We're going to have a ladies night."

"But it's a school night."

"I know, but it's a special school night."

"What's so special?"

Sometimes she wished her daughter weren't so inquisitive. "I love you. Can't that be reason enough to celebrate?"

Rebecca shrugged. "I guess so."

"Okay. Let's get into our pajamas, order a pizza and watch cartoons until bedtime."

Rebecca ran off to her room. Brooke needed a few minutes alone to digest what had happened in Mr. Cavalier's office. As crazy as his idea was to let Damon have custody it was even more bizarre for Damon to think it was a good idea. He had to know she'd never go along with it. Maybe he did have better resources. Money didn't matter. Rebecca was her daughter and she wouldn't hand her over to Damon any more than she would Neal. After changing into her pajamas, she pulled on a pink terry cloth robe. Just as she was looping the belt, the doorbell rang.

"Mom!" Rebecca yelled from her bedroom.

"I've got it." She made her way across the living room. Damon was standing on her porch still dressed in the suit she'd seen him in earlier. If he'd come to persuade her to go along with Mr. Cavalier's scheme, he was wasting his time. "What are you doing here?"

"You were so upset when we left Cavalier's office. I didn't think you wanted to be alone."

She didn't want to be alone. She needed him beside her, helping her through this difficult time. They'd always been able to talk, and she needed to be able to work out her fears with him. Her hesitation came when she thought he might try to give him custody.

"You aren't still mad at me, are you?" he asked. "I brought Chinese." He held up the bags.

"I'm not mad at you."

"Can I come in?"

She stepped aside so he could come in.

"I know you want to forget today, but we need to talk. I think I have a solution."

Rebecca rounded the corner, her feet pattering over the carpet. "Hi, sir."

Damon's face lit up when he saw Rebecca. "You're ready for bed." He looked back at her. "You're both ready for bed."

"We're having a ladies' night," Rebecca told him.

"Can I come to your ladies night?" He showed her the Chinese food. "I brought dinner."

They both turned to her with hopeful expressions. If there had ever been a doubt about Rebecca's parentage, it was put to rest by their matching grins. "Fine. Damon can stay."

They camped out in front of the television, laughing at cartoons while they ate Chinese. Damon had peaked her interest by telling her he'd found a solution. She'd have to wait until Rebecca was asleep before she learned what it could be. She had to admit it was nice having Damon around. They laughed and found joy from the simplest things. Rebecca fell asleep in his arms, and he tucked her in for the night. Brooke watched from the doorway of Rebecca's room, observing how attached he'd become to her by the care he took in putting her to bed.

She waited until they were in the living room before she brought up the subject of Rebecca's custody case. "I lost it in the parking lot today. I can see you only want what's best for Rebecca. I shouldn't have snapped at you."

"It's understandable. We're both edgy right now."

They sat together on the sofa and she burrowed into his chest, absorbing the strength he offered as he held her close. "You seem to be holding it together well."

"That's because I have no doubt everything will turn out just like you want it."

She looked up at him. "You said you'd found a solution to this whole mess."

"I did." A huge smile bloomed. "Marry me."

Her eyes widened in disbelief.

"Don't look so shocked."

"I can't believe you sprang that on me."

"Well?"

"Well, what? You aren't serious?"

The wounded expression on his face told her he was. "It'll solve our problem."

"And create another."

"How will marrying me create problems?"

"Neither one of us is ready for marriage. I just ended a long-term relationship. You haven't been divorced six months. We can't get married just to solve our problems."

He inched away from her. "I wasn't prepared for this reaction."

"C'mon, Damon. Did you think I'd go along with something as radical as marrying you to win my custody case?"

"No," he clipped. "I didn't know you'd consider marrying me radical at all."

"I wouldn't say—"

He shifted so he faced her directly. "What are we doing here? I thought us getting back together meant we were back together—for good."

"You have to admit this came from out of nowhere."

"No, I don't have to admit that, Brooke. It was only a matter of time before I asked you to marry me. All we're doing is moving up the date."

She watched him, searching for a hint of doubt in his eyes. He had thought this through. Maybe not today, but marrying her had been on his mind.

"I love you, Brooke."

"I love you, Damon."

He took her hands in his. "We can be a family. Don't you want it as badly as I do?"

The telephone rang, saving her from answering. The idea of making a family with Damon was intoxicating, but she couldn't marry him because it was convenient. They had to be certain it was the right thing for both of them. She couldn't let her love for him cloud the issues.

"What is it?" Damon asked when she hung up the phone.

"Aunt Foster fell. She's in the hospital with a broken hip." She jumped up and raced to her bedroom.

"How bad is it?" Damon called after her.

"She says it's fine, but they'll probably have to operate."

"I'll drive you to the hospital."

"No. I need you to stay with Rebecca."

"Are you sure?" He stood in the doorway, watching her change.

"She's too young to visit."

"You shouldn't go alone. We can take Rebecca to my parents."

"No. I don't want to wake her or your parents." She pulled a sweater over her head. "You stay. If you don't mind."

"Of course not." He grabbed her coat and gloves while she pulled on her boots.

"It'll probably be pretty late when I get back."

"Don't worry about what time it is." He helped her on with her coat. "Call me and tell me how she's doing as soon as you know."

"I will."

He followed her to the front door. "And call me when you're on the way home so I can watch for you."

"I will." She grabbed her keys and her purse. "You're blocking me in."

He dug his car keys from his pocket and exchanged them for hers. "Take the Land Rover."

"Okay."

He pulled her into his arms and gave her a hard hug. "Drive safely."

—◦◦◦—

Kurtis was bold enough, angry enough to park his car right in front of Brooke's townhouse after he witnessed her kissing Damon good-bye and then taking off in his Land Rover. She had never, ever let him stay overnight because of Rebecca. *I guess the rules are different for Damon. He's Rebecca's father.* He considered marching up to the door, snatching Damon outside and pounding him into the ground. He was a man. He had his pride. Brooke had tossed him aside and changed partners before his heart had a chance to recover. He'd worked hard to win Brooke, but Damon just waltzed right in, declared his fatherhood, and make his place in her heart—and in her bed. Barbara had been right about everything.

He might have pushed marriage a little too hard. But Brooke was the kind of woman who needed her man to make all the important decisions in her life. Or so he'd always believed.

Meeting with Neal's attorney was way out of line, but Barbara had worked him up. It was her frantic call tonight that made him drive by Brooke's place. Barbara had gone to try to win Damon back, but he wasn't home. She had told Kurtis she had waited for hours, but he never showed. When Kurtis wouldn't give her Brooke's address, she'd insisted he go see for himself. She had been right on the money. She was waiting at her house for him to tell her what he'd found out.

She's going to flip when I tell her this, he thought as he pulled away from Brooke's townhouse. *I wonder what she'll want to do next.*

—◦◦◦—

Brooke sat next to Aunt Foster's bedside as she slept. The doctor had medicated the pain. In the morning, an orthopedic surgeon would evaluate Foster's need for surgery. The emergency physician had said it was inevitable. The nurse had spoken to them at length about the high incidence of falls among the elderly. She'd also told Brooke that Foster might need help performing her daily chores after the operation. Foster had refused to hear it. She'd been independent all her life. She wouldn't need anyone to care for her because of a little fall.

Brooke held her aunt's hand, contemplating how her future was changing. This included Damon's proposal. She prided herself on being honest in her relationships. She didn't lie, and she didn't use people. Her heart wanted her to accept his proposal, but her mind told her to mull over all the possible angles. Her limited experience with dating had not jaded her belief in true love. Actually, she'd only been involved with three men—Damon, Neal, and Kurtis—and all three were still a part of her life. The largest dating drama had been her breakup up with Damon, and he had forgiven her for it.

Until recently, she had led a charmed life. All things considered, she was still very lucky. Damon had returned without placing blame or making accusations. Kurtis had stood by her—she had been the one to end their relationship. Neal was very good to Rebecca—although his reasons for wanting total custody was negatively skewed. She was fortified with Aunt Foster's iron will. "I'm fortunate to have my life," she thought aloud, "but I have this nagging feeling that something's missing."

"Love," Aunt Foster answered groggily.

"What?"

"I heard you. Love. Love is what's missing."

"You love me." Brooke stood and kissed her aunt's forehead.

"You can't see it because you're too close. When Damon comes around, you're different. Happier. He's good for you and Rebecca."

She pulled her chair closer. "I can't believe you're finally admitting Damon is good for me." She smiled. "It must be the pain medicine."

"Hold on. Damon is good for you *now*. You're adults. When you were in high school, he wasn't the best thing for you. You were distracted, and reckless in your relationship with him. Your future was taking second place to your hormones. It wasn't the right time for such an all consuming relationship."

"But now is the time?"

Foster shrugged. "Only you know for sure."

"My attorney suggested letting him have custody of Rebecca and having him fight Neal. Damon thinks it would be better to get married."

"Married? He moves fast. What did you say?"

Brooke ran her hand across her face. "I haven't answered. We were talking when the hospital called."

"What are you going to tell him?"

She moved to the edge of her seat. "I don't know. On the one hand, I wanted to jump up and shout yes. On the other, I've loved him so long, I don't want to chance messing it up again."

"How would marrying him ruin anything? Especially if it's what you both want."

"I can't be sure he really wants to marry me because he loves me. He could be doing this to help me keep Rebecca."

Aunt Foster reached for her hand. "Talk to Damon. Ask him why he wants to marry you."

⚮

Brooke called Damon from the hospital and he assured her he could get Rebecca off to school. Wanting to be there when the orthopedic surgeon arrived, Brooke made arrangements to speak with him by noon. Aunt Foster refused the surgeon's diagnosis—until she tried to walk to the bathroom and the pain knocked her flat on the back. The surgery was scheduled for late afternoon. Brooke headed to Aunt

Foster's to pick up essentials, and then home to change and get Rebecca settled before she needed to get back to the hospital.

"Damon," she called when she arrived home. She found him in the kitchen, surrounded by paperwork. "You're still here?"

"I didn't know if you'd get away from the hospital in time to pick up Rebecca from school." He greeted her with a kiss.

"So you stayed? What about work?"

"I'm the boss. Have you eaten?"

"I didn't realize I was hungry until you mentioned it."

He moved to the refrigerator. "I'll make you an omelet and toast. Has the surgery been scheduled?"

"This afternoon." She kicked off her shoes and sank down at the table. Sleeping in a chair at the hospital was exhausting.

"I'll get Rebecca from school. Do you need me at the hospital? My parents are able to keep Rebecca."

Brooke watched him move around the kitchen cooking her breakfast, managing the household during her aunt's crisis. These were the actions of a man who knew the importance of a family. Without being asked, he had stepped up and taken charge, all the while offering her the emotional support she needed.

"Brooke?" He looked over his shoulder. "Should I tell my parents we need them to keep Rebecca?"

"No. I'd appreciate it if you stayed with Rebecca. I don't want her routine upset too much."

"I told her about Aunt Foster. I hope you're okay with it. She wanted to know why you weren't here."

"How'd she take it?"

"She's worried, but not scared."

"Good." She watched him butter toast and place it on the oven rack. "Damon, we need to talk."

He turned to her, mixing the eggs in a bowl. "Later."

"Things have been so crazy since I came back into your life. I don't want you to look up one day and realize you made a mistake."

SWEET REPERCUSSIONS

"We'll talk when Aunt Foster is better. Concentrate on her right now. Eat and get some sleep before you have to go back to the hospital. I'll be here when you get home."

While Brooke ate the breakfast he'd prepared, Damon drew her a bath. He gave her privacy while she slipped into the warm water. His voice carried from the kitchen as he went back to work. It was comforting to have him near. Knowing he was steps away made her feel safe.

"Are you asleep?" Damon appeared in the doorway.

"No. Thinking."

He sat on the edge of the tub. "About what?"

"I want Aunt Foster to live with me." She told Damon what the nurse had explained about Foster needing help once she was discharged.

"Do you think she will go for it?"

She stepped from the tub, and he helped wrap her in a towel. "Not at first, but she'll realize she needs help."

They moved to the bedroom where Damon had her climb into bed while he rubbed oil into her back. "What's the plan?"

"I'll talk to my aunt before surgery and try to convince her. If I can get her to agree, I'll move her things, and she can come here directly from the hospital."

"Hmmm," Damon agreed.

"I can move upstairs. She can take my room so she won't have to use the stairs. Of course, getting the upstairs ready will be a big job."

"Don't worry about the details. Just get Aunt Foster to agree to it."

Her lashes dipped. "You take very good care of me."

He kissed the back of her neck. "What time should I wake you?"

She glanced at the bedside clock. "Give me four hours."

He nestled his nose in the crook of her neck. She rolled onto her back and wrapped him in her arms, pulling him against her naked body. His lips devoured her, finding the inlet to her soul. She loved his kisses. He conveyed all his true feelings through his kisses. He offered emotional closeness, not a prequel to sex. He showed her intimacy by giving all of himself. Damon pulled back, reading her reaction.

"Okay."

"Okay, what?" he asked, enjoying the dizzying effects his kiss had on her. He pressed his forehead to hers. "Okay I do this?" He pressed his lips against her shoulder. "Okay I try this?" His lips burned her cleavage. "Okay I share myself with you?" His mouth found hers again. "You better tell me exactly what you mean by okay before we get into trouble."

She stared into his inviting green eyes still speechless.

He caressed her cheekbone. "If you could have anything you want, what would it be?"

"I would want you to stay with me. I want to sleep with you holding me, knowing you'll watch over me and make everything all right."

"You give me too much credit. I can't fix everything in your life." He chuckled. "When I tried, it didn't turn out too well. What I can do is hold you and take away some of the burdens you're carrying."

He removed his shoes and climbed into bed with her. He molded his front to her back and covered them with the comforter. His arms secured her waist.

"I am glad you're here. Thank you."

"Brooke?"

"Yes?"

He laughed. "Watching you in the tub was torture, but holding you while you're naked is agony."

She laughed with him. "Not up to the job?"

He wiggled his hips against her bottom. "Very up to the job. That's the problem."

CHAPTER 29

It wasn't until Brooke was sitting in the surgery waiting room that she pulled out the statements Mr. Cavalier had given her. Two lines into the document, she recognized Kurtis's stamp all over it. She wanted to kill him. He told stories about their relationship ending because she'd cheated on him. He even had made-up proof. She knew it was Kurtis because she'd only had three relationships in her life. Neither Damon nor Neal would make up these stories. Neal wouldn't jeopardize his position at the University. Damon loved her too much. How could Kurtis stoop to making up lies about her heiress promiscuous to punish her for not wanting to marry him? She had foolishly believed he really cared about Rebecca. But how could he if he were willing to insinuate himself into the middle of her custody case with his lies?

How could she have considered marrying Kurtis? Everything good he'd ever done would be overshadowed by this. He had to know it wasn't a game. She could lose Rebecca because of his bogus statements. If he hadn't interfered, it wouldn't be necessary for her to consider giving custody to Damon.

She didn't know Barbara well, but something told her she had been involved in some way. The last time she'd talked to Kurtis he'd admitted to spending time with her. She'd never suspected their time together would be used plotting against her. She had to talk to Damon about this.

"Ms. Foster?"

"Yes." She stuffed the documents back into their envelope.

The doctor approached. "Your aunt came through the surgery just fine." He gave her the details of the surgery, telling her Aunt Foster's recovery would take weeks. She would be released from the hospital as soon as she could walk with the assistance of a walker. "You can see her in a few minutes."

"Thank you, doctor."

It might not have been fair, but Brooke needled Aunt Foster into agreeing to moving in with her while she was still under the effects of the anesthesia. They'd discuss it again, but she needed her aunt to realize her age and her weight put her at risk for injuries. Living with Brooke meant having someone around to help out.

"I'm only agreeing to this," Aunt Foster said, "because Rebecca needs me." She swiveled her head around to the nurse. "My niece has a good man wanting to marry her and she can't decide what to do. Don't that sound like she needs my help, and not the other way around?"

<hr />

Damon and his lawyer were already seated at the conference table when Barbara and her attorney walked in. Damon was beginning to dislike lawyers. Lawyers were driving every negative action in his life. It was an honorable profession, but he sincerely hoped Rebecca would pursue astronomy like Brooke wanted, and steered clear of the judicial system. Lawyers always meant bad news and he couldn't imagine why Barbara was calling this meeting. The terms of their divorce were final. She'd received a good settlement, considering she'd never loved her husband.

"I really need to wrap this up," Damon whispered to his attorney. "I have to pick my daughter up from school."

"We'll move it along."

Barbara was dressed for war. Her legs flowed from beneath a red leather miniskirt. The matching jacket barely covered her heaving breasts. Her hair was coiled into a tight bun, calling attention to her flawless face. Damon could hear the men in the room swallow—

hard—as she slid into her seat. He wanted to scream a warning. This woman was a black widow.

"Stanly, this will be an easy one." Barbara's lawyer passed a set of papers to Damon's attorney. Barbara's nose wrinkled at their familiarity.

"Good, Stanley, my client appreciates it. She's wasted enough of his time during their marriage."

Damon saw Barbara cringe. He had selected Marty as his attorney because he could be ruthless, but only if provoked. Obviously, he felt provoked by this bogus meeting.

Marty addressed Damon directly. "Mr. Richmond, my client doesn't want to hold you captive by this marriage. She realizes her mistake."

"Why are we here?" Marty asked. "He's given you the house and all its contents. He's paid the mortgage and car note for six months. My client has been more than generous—all to make it easier on her and the kids. What more could she want?"

"I want half the business," Barbara blurted out.

Damon was so stunned he shouted, "What business?"

"Employment Network Unlimited. We were married. I'm entitled to half."

Damon raised his voice. "Are you out of your mind? I've given you everything I'm going to give you." He turned to his attorney. "She can't ask for more after the settlement has been reached, can she?"

"Absolutely not." Marty stood and grabbed his briefcase. "Let's go."

"Employment Network Unlimited was started before you came along. You haven't even come to the office more than once. How dare you ask me to give you half of it?"

"You might want to take a look at the motion, Marty." Stanley sounded too sure of himself. "The settlement isn't valid if your client was hiding assets."

Marty fell silent.

"What is he talking about?" Damon asked.

"My client found proof of his deception when she packed the last of his things. You'll find the evidence in my disclosure."

Damon hated lawyers. He cursed underneath his breath.

Marty grasped his arm. "We'll get back to you after I look over your motion and confer with my client."

Marty took Damon down the hall to another conference room. "Do you have any idea what's going on?"

"None. I've never hidden any assets. The business never came into play during the divorce because I gave Barbara everything she wanted."

"Well, something has put her back on your trail. Have you been fighting?"

"We don't have occasion to speak very much. The times we've talked, we didn't fight. I can't believe this."

"Barbara is angry about something, and she's expressing it by trying to take your business. She's expecting a fight—probably wants one. She's trying to get you riled up. Let's just stay cool until I sort through this."

"I won't give Barbara one cent from my business. She never showed any interest in it. She never supported my efforts to build it. The only thing she wanted was my money. I don't know why she's doing this, but I won't give in to her. I need the income stability. I'm fighting for my daughter. If she wants a fight, give her a fight."

<hr/>

"This is going to be a lot of work, sir." Rebecca struggled with an armload of baby clothes she'd outgrown.

"Sure, it's a lot of work, but it's worth it to make your mom happy, right?" Damon took some of the clothes away and made a second pile.

"Yes, but we never come up here."

"I know, but your Aunt Foster is coming to live with you for a little while. Remember I told you she hurt her hip?" He carried a large box of Christmas decorations downstairs with Rebecca on his heels.

"She's still in the hospital."

"Right. Well, when she gets out of the hospital she'll come here until she's better. Since her hip is broken, she can't climb up the stairs. It'll be better for your mother to sleep upstairs, and Aunt Foster to sleep in her room."

Rebecca ran back upstairs. "So we have to clean up so Mom will have somewhere to sleep."

"You've got it, sweetheart." He gathered the last storage box. "If we can clean all this stuff away, the only thing your mom will have to do is arrange her furniture." He looked around at the large, open space. There was one huge bedroom, a small bedroom and a bathroom on the second floor of Brooke's townhouse. Once they had removed all the clutter stored in the two bedrooms, it was a prime space with large windows and dark hardwood flooring. While Rebecca boxed the old clothing in the second bedroom, Damon found Brooke's limited tools and tinkered in the bathroom until it was up and running. With a woman's touch the upstairs would be a real showcase.

Brooke had been at the hospital all day with Aunt Foster. He'd sworn Rebecca to secrecy about their cleaning project. He wanted to make things a little easier for Brooke if he could. She was going through a rough time, which wouldn't be made better once he told her about Barbara's new demands. He hoped to help Brooke with Rebecca until Aunt Foster was released. If he couldn't settle things with Barbara by that time, he'd have to tell Brooke about her quest to take half of his business.

He'd never been one to fight over possessions or money, but he needed his financial stability right now. The custody fight with Neal sounded as if it would be a long drawn out, expensive venture. If Brooke did decide to follow Mr. Cavalier's suggestion and let Damon have custody of Rebecca until the fight was over, he needed a stable income. If Brooke decided she wanted to marry him, he couldn't go into a new life with her and Rebecca while fighting with Barbara about the old one.

"Sir, I'm hungry." Rebecca stood in the bathroom doorway covered in dirt.

"You're a mess." A cutie, but still a mess.

"Mom is going to be mad if she sees my hair."

Dirt and dust covered her thick braids. She had to go to school tomorrow. In his attempt to help Brooke, he'd inadvertently made more work for her.

"I have an idea." He started packing away the tools. "Go change into something clean. We'll get something to eat, and I'll take care of your hair before your mom sees you."

While Rebecca washed up and changed her clothes, Damon hauled the last of the storage boxes into the storage closet. What didn't fit, he took to the basement. After washing up, he took Rebecca to Burger King. She told him about her day at school. Brooke called his cell and he watched Rebecca's face light up when she spoke to her. What Neal was doing was cruel. Brooke and Rebecca were close. No one should try to break their bond.

"Your mom says she'll be home in a couple of hours. Let's do something about your hair."

"What?"

"We're going to seek professional help. Eat up."

She dug into her burger and fries.

"Rebecca?"

"Yes, sir?" She looked up at him with sparkling green eyes.

"Do you understand I'm your father? Your Dad?"

"Yes, sir."

"Can we be friends, too?"

"Yes, sir." Her little hands stuffed fries into her mouth.

"Do you think you could call me something other than sir?"

She used two hands to drink her juice.

"Dad?"

"I have a dad."

"How about Daddy?"

"Okay." She went back to her fries. It didn't matter what she called him. In her eyes she was his *other* dad. He realized it would take a long time to prove his importance in her life. All things considered, the development of their relationship was going well. Still, it hurt to be referred to as the "other dad."

"Sir," Rebecca corrected her mistake, "Daddy, I have to use the lavatory."

He smiled at her attempt at proper manners. Maybe words weren't so important after all. He should cherish the relationship they were building and forget what label she attached to him. Damon had one of the employees watch over Rebecca while she used the ladies' room. After they finished dinner, they climbed into his Land Rover and headed to the beauty salon.

Damon had his dreads washed and oiled while a short woman charmed Rebecca into letting her place a neat ponytail down the middle of her head. It wasn't the elaborate braiding style Brooke had done, but it was neat. Rebecca smiled over at Damon as the beautician spun her aroused in the chair next to him. He watched over his magazine as they chattered like two adults, consulting on Rebecca's braids.

"Beautiful." Damon lifted her from the chair and gave her a big hug.

Brooke had made it home when Damon pulled into the driveway of her townhouse. Rebecca couldn't wait to tell her about the day's adventures.

"Oh, my goodness." Brooke whistled. "What did you do to my daughter? She's gorgeous."

Rebecca giggled as Damon twirled her around in a circle.

"Is it okay?" he asked.

"It's fine. Very pretty." She asked Rebecca, "Why'd you need your hair washed?"

She led Brooke by the hand up the stairs to show her what they had done.

Brooke's hands went over her mouth. "You did all this today?"

Rebecca gave her the details while Damon stood off watching their interaction. They were happy. They were a family.

Brooke gave Rebecca a tight squeeze. "Go get ready for bed. I'll come tuck you in."

Rebecca ran down the stairs to her room.

Brooke came over and hooked her arms around Damon's waist. "I can't believe you did all this."

"I wanted to help, but didn't want you to think I was overstepping my boundaries."

"When you possess my heart, there are no boundaries." She tilted her head up for his kiss, and he happily obliged.

"This is all mine?" He outlined her heart with his fingertip.

"Every inch. Or should I say every artery and vein?"

"Silly."

She pulled away and floated around the room. "First thing, I'm going to go shopping for drapes and rugs. This will be my haven. Can you imagine making love up here with the sun pouring in from these big windows?"

"The picture is becoming more and more vivid."

"I have an idea." She sashayed up to him, pressing her body against his. "Why don't we get some blankets from downstairs and try out some new positions."

"Brooke." He smiled, enjoying her sauciness.

"I need to find the best place to put my bed."

"I have a suggestion. Away from the vents."

They laughed together. With all the stress surrounding the custody case, they hadn't laughed much lately.

"Aunt Foster would have a fit," Brooke said, starting downstairs.

"We don't have much time. We better find the best position before she's released from the hospital."

"My thought exactly." She waited for him at the bottom of the stairs. "You grab some blankets from the closet in my bedroom. I'll tuck Rebecca in."

He gave her a quick kiss. "Meet you upstairs."

Damon brought the blankets upstairs and arranged a soft pallet. He undressed, and waited for Brooke beneath a sheet. If she would accept his proposal, they could have many more days like this—being a family. How would their relationship change if she didn't agree to marry him? He couldn't remain her boyfriend forever. They were much too old to continue playing the dating game. Besides, he doubted his heart could take it if she didn't love him enough to marry him.

"Mr. Richmond, you are bad." She started undressing.

"You've been teasing me since I had to watch you step out of the tub."

She smiled, remembering his reaction.

"Get over here."

She removed her clothing with tantalizing movements that made him want to spring from the makeshift bed. She had a perfect body that had not been altered by childbirth. As he watched her discard her blouse, he imagined what she must have looked like when she was nine months pregnant. He pictured her skin stretched across the belly nurturing his child. He pictured her thighs, thickened by the weight of carrying Rebecca. She would have been full in the face, her cheeks blushing with the prospect of becoming a mother.

"Why are you looking at me like that?" she asked, climbing beneath the sheet with him.

"I'm picturing you pregnant."

She burst into laughter. "It wasn't a pretty sight."

He covered her body with his. "One day."

"One day, what?" she pressed her lips to his neck.

"One day, I'll see for myself just how lovely you are when you're pregnant." Before she could respond, he pressed his mouth to hers. He sank into the softness of her curves. Her skin was smooth and warm, inviting him to seek refuge. He touched her tenderly and kissed her wildly. He tasted every inch of her body as if it were the first time. He drank her up—mind, body and soul.

He had learned her body and knew it better than his own. He touched her where her body needed it most. He kissed her when she craved the intimate connection. He licked her where it made her cry out in ecstasy. And he knew when it was too much for her to bear. He surged forward with her hands gripping his buttocks and pulling him deeper. They came together in a wash of emotions, and he was more fulfilled than he had ever been.

He held her in his arms for a long time before she broke the silence. "Kurtis gave Sam Markowitz a statement against me."

"What?" He sat up on his elbow, looking down into her sad eyes.

"I read the statement. He gave a fake name, but it was him."

"If it was, he'll have to identify himself soon. It's your right to question him. Are you sure it was Kurtis?"

"Positive. He says I'm promiscuous and left him to be with you."

Everything fell into place. "I met with my attorney today. Barbara wants half of Employment Network Unlimited."

"I thought your divorce was settled."

"It is. She's claiming I hid assets and wants to renegotiate."

"Do you think Kurtis put her up to it?"

He stroked away the wrinkle on her forehead. "No. I would bet Barbara put Kurtis up to it."

"Why?"

He tilted his head to the side. "Jealousy." "They're feeding off each other's jealousy. I'm not giving in to Barbara, and I won't let Kurtis get away with lying, either. No one will take Rebecca away from us." He kissed her forehead, gathering her in his arms. "And no one will come between us."

CHAPTER 30

"Mr. Richmond," Mrs. Friedman announced, "Brooke Foster is here to see you."

"Brooke's here?" He started around his desk, but Brooke burst in, stopping him. "Hold my calls, please," he dismissed Mrs. Friedman. "This is a surprise."

"I have news." She pulled a chair up to his desk.

"Aunt Foster?"

"She's fine. On schedule to come home tomorrow."

"What's the news?"

"I'm coming from Tom Cavalier's office."

"Why didn't you call me to go with you?"

She waved away his question. "Neal rejected our offer of mediation. Tom told his attorney about the possibility of you taking custody of Rebecca, and Neal blew his top. He was being completely obstinate."

"If the meeting was so bad, why do you have a big grin on your face?" He resisted the urge to go to her and kiss the corner of her mouth.

"Finally, after intense bickering, Tom said it would be best for both sides to think about the suggestions made and reconvene next week. As soon as we ended the conference call, he left me to get myself together. Needless to say, I was a wreck by then. When he returned, a call came through. After he hung up, he was smiling like the cat who ate the canary."

"Because?" Her happiness was contagious, spilling onto him.

"*Because*," she mocked him with a smile, "he had just spoken with the private investigator who assured him there was something we needed to see. We met with the investigator over lunch. I should add that the investigator is a woman." She pumped her fists above her head with female solidarity.

"Bring it down a notch, Norma Rae." He laughed. "Go on with the story."

"*My sister* did good work. She had tapes, notes and pictures of Neal that would make even you blush."

"What does this mean?" Her mood was too good not to be infectious.

"It seems Neal has slept with many more coeds since I left campus. There are pictures of him with women as recent by as a week ago. Tom feels Neal won't want Ella finding out about the infidelity—let alone the university board and the public."

"Talk about an unfit parent," he added.

"All of his high class friends at the courthouse would see firsthand what kind of man he is. They won't look kindly on all of his affairs with his students. The information I gave Tom about Kurtis and Barbara gave him more ammunition. Tom is scheduling a meeting with Neal and his attorney right now. He's sure Neal will agree to a quiet ending to this whole custody mess."

"I can tell Barbara what we've found out?"

She nodded.

"I don't have to give her one cent from my business."

"Nope. We have to celebrate. Rebecca's birthday party will have to be special."

"This will be over soon?"

"Looks like." Brooke beamed.

Damon rounded the desk and pulled her into his arms for a kiss. "This is good. We'll both have our lives back soon."

⸎

"This is no more than blackmail." Neal tightened his fist around the 8 X 10 color glossy. He threw his eyes in the direction of his attorney. "What kind of person are we dealing with here?"

Sam Markowitz placed a firm hand on his shoulder. "It's your choice. If you want to keep fighting, I will. But this is sure to get out."

"Can't you exclude it as evidence? Discredit it?"

"I don't see how. You opened the door when you claimed Brooke is an unfit mother. She has the right to prove you're the unfit parent. There are tapes to corroborate the pictures. There's no way I can keep your affairs from becoming public news."

"Do you get a perverse pleasure from these?" He waved another photo in front of Sam's face before crumpling it and throwing it across the room.

Sam remained cool, angering Neal further. His case was disintegrating in front of him. Brooke was getting away, and he was losing Rebecca.

"How do you want to handle it?"

Neal shrank back in his chair. He had been prepared to verbally spare with Brooke's lawyer. He could produce several witnesses to discredit Brooke. As long as she kept seeing Damon he could claims she was promiscuousness against her. He wasn't prepared to have to defend his own actions. "I would be forced to admit to seeing these women?"

"Lying under oath wouldn't be the action of a good parent."

His extra credit activities with the young coeds would be the end of his career and his marriage. His career defined him as a man. Ella was his backbone. He couldn't lose either. If there were a way for him to still see Rebecca, keep his job and save his career, he had to take it. "What are they offering?" he asked, admitting defeat.

<hr />

"You're planning a party for a princess," Aunt Foster teased Brooke.

"She is my princess."

Rebecca giggled. "Everything is going to be Barbie."

"Barbie, huh? Clear the table so your mother can set out dinner." Aunt Foster was getting around well with the use of a three-legged walker, but Brooke didn't want her to overdo it. The three had divided the household chores making it easier on everyone. They had fallen into a comfortable routine when Aunt Foster moved in, and Rebecca definitely benefited by having her around. Brooke was able to sneak away to see Damon without guilt, because Aunt Foster and Rebecca truly enjoyed each other. She suspected Aunt Foster would be thrilled if the arrangement were permanent, despite her grumbling when Brooke suggested it.

After dinner, Rebecca ran off to finish her homework. Brooke cleaned the kitchen while Aunt Foster sat at the table, clipping coupons and making the weekly shopping list.

"I suppose you didn't accept Damon's proposal since you're not wearing an engagement ring," Aunt Foster said.

"Actually, I didn't accept or refuse. It never came up again, and once Neal agreed to my visitation terms, it didn't seem necessary to talk about it."

Foster shook her head. "I don't understand kids today. And you and Damon are the worst. Since you were in high school, you've been fighting to be together. Now you have the chance and 'it never comes up.'"

"It's complicated."

"You don't think he really meant to propose. You think he only did it to help you keep Rebecca. Let me tell you something, niece, men don't do anything they don't want to do. If he asked, he wants to marry you."

"Then why hasn't he brought it up?"

"Maybe because you all but refused the first time. Damon isn't the type of man to push or beg. He thinks you're avoiding the subject because you don't want to marry him."

She had never looked at it from that perspective. She'd assumed Damon had not mentioned his proposal again because the custody case had been settled. Was it possible he was waiting for her to broach the subject?

"And about Rebecca's party," Aunt Foster went on. "How come Neal and Kurtis aren't on the invitation list?"

"After what Neal tried to do? And Kurtis with his butting in? I don't want them here."

"That would be important if it were your party, but since it's not, you should have the people Rebecca wants here at her party. She keeps talking about them coming. How are you going to explain it when they don't show?"

She'd done a good job of keeping the custody battle from Rebecca, but Rebecca had sensed the tension between her and Neal. But she understood the visitation arrangements had changed. She didn't know how badly Neal had acted, or how much of a snake Kurtis had turned out to be.

Aunt Foster hoisted herself up using the edge of the table. "You should do the right thing." She grabbed her walker and left Brooke to ponder her advice.

———∞∞———

Kurtis entered Brooke's office, hidden behind a bouquet of yellow roses. "Truce?" He bowed his head and presented the flowers with an outstretched hand.

She took a deep breath, preparing to confront him for the last time. She took the bouquet. "Flowers weren't necessary."

He handed her a pink gift bag with Barbie on the front. "This is for Rebecca. I know her birthday is in a few days." He rushed on. "My secretary's little girl assures me it's the coolest new Barbie doll." He smiled, trying to break the tension in the room.

"You can give Rebecca your present yourself." She went into her drawer and handed him an invitation to Rebecca's birthday party.

He gathered his slacks at the knee and sat down. "Then you forgive me?"

"Do you think flowers and a Barbie doll are enough to right what you did? You tried to help Neal take my daughter away from me. I knew you were hurt, but I never imagined you would betray me. If nothing else, I believed we were friends."

"You're right." He slid to the edge of his seat, placing his hands firmly on the corner of her desk. "You hurt me. I wanted to hurt you back. I should have never gotten involved with Barbara's scheme. I regret ever talking to Neal's attorney."

"No, you shouldn't have. I can never trust you again."

"In time—"

She glared at him, making him shudder. "If I did ever want to get back with you, I couldn't do it after what you've done."

"I understand."

She was almost speechless, but pressed on. "I don't want to have to worry about you getting mad and doing something vindictive to ruin me. You know how much Rebecca means to me—I just can't believe what you did."

"I understand everything now. I know why you couldn't marry me. I won't deny what I did was wrong. In time, maybe we can be friends. I'm trying to make things right."

"How are you doing that?" She didn't want to be surprised by any more of his schemes.

He squirmed, uneasy. "I talked Barbara into dropping her claim to Damon's business."

"Really?" She was still suspicious. "Exactly how did you accomplish that?"

He squirmed again. "We're kinda seeing each other."

Brooke listened with morbid fascination as he told her how his relationship with Barbara had evolved from the first dinner at Sinbad's restaurant. He liked the idea of keeping Barbara at home, draped in luxury. She would surely accept his proposal of a carefree lifestyle. Somehow, Brooke knew they were made for each other.

"I have to get back to work." She still found it difficult to look at him. Eventually, the anger would wear away, but right now she still couldn't forgive him for his part in the custody case.

"Sure. I should be going." He stood, but stopped once he reached the door. "Can I call you—as friends? Just to check on you and Rebecca?"

"If we need anything, I can handle it. You're invited to the party because Rebecca wants you there. After it's over, I don't want to speak to you again."

He nodded, and left her office with his head hanging.

It took Brooke most of the afternoon to put his visit out of her mind. She had practiced what she would say to him. She took full responsibility for her part in their break up, but what he'd done was so far over the line there was no way to erase it all and have a friendship. She truly saw him for the first time. He was controlling because he had no confidence. He conspired against her because he couldn't deal with a strong woman rejecting him. She had avoided all the curse words, and handled herself with dignity. Her victory had come in the way he slithered out of her office.

"How did it go?" Ella was waiting in the living room when Neal walked in that evening.

He shrugged as she helped him out of his suit jacket.

"Tell me what happened. You don't look pleased."

"After I tried to do the right thing and drop the custody case, Brooke threw me a bone and acted like she's doing me a big favor." He sank down in his leather chair.

Ella poured him a glass of brandy. "What kind of favor?"

He dug the party invitation from the jacket of his suit.

She handed him the glass and returned to her seat to read the invitation. "It was nice of Brooke to invite you."

He gulped his brandy. Trying to keep the reasons behind the settlement a secret from Ella was exhausting. He'd gone along with Brooke's one weekend a month visitation plan. He deserved more than an invitation to his daughter's birthday. "The visitation agreement states I keep Rebecca for two weeks over the summer. I'm taking her to Disney World next July."

"Be nice, Neal. Brooke doesn't have to let you take Rebecca out of the state. It's at her discretion. Plus, you want her for some of the upcoming holidays."

"I don't like begging for time with Rebecca." He swirled the liquid in his glass before placing the rim to his mouth.

"Go to the party. Show you're the bigger person. Rebecca wants you there, I'm sure."

"We don't want to interfere with the bond *Damon* is trying to build with Rebecca," he said sarcastically.

"Don't be this way. Brooke did compromise. She agreed to leave Rebecca in Cambridge until graduation, even though Damon wanted to put her in a more conventional school. Your legacy at the school continues. She even offered to make arrangements to pay back the money you've contributed to raising Rebecca."

"I don't want her money. I gave her money because I wanted Rebecca to have the best. I still want that. I don't want her money." He paused to take another sip of brandy. "Damon insists on paying half of Rebecca's tuition from this point on—his way of flexing his muscle in my daughter's life. It's foolish, I told Brooke, but she says he insists."

"Oh, Neal." Ella kissed his temples. "It'll all work out. Go to the party and celebrate Rebecca's birthday. She loves you. She'll be hurt if you don't come."

CHAPTER 31

Damon sat at the writing table in his master bedroom and signed the last check he would be writing to cover Barbara's mortgage. He had agreed on paying another two months in exchange for her dropping her claim against his business. He didn't understand her sudden cooperativeness until Brooke told him she was seeing Kurtis. With that check his tie to Barbara was broken. There should be a ceremony with the presentation of the final check. Brooke had promised him something special this evening, and his body became tighter by the minute, waiting for her to arrive.

Instead of relying on the postal carrier to deliver the check, he would do it himself. He would apologize for it not working out between them, and wish her a good life. He would also ask about Roger and Lisa. Then he remembered their last conversation and thought it better of visiting her. He closed the envelope, placed a stamp on it, flipped it over on the reverse side and penned very neatly, *Be Happy. D. W.* He grabbed his jacket and walked down the street in the crisp winter wind to drop the envelope in the mailbox. The walk cleared his head and allowed him to let go of any grudges he had against Barbara. He had a chance at a future with Brooke. He was building a relationship with Rebecca. Even Aunt Foster seemed to have finally accepted him in her niece's life.

The mailboxes were located outside the Briarcliff Elementary School. He hadn't been able to persuade Brooke to put Rebecca in the school built exclusively for Briarcliff residents. He'd given up when she pointed out his wanting Rebecca there was for his ego not because it was the better school. Cambridge Academy had a solid reputation and Rebecca would benefit for a lifetime from attending.

A woman walking her dog across the school lawn caught his attention. Damon zipped his jacket against the falling temperatures and watched the woman. A little boy ran up and chased the dog, setting off a barking frenzy. The woman scolded him, but couldn't keep the joy out of her voice. Damon started back to his house, but couldn't get the picture of the woman and son out of his head. The dog's barking followed him. The overwhelming urge to see Rebecca warmed his chilled hands. She would love a puppy. He'd discuss it with Brooke. He could keep the puppy at his place for when she visited.

More than anything, he wanted them to be a family. He wanted to take Rebecca on walks in the park. He wanted to spend time with Brooke, sharing intimate secrets. He hadn't given up hope on his proposal. They hadn't discussed it since he'd asked, but at least she hadn't said no. He wouldn't push—that had been Kurtis's mistake. He wouldn't give her too much room, either—that had been his mistake the first time around. He knew they were meant to be together. They had been through so much, and they still loved each other. He had to let Brooke come around and when she did, he'd be waiting. As he had been waiting all his life.

CHAPTER 32

"Did you get it? Did you get it?" Rebecca jumped up and down at Damon's feet trying to see what was contained within the white baker's box. The tiny braids cascading down her shoulders bounced around her face.

"I've got it. Of course I did. I couldn't let my birthday girl down."

"Can I see?"

Damon made a grand show of lowering the box within her view. "One chocolate Barbie doll cake for the birthday princess."

Her smile broadened, warming his heart.

"What's all the noise out here?" Aunt Foster maneuvered her walker through the door of Brooke's kitchen.

"Sorry. My fault." He winked at Rebecca.

Aunt Foster put both of her hands on her waist. "Go finish getting dressed, young lady. Keep spoiling her, and you'll be sorry one day."

"Aunt Foster, you're the worse." He kissed her cheek as he moved past her into the kitchen.

"Don't be smart," she called after him.

"Yes, ma'am."

Every year Brooke vowed to downsize Rebecca's birthday party. This year's excuse for not keeping the promise was the fact that Damon had missed so many of Rebecca's birthdays. He wanted this one to be special for his daughter. Aunt Foster huffed, rambling on about the danger of giving a party for the adults and not for the child. True, Brooke and Damon had both invited work acquaintances, but only those with children. And at the final hour, they had decided to have the party at Brooke's townhouse instead of the hall they had rented.

Damon had spent the entire morning shifting the furniture in the living room, hanging streamers, and blowing up balloons. Brooke and

Aunt Foster took over the decorating when they saw the work he and Rebecca had done. They were proud, but Brooke and Foster's faces dropped and a shopping list was quickly thrown together to get him out of the house. "You're great at some things," Brooke whispered, "but decorating is not one of them." When he returned, the living room had been transformed into a pink and white Barbie palace. He had never seen so many Barbies in his life.

Rebecca had described her room at Neal's house. It saddened Damon with jealousy to know Brooke and Neal had parented so well together. They had been a team. He wanted to take Rebecca on her first trip, but Neal and Ella had already made plans to take her to Disney World next summer. He had to be honest and admit his jealousy was about more than Neal's role in Rebecca's life. It was hard for him to accept Neal's importance, but his place in Brooke's life bothered him more. He had come between them once. Damon wouldn't let it happen again. Even after the custody fight, Neal had managed to keep his place in Brooke's life. He would be at Rebecca's party, throwing his weight around. With Kurtis in attendance, it would be dinner at Sinbad's again.

Damon's parents were the first adults to arrive at the party. Rebecca embraced Grandma and Grandpa, but her attention was locked on the large, red package under her Grandpa's arm. Having grandparents was new for her, but she had quickly adjusted when she found out their purpose was to buy her whatever she wanted. Whenever Damon's father went near Rebecca he teared up, and today was no exception. He said Rebecca reminded him of his wife when they were younger. "Now don't those green eyes make you the prettiest girl I've ever seen," he'd tell Rebecca while winking at his wife.

The guests started arriving quickly. Kurtis scooped Rebecca up in his arms and she giggled with delight. Neal and Ella came fashionably late, interrupting Rebecca's pummeling of the piñata. Damon kept his cool, remaining cordial to Neal and Kurtis, but finding ways to keep busy and stay away from them.

Neal observed every word passing between Damon and Brooke. He leaned over and whispered extra loudly into Ella's ear, "The least they can do is try to keep their hands off each other in front of Rebecca."

"Oh, Neal," Ella admonished. "They haven't touched each other once."

Damon busied himself with the kids, trying to ignore Neal's verbal insults.

"They keep going off together in corners, whispering. It's the same thing. I had no idea his mother was *white*. His eyes are that crazy changing color, but I attributed it to colored contact lenses. Anything to make Rebecca his."

"Neal," Ella said, trying to keep her voice down. "It's Rebecca's birthday. Don't spoil it by sitting here pouting and spewing venom about her father. Kids pick up on tension between adults."

"Are you accusing me of trying to ruin my daughter's party?" He was on edge, and his voice rose, getting the attention of the adults at the party.

"Listen to you, *my daughter's party*. It's *his* daughter's party. We're lucky we were even invited. Let's just relax and enjoy this for Rebecca's sake. Or I'm leaving."

"You have never supported me on this. Never. You pushed me into getting a paternity test. If I hadn't given in to you, I would still have my daughter."

"This is not the time or the place." Ella lowered her voice, hoping he would follow suit. Neal propelled himself up from the sofa and joined Rebecca, pulling her away from Damon.

Brooke rubbed his back. "Let it go. He's had his moment of rebellion."

"Why is he doing this at Rebecca's party?" he asked through clenched teeth. He had agreed to go along with Brooke and Aunt Foster when they'd insisted on inviting Neal and Kurtis, but he wouldn't allow them to ruin Rebecca's birthday.

"It's okay." She handed him a bowl of chips. "Put this on the table for me, please." She offered him a reassuring smile.

"Everyone gather around," Neal shouted. "It's time to cut the cake."

The kids roared, running toward the table holding the cake.

Damon swung around, ready to erupt. He had intended to announce the cutting of the cake and opening of the gifts.

Brooke suddenly appeared at his side, taking his hand in hers. "It's only the cutting of the cake. Don't make a big deal out of it."

"It *is* a big deal. Rebecca and I spent all day picking out the cake. Blowing out the candles and singing 'Happy Birthday' is the most important part of the party."

"You're pouting." She smiled up at him, trying to smooth it over. "You'll help her open her presents. *That's* the most important part of the party."

"As soon as he's finished with his little show, I'm going over there."

"No, Damon. C'mon. Don't do anything to make Rebecca feel uncomfortable at her own party. This is hard on all of us, but we're the adults. We need to handle ourselves the right way."

He backed down, knowing she was right, but knowing he had a valid argument too. She moved through the chaos to stand on the other side of Rebecca while she blew out the candles on her cake. Damon simmered watching them. Neal had won again. He and Rebecca and Brooke, cutting the birthday cake like the perfect blended family.

"She looks happy." Kurtis slithered up to him, making an awkward situation worse.

"Brooke and I have tried to keep this craziness from her."

"Oh, I meant Brooke." He clasped Damon's shoulder. "I see you're fighting the same battle I had to fight. It's always the three of them. The perfect little family. The rest of us are just casualties of their relationship."

Damon turned to him, fuming and fighting to keep his anger under control. "Brooke said you promised not to make trouble."

"I don't mean to. I'm just warning you. I wish someone had warned me." He walked away whistling, and Brooke appeared to soothe Damon anger again.

"Remind me again. Why is *he* here?" he asked.

"Rebecca adores him. She wanted him here on her birthday."

"How long is he staying?"

"Damon."

Aunt Foster stepped in. "Don't let Neal and Kurtis crowd you out."

"Aunt Foster!" Brooke said, shocked. "Don't egg him on."

"How would you feel if you missed five years of your daughter's life, and these two were throwing it up in your face?" She motioned between Neal and Kurtis.

"Exactly. Thank you, Aunt Foster."

"Hush, child. I expect you to behave better than those two." She hobbled away on her walker.

Brooke shrugged and followed her aunt into the kitchen.

What place did he have here? Neal was prancing around as of he were the king of Brooke's castle and fawning over Rebecca. Kurtis was grinning at him from across the room and making eyes at Brooke whenever he thought Damon wasn't watching. He didn't like being played down in his daughter's life. Especially in front of his parents and the woman he loved. He and Brooke should be standing next to Rebecca while she cut her cake.

Never had a child's birthday party been so ensnared in controversy. But if he could get through the next hour, the party would end and he wouldn't have to see Neal or Kurtis again. Aunt Foster was right; Neal and Kurtis were not respecting his place in Rebecca's life. If everyone would take a step back, they would see the only person who would be hurt was Rebecca.

As soon as the cake was served, Damon announced Rebecca would open her gifts. Brooke joined them as Rebecca tore at her presents, ripping the paper away. She squealed with delight at every new toy. She held each present held high for all the guests to see. Damon's mother snapped pictures, thoroughly enjoying her granddaughter.

Damon wasn't happy when Rebecca opened Kurtis's gift. He had given her a new doll and a complete Barbie wardrobe. Consisting of a mink coat, a skiing outfit, and a wedding dress. There was even a pre-assembled closet with tiny hangers. It was too costly. Not appropriate coming from Kurtis. The gift warranted a hug and kiss from Rebecca. Kurtis beamed as he looked at Damon with depraved satisfaction.

"Maybe you should save Dad's gift for last." Neal stepped up to the table with his chest stuck out and a grin on his face.

"No, sweetheart." Damon guided Rebecca to the tall box on the floor next to the gift table. "You can open Neal's gift next." Rebecca wanted to open the jumbo box next, and he would allow her. Neal was trying to take a direct shot at him. There were only two gifts remaining to be opened—his and Neal's. Obviously, Neal wanted his to be the finale.

Rebecca ripped off the paper with the help of Brooke. All the children gasped. A picture of a motorized pink and white Barbie jeep was on the outside of the box. Rebecca giggled, jumping up and down. "Thank you, Dad." She jumped into Neal's arms. "Can I ride it now?"

She continued to plead with Neal to open the box. A three hundred dollar toy definitely wasn't an appropriate birthday gift for a six-year-old, and Neal knew it. He was trying to show Damon up. Neal wanted him to look bad in front of his daughter. Damon's fuse was lit, his patience gone.

"Rebecca." Damon's father held up the last present in full view of the audience. "You have one last gift to open. This one's from your father."

Damon silently thanked his dad for giving him time to compose himself. He redirected his focus to his daughter. She slashed through the paper of his gift. A squeal of happiness cut across the room, visibly slaying Neal.

"Mom, it's a video game."

It wasn't exactly a video game system. It was a learning toy, meant to help her grasp French. She'd been struggling with the class and he thought it would help her to catch on.

"Thank you, Daddy." Rebecca threw her arms around his neck and he held her close. Neal's mouth fell open in astonishment.

"Daddy?"

Damon released Rebecca back to the party. The kids quickly gathered around, itching to get a chance to play with her toys.

Neal spoke up harshly, quieting the crowd. "Brooke and I decided Rebecca should not have a video game system. We prefer educational toys. Sorry no one told you. Rebecca, you know better."

Damon's father guided Rebecca away from the scene.

Damon had enough. It was time. He'd spent the entire afternoon being run over by two arrogant men trying to push their way between him and Brooke and Rebecca. "Educational? Do you mean educational like the toy jeep you gave her?" Before Neal could answer he added, "And don't ever chastise my daughter."

"Brooke and I have spent many years instilling certain values in Rebecca and we don't want those to be abandoned so you can win brownie points with her."

Brooke stepped between the two men. "Neal, it's all right for Rebecca to have the game."

"Have you discussed this with Damon already, or are you just taking his side?"

"Neal, you're making a scene."

Ella was at Neal's side, unsuccessful at keeping him quiet. Aunt Foster distracted the children, moving the party away from the escalating scene.

Brooke defended Damon. "Damon is Rebecca's father, and he has the right to buy her the gift he feels is appropriate for her to have."

"I should have expected this." Neal slapped Ella's hand away. "Since you're sleeping together, my opinion doesn't matter anymore."

"Neal!" Ella shouted.

Neal raised his voice. "We have a legal and binding agreement, Brooke." He addressed Damon. "You can't interfere with it. I have the right to make certain decisions in Rebecca's life."

Rebecca sobbed, catching Damon's attention. His mother was holding her against the skirt of her dress. She lifted Rebecca and carried her out of the room. Brooke went to comfort her daughter. Damon wanted to follow, but he wasn't finished with Neal. Aunt Foster started seeing everyone out the front door.

The room grew quiet as Damon and Neal stared eye to eye.

"This has been a long time coming," Damon said, ready to do battle.

"Neal, let's go home. We can all talk about this later when tempers are under control."

"We're going to settle this right here, right now." He moved away from Ella. "I won't be the one to back down."

Damon exploded "*I* am Rebecca's father. I will give the final word on how her she lives her life. I appreciate what you did in my absence, but I'm here now. I know what's best for my daughter without any interference from you."

"How would you know? You haven't been here for the last five years. Do you think you can dismiss me so easily? Don't step in trying to take over now. I'll reopen the custody case if I have to."

"You go right ahead and do that if you want. But if you do, remember, it will be me you're dealing with, not Brooke. I don't have a soft spot for you. I'll use anything and everything I get my hands on to win my daughter—and keep you away from her. You're like poison to anyone you get involved with. I will no longer allow you to use my daughter as a pawn in your sick attempt to win Brooke back."

Ella's mouth dropped. She didn't know why Neal had had a sudden change of heart in his custody fight. "You told me you dropped the case because you wanted the best for Rebecca. What is Damon talking about?"

"Don't let him get to you."

"Am I the only one here who doesn't know what Damon is talking about?" Ella looked around the room and everyone avoided her eyes. "Was Kurtis right? You still want Brooke?"

"Don't do this here," Neal told her.

"I know about the rumors about other women, but I never suspected…The only reason you were fighting for Rebecca was to keep Brooke in your life?" Having heard enough, Ella snatched up her coat and raced out the door.

"This is not over." Neal went after his wife.

Damon stepped in front of him. "Neal, this is over. I don't want you around Rebecca anymore."

"You don't have the right—"

"But I do," Brooke said. She walked up to him. "Damon and I will talk, and if we decide you can see Rebecca again, I'll let you know. For now, consider our agreement null and void. You can challenge me in court if you want to, but I think your reputation at the university is too precious to you to do that."

Neal looked between Brooke and Damon. He mumbled a curse word before racing to catch up with Ella.

Damon towered over Kurtis who was watching the action from the sofa. "And what the hell are you doing here?"

"I was hoping you wouldn't forget about him," Damon's father said. "Lay into him, son. He's after your woman."

"Shh," Damon's mother grabbed his arm, pulling him away.

Kurtis stood to Damon's challenge. "Rebecca wants me here."

"I don't want you here," Damon informed him.

"This is Brooke's house."

"But I'm telling you to leave."

"I need to be sure Brooke and Rebecca are all right."

"They're fine. If they weren't it would be my responsibility to take care of them, not yours."

Kurtis held up his hands in surrender. "Hey, I'm not the professor."

"I know exactly who you are and what you want. Listen up. *I love Brooke*. I love her and my daughter. I *am not* moving aside. I'm here to stay—forever. Go about your business, and we'll have no beef with each other."

Kurtis looked to Brooke for validation, but her eyes were pasted on Damon. "Brooke?"

"Good-bye, Kurtis."

<hr />

"I don't want my dad to go away." Rebecca buried her face in the bosom of her grandmother.

"Your dad is not going away." She rubbed Rebecca's shoulders, trying to stop the tears from flowing. "Do you understand what is going on, baby?"

Rebecca shook her head. She looked up at her grandmother for an explanation that would make everything all right again.

"Your father," she clarified, "Damon, loves you and he wants to make sure he's as important to you as everyone else is."

"I like both my dads."

"I know you do, baby." Damon's mother looked up just as her son walked into the room.

"Dad is waiting for you in the car." Shame kept him from making direct eye contact with his mother. He'd made a scene at his daughter's birthday party. His mother detested people who argued in public. Private matters should be dealt with at home, behind closed doors. In all the years she'd been married to his father, not once had he witnessed a disagreement between them.

"Everything is going to be okay, baby." She kissed the top of Rebecca's head before releasing her embrace. She brushed Damon's cheek as she moved past him.

He closed the door and sat next to Rebecca on her bed. "I really messed up your party. Are you mad at me?"

"I don't want my other dad to go away."

"He won't go away."

You told him to. I heard you."

He ran his hand through his dreads. "Come here." He pulled Rebecca onto his lap. "I want to tell you the truth because I'm your father and I should never lie to you. Do you understand?"

She nodded.

"Sometimes, don't you want your mom all to yourself? With no one else around? So you can do stuff together all alone."

She nodded.

"I feel the same way about you. Sometimes, I want to have you all to myself so we can learn to be friends. I know you don't understand everything that's happening around you, but one day you will. For right now, I want you to know I love you because you're my little girl. I want you to love me because I'm your father. One way for that to happen is if we spend time together—just the two of us." He wiped away her tears before he went on. "When Neal comes around, I can't spend time with you. It's okay to go places with him, but I want to take you places too. It may not be fair, but I have more of a right to do that than Neal does. I got mad today because I wanted everyone to know it's time for you and me to spend time alone together."

"Are you going to take me away from Mom and Dad?"

"No way." He smiled reassuringly. "Can you keep a secret?"

A grin began to form. She nodded.

"I'm hoping I can get your mom to spend time with us. I want to spend special time alone with her too."

"I heard Dad tell Ms. Ella you want Mom, but you don't really want me around."

Damon suppressed his anger at Neal's attempt to turn his daughter against him. "Neal made a mistake, but I think I straightened it all out just now. I want to spend time with you. I want to spend time with your mom. I want to spend time with you and your mom together. Sometimes, grown-ups like to do things kids don't want to do so your mom and I might go out alone. But that's okay isn't it?"

Rebecca nodded.

"Do you feel better?"

She smiled.

"Want to go play with your toys?"

"Grandma said I could take some of my toys to her house for a sleepover tonight," she hedged.

"Let's go ask your mom."

⸎

Brooke stood on the front lawn, watching the taillights of Damon's father's car grow dim as they moved away. The Richmonds would take good care of Rebecca. After Damon's talk she'd calmed down and was actually excited about spending the night with her grandparents. The birthday party had been a disaster, and Rebecca had probably been scarred for life—she'd never want another birthday party. Brooke didn't doubt there would be more fallout from Damon's tirade. Just when she believed things were back on track, the men in her life had had a testosterone surge. She turned to find Damon standing inside the door watching her. Aunt Foster quickly disappeared, leaving them alone in the living room.

"What was that scene all about?" she asked.

"Neal and Kurtis have been disrespecting my place in Rebecca's life from the very beginning. It was time I stood up for myself."

"Maybe, but at Rebecca's birthday party? In front of our family and friends?"

"It was about me claiming my place in Rebecca's life—in your life. I walked away once without a fight and lost everything important to me. I'm not going to let it happen again. Not without a fight." He took her hands and pulled her down onto the sofa with him. "Can't you understand what I've had to put up with from those two? I had to assert myself. I was standing in the room with the only other men who have played a part in your life. Any other man would have complained about this situation a long time ago. I've spent my life trying not to cause a commotion. This time I had to make some noise."

"It's not only about your and Rebecca's relationship. It's about you and me."

"It's about you, me, and Rebecca as a family."

"When were you going to ask me how I felt?"

"I love you. I thought we were on the same page."

"Damon, I do love you. Right now there's your relationship with Rebecca. There's your relationship with me. We haven't merged into a family. You can't force this on me."

"I don't understand what you're saying."

She took Damon's hands in hers. "It has to be my decision."

"I know I did the right thing. I know it right here." He placed a fist over his heart.

"I need to sort through all of this."

"No."

"No?"

"No."

"This is my house."

"This is our life together."

"Damon, I love you. You're good with Rebecca. I don't want us to rush into anything we're not ready for."

"We've been in love since we were kids. What exactly is confusing you? Why do you need to be alone? What is there to think about?"

"Us."

"Do you love me?"

"That's not the point."

"Do you love me, Brooke?"

"Yes."

"I ask again, what do you need to think about?"

"Damon, it's not simple."

"Why not? Why do you have to make it complicated? You've been searching for something else ever since we were at the university. You never found it. You always end up right back with me. Do you want me to wait another five years for you to figure out we should be together?"

Brooke couldn't deny her feelings for him. She loved him and wanted to build a life with him. She didn't want to be with him to prove a point or to win a custody case. She wanted him to want her because they belonged together. "Is this your way of winning me over?"

"I've already won you over." He smiled, his eyes warming to hazel. "Weren't you paying attention? I know why you left me all those years ago. It wasn't about your fascination with Neal. It was about your fear of making a life with me."

"You're wrong. I've always wanted a life with you."

"Then why are we having this conversation? Why are we stuck, spinning our wheels? I never lied to you or did anything to hurt you, but for some reason you were always afraid—you're still afraid of committing to me. Months ago you were going to marry someone you didn't even love. If marrying Kurtis was so easy, this should be a piece of cake for you. But it's not, is it, Brooke?" He pushed a tendril of hair behind her ear. "Talk to me, Brooke. Tell me why you're so hesitant about being with me?"

"I'm not going to let myself love you so you can hurt me."

"What? I'd never hurt you. I love you."

"I want you to be certain I'm what you want. I need to know you love me, Damon. I have to feel our relationship isn't a way for you to be close to Rebecca."

"Why are you denying me your love? I'm fighting to keep you in my life. I'm talking about the long haul. Marriage, more kids. I can't let you walk away again. I don't care if you're scared. You have to give me a chance to prove myself. I'm coming off a failed marriage. You've had a hard time lately. It doesn't matter. I don't have any doubts. Not one because I've loved you since the day you noticed my intelligence and not my eyes. Don't you see? We went down separate roads, but still we came back to each other. I wish we could have spared Rebecca the pain and confusion. She shouldn't have to deal with repercussions from our mistakes, but there's nothing we can do to change the past. When you think about it, isn't falling in love again the sweetest repercussion for our transgressions?" He pulled her to him, kissing her with all the emotion he couldn't convey with words. "Is there any doubt about how I feel about you?"

She searched his eyes. "No."

"I'm at home. Here. With you. This is our fate." He smiled. "It's meant to be."

He was right. They were meant to be. She had loved him since she first saw him standing in the front of her English class reciting Shakespeare. He understood her. He cared for her, always making sure her needs were met. He hadn't blamed or made accusations when he learned about Rebecca. He'd stepped up and become the father she needed. He was handsome and worshipped her body when they made love. How could she allow unfounded fears to stand in the way of her happiness? She'd made herself a promise at the start of the custody case. She would fight to keep Rebecca, and she would fight to have Damon in her life.

Brooke pulled him by the collar to meet her lips. She kissed him with enough emotional energy to make his eyes simmer. "You proposed to me. Remember?"

He smiled. "Yes."

"Is the offer back on the table?"

He laughed. "Never took it off."

She started unbuttoning his shirt.

"What are you doing?"

"Making you comfortable. You're going to be here for a long, long time."

Aunt Foster cleared her throat as she entered the room. Rebecca had suggested putting tennis balls on the legs of Foster's walker to quiet the noise when she moved across the kitchen floor. They'd have to rethink that move if Damon was going to be around.

"Okay, you two, spill it."

"Ma'am?" Brooke and Damon answered together, igniting a round of giggles between them.

"You're too quiet in here. Why are you giving each other goo-goo eyes? What's going on?"

"Nothing, Auntie. We're just happy. Nothing more."

"Are you still together?"

Damon nodded, giving Brooke the okay to share the news.

"You couldn't get anything over on me while you two were in high school, and you can't get anything over on me now. Spill."

"We're getting married," Brooke blurted out.

"As soon as possible," Damon added.

"It's about time you two get it together." Aunt Foster waddled into the kitchen with a smile.Epilogue

"Daddy, I'm home!" Rebecca ran into the study, falling down into her father's lap.

Damon showered her with kisses. "You're too old to be sitting in my lap."

"You told me I'd never be too old to sit on your lap."

"Did I say that?" He held her tight. "We've missed you. Have you seen your little brother?"

"Mom and I picked him up from school together."

"Get up and let me take a look at you." Damon stood and circled Rebecca. At twenty, she was the spitting image of Brooke at the same age. "My daughter is studying philosophy at the *Universite Paris Sorbonne.*"

Rebecca replied in French, moving her head saucily as she dramatically waved her hands.

"You're so grown-up. Mom and I are so proud of you. How long are you staying?"

She sat behind his desk. "Until the end of the semester. Someone needs to get junior in shape. You guys have spoiled him terribly."

Damon laughed. "I wouldn't talk, young lady. You're spoiled rotten." He and Brooke had indulged all her whims, although they were a bit more strict with Damon junior.

"I'm not spoiled. Just thoroughly loved."

"Is there a boyfriend?"

Her face bloomed into a bright smile. "Don't tell Mom. She freaks about such things."

"Is he a good guy? Because if he's not, I'll be on the first plane to Paris."

"You'd like him. He's a lot like you."

Damon warmed inside. He'd never hoped to have such a close relationship with his daughter. It had taken some work, and they had crossed many rough roads, but they'd made it through. Junior had come along four years after he married Brooke, completing their family. Damon was crushed to see Rebecca go to the university in Paris, but he didn't hold her back. It had been hardest on Brooke, especially when Aunt Foster passed away, but she found comfort in loving Junior.

"Have you called Neal?" Damon asked.

"I spoke with him before I left Paris. We're going to have lunch while I'm here." She spun back and forth in his chair. "I feel bad for him. He's so lonely. Maybe if he could still work at the university, he'd be okay."

Ella had divorced Neal shortly after Rebecca's sixth birthday party. Years later, his health had failed and he had been forced to leave the university. He didn't call Brooke much after Damon and Brooke were married. Once Rebecca went off to school, there was no contact with him.

"Guess what?" Rebecca beamed. "Kurtis sent me a birthday card."

"Really?" Damon wasn't aware they were still in touch.

Kurtis had married Barbara two years after Damon married Brooke. From what he understood, they were very happy together. Kurtis had a trophy wife. Barbara had a bottomless bank account. They were made for each other.

"Daddy?"

"Yes, sweetheart?"

"I'm glad I'm home."

"I love you. If you ever get lonesome flitting all around the world, you always have a home here."

⚮

ABOUT THE AUTHOR

Kimberley White is the author of many sensuous romance novels. She is a registered nurse pursuing her master's degree. She enjoys teaching writing courses and speaking at conferences. Ms. White loves to hear from her readers:

P.O. Box 672
Novi, MI 48376
kwhite_writer@hotmail.com.

Excerpt from

A DRUMMER'S BEAT TO MEND

BY

KEI SWANSON

Release Date: November 2005

CHAPTER ONE

With a visible rhythm in his step, Tetsuro Takamitsu walked through the shadowy hallway behind the stage, his fingers tapping out the gentle cadence of his soul against his jean-encased thighs. A beat had always been there. It had been awakened by the pulse of rock and roll in cosmopolitan Tokyo, then refined by the tradition of feudal Japan and its ancient drummers.

Curtains at the wings swung, brushed by Tetsuro's fellow performers who arranged the drums on the stage for practice the next morning. The backstage area teemed with stagehands going about their work without regard to the Japanese performers helping them.

Whenever the group arrived early in the performance city, Tetsuro enjoyed taking in the city's sights instead of crashing at the hotel and seeing only the auditoriums. Taiko Nihon, the drummers' troupe, would give two night performances in Cleveland. He had the afternoons free to attend baseball games of the Cleveland Indians. Tetsuro was not alone in his passion for America's favorite pastime. No matter how far away from the shores of Japan her drummer-sons strayed, the lure and love of baseball was always present. The Japanese love for the game was renown, at times surpassing that of Americans. Tetsuro looked forward to seeing Kentaro Ikuta pitch for the first time since the phenomenal pitcher from Nagasaki had defected, as the Japanese press called it, to the U.S.

Pulling sunglasses from his jeans' hip pocket, Tetsuro unfolded them around his eyes and exited the theater. The fresh air was energizing after the four-hour plane flight. A gentle breeze stirred the loose strands of straight raven hair draping his neck and shoulders. He ran a hand through his hair as he paused to breathe in the scent of grass and flowers. The heavy hair settled back around his shoulders seconds later.

From behind him, a sultry feminine voice spoke, "*Ohayo, Te-chan.*"

"*Ohayo.*" Tetsuro turned to the petite woman in her late twenties who leaned against the wall beside the door. "Are you not supposed to be unpacking wardrobe?"

"I am taking a break." She pushed from the wall and dropped her cigarette.

Tetsuro wondered whom she thought she was fooling since she merely took the smoke in her mouth before almost immediately blowing it out. He was glad he'd given up the habit before he was twenty. *Man! Had it been twelve years?*

"I absolutely hate caring for those old-fashioned kimono! Have you been stuck with unpacking the drums?"

"It is my turn." Tetsuro kept walking and she fell into step with him.

"Are the truck drivers and stagehands not hired to unload the drums? I do not understand why we have to unload and unpack."

"It is so you respect every element of performing, from the work of the lowest to the highest."

"Yeah, yeah, yeah."

Tetsuro stopped and looked at the woman.

"Kifume-*san*, if you do not like it, why do you study? *Taiko* is an art...every part of it. If you can not respect one element, how can you honor another?"

Kifume snorted softly, then said, "You make it sound like a religion."

"It is...almost." With his rhythmic walk Tetsuro continued down the sidewalk toward the eighteen-wheeler backed to the curb.

"I like the performing!" Kifume trotted to catch up with him. "And, I like one of the drummers!"

"Well, *that* has been over for a while." It was Tetsuro's turn to scoff.

"Not soon enough." Kifume stopped moving.

Tetsuro took three more steps ahead of her, then halted. He'd heard such a tone before when he was twenty. He turned back to look over his shoulder, pulling his sunglasses down his nose to see her clearly.

"What do you mean?" He jerked the sunglasses off in anger.

"I am pregnant."

The tone *was* the same. Rage flooded through him.

"You said you were on the pill." Hadn't Emiko taught him not to be too trusting?

"So...I lied." Kifume stared straight at him as she spoke. At home, her eye contact would be considered bold. Japanese women, even in the twenty-first century, weren't brazen enough to confront a man thusly. Kifume's youth, exposure to America and its customs, and the familiarity grown from studying *taiko*, gave her the confidence to be so direct with him.

"We also used protection," he continued.

"Maybe it slipped." Kifume gave a slight shrug of her narrow shoulders.

Furious, Tetsuro turned on the heels of his black leather boots and stomped to the truck. The back door was open and half of the equipment was already in the theater. He hung his sunglasses by the earpiece in his back pocket and stepped into the dark cavern. At the midpoint sat a large crate with the *O-Daiko,* the largest drum, and the centerpiece of the show. He should have help to move it, but anger and ego clouded his judgment. Once he moved it to the end of the van, the others would be there to help.

Kifume followed. "Are you not going to say anything?"

"I think you have said enough for the moment. Besides, how do I know you are not lying now?" Tetsuro put his hands on the edge of the huge, heavy crate. "What makes you think it is mine? You *like* a lot of drummers."

He wiggled the crate forward. The rollers of the pallet below the large crate allowed it to move easily, almost on its own.

Kifume moved behind the crate and unhooked a strap.

"This will make it easier."

"No! I have had enough of your help." Too late Tetsuro's words ricocheted off the walls of the truck.

The great crate lunged, surging without warning toward the left. Tetsuro gripped the edges, spreading his feet apart to brace himself. Extending his arms wide, he clutched the rough planks with his long fingers, but his attempt to hold the heavy object in place was futile. The crate shifted in the unleveled truck and the edge of the heavy box slammed his left hand into the truck wall. Monstrous pain ripped through his arm and his deep-throated scream echoed in the cavernous truck.

"Tetsu!" Kifume threw her slight weight against the crate. Unable to move it, she clutched the rope strung across the back and pulled. Still unable to relieve any of the pressure on Tetsuro's hand, she shouted in English, "Help! Somebody! Help!"

"What the…?" The returning driver jumped into the truck and grasped one side of the large crate and heaved.

More performers arrived, returning to continue unloading the truck. Seeing the situation, some of them rushed to shove the drum crate away while others bent over Tetsuro. His hand was pinned between the crate and the wall four feet above the truck floor. His body turned into the side of van. Pain ran from his fingers to his shoulder and echoed in his chest with the bounding beat of his blood. His scream gargled back into his throat as intense agony took all the breath from him.

Once the pressure was removed, Tetsuro slid down the wall. Folding his legs beneath him on the floor, he cradled his left hand in his right. Blood throbbed to the injury in a painful rush and a nauseous knot balled up in his stomach, threatening to force the airline meal up. He fought the wave of sickness and struggled not to lose consciousness.

"Te-chan, sumimasen." Kifume wept as she reached toward his hand.

"Get away from me!" he growled, refusing her apology.

"We need to get you to a hospital," said a male performer who kneeled to help Tetsuro when Kifume moved away.

"I think you are right, Susu-*san.*" Tetsuro battled the pain striving to overtake his consciousness.

Susumu, his best friend, put a supporting arm around his back and helped him stand as Tetsuro held the injured hand higher than his fast pounding heart. He'd already discovered that blood flowing downward increased the pain.

"What about the performance?" Tetsuro groaned, his voice barely audible.

"Do not worry. We will get along without our beloved artistic manager," Susumu ribbed him. "While we are drumming before a nameless audience, you will be making new friends."

"Are you trying to make me feel better?" Tetsuro attempted a smile, but the cutting pain made it difficult.

"Trying to, my friend."

Leave it to Susumu to see the bright side of things. Tetsuro leaned heavily on his friend, happy to have the support. Who knew what the next few hours would bring, much less the following day?

SWEET REPERCUSSIONS

2005 Publication Schedule

January

A Heart's Awakening
Veronica Parker
$9.95
1-58571-143-8

Falling
Natalie Dunbar
$9.95
1-58571-121-7

February

Echoes of Yesterday
Beverly Clark
$9.95
1-58571-131-4

A Love of Her Own
Cheris F. Hodges
$9.95
1-58571-136-5

Higher Ground
Leah Latimer
$19.95
1-58571-157-8

March

Misconceptions
Pamela Leigh Starr
$9.95
1-58571-117-9

I'll Paint a Sun
A.J. Garrotto
$9.95
1-58571-165-9

Peace Be Still
Colette Haywood
$12.95
1-58571-129-2

April

Intentional Mistakes
Michele Sudler
$9.95
1-58571-152-7

Conquering Dr. Wexler's Heart
Kimberley White
$9.95
1-58571-126-8

Song in the Park
Martin Brant
$15.95
1-58571-125-X

May

The Color Line
Lizzette Grayson Carter
$9.95
1-58571-163-2

Unconditional
A.C. Arthur
$9.95
1-58571-142-X

Last Train to Memphis
Elsa Cook
$12.95
1-58571-146-2

June

Angel's Paradise
Janice Angelique
$9.95
1-58571-107-1

Suddenly You
Crystal Hubbard
$9.95
1-58571-158-6

Matters of Life and
  Death
Lesego Malepe, Ph.D.
$15.95
1-58571-124-1

2005 Publication Schedule (continued)

July

Class Reunion
Irma Jenkins/John
  Brown
$12.95
1-58571-123-3

Wild Ravens
Altonya Washington
$9.95
1-58571-164-0

August

Path of Thorns
Annetta P. Lee
$9.95
1-58571-145-4

Timeless Devotion
Bella McFarland
$9.95
1-58571-148-9

Life Is Never As It Seems
J.J. Michael
$12.95
1-58571-153-5

September

Beyond Rapture
Beverly Clark
$9.95
1-58571-130-6

Blood Lust
J. M. Jeffries
$9.95
1-58571-138-1

Rough on Rats and
  Tough on Cats
Chris Parker
$12.95
1-58571-154-3

October

A Will to Love
Angie Daniels
$9.95
1-58571-141-1

Taken by You
Dorothy Elizabeth Love
$9.95
1-58571-162-4

Soul Eyes
Wayne L. Wilson
$12.95
1-58571-147-0

November

A Drummer's Beat to
  Mend
Kei Swanson
$9.95
1-58571-171-3

Sweet Reprecussions
Kimberley White
$9.95
1-58571-159-4

Red Polka Dot in a
  World of Plaid
Varian Johnson
$12.95
1-58571-140-3

December

Hand in Glove
Andrea Jackson
$9.95
1-58571-166-7

Blaze
Barbara Keaton
$9.95
1-58571-172-1

Across
Blue Dawson
$12.95
1-58571-149-7

Other Genesis Press, Inc. Titles

Acquisitions	Kimberley White	$8.95
A Dangerous Deception	J.M. Jeffries	$8.95
A Dangerous Love	J.M. Jeffries	$8.95
A Dangerous Obsession	J.M. Jeffries	$8.95
After the Vows	Leslie Esdaile	$10.95
(Summer Anthology)	T.T. Henderson	
	Jacqueline Thomas	
Again My Love	Kayla Perrin	$10.95
Against the Wind	Gwynne Forster	$8.95
A Lark on the Wing	Phyliss Hamilton	$8.95
A Lighter Shade of Brown	Vicki Andrews	$8.95
All I Ask	Barbara Keaton	$8.95
A Love to Cherish	Beverly Clark	$8.95
Ambrosia	T.T. Henderson	$8.95
And Then Came You	Dorothy Elizabeth Love	$8.95
Angel's Paradise	Janice Angelique	$8.95
A Risk of Rain	Dar Tomlinson	$8.95
At Last	Lisa G. Riley	$8.95
Best of Friends	Natalie Dunbar	$8.95
Bound by Love	Beverly Clark	$8.95
Breeze	Robin Hampton Allen	$10.95
Brown Sugar Diaries &	Delores Bundy &	$10.95
Other Sexy Tales	Cole Riley	
By Design	Barbara Keaton	$8.95
Cajun Heat	Charlene Berry	$8.95
Careless Whispers	Rochelle Alers	$8.95
Caught in a Trap	Andre Michelle	$8.95
Chances	Pamela Leigh Starr	$8.95
Dark Embrace	Crystal Wilson Harris	$8.95
Dark Storm Rising	Chinelu Moore	$10.95
Designer Passion	Dar Tomlinson	$8.95
Ebony Butterfly II	Delilah Dawson	$14.95

Erotic Anthology	Assorted	$8.95
Eve's Prescription	Edwina Martin Arnold	$8.95
Everlastin' Love	Gay G. Gunn	$8.95
Fate	Pamela Leigh Starr	$8.95
Forbidden Quest	Dar Tomlinson	$10.95
Fragment in the Sand	Annetta P. Lee	$8.95
From the Ashes	Kathleen Suzanne	$8.95
	Jeanne Sumerix	
Gentle Yearning	Rochelle Alers	$10.95
Glory of Love	Sinclair LeBeau	$10.95
Hart & Soul	Angie Daniels	$8.95
Heartbeat	Stephanie Bedwell-Grime	$8.95
I'll Be Your Shelter	Giselle Carmichael	$8.95
Illusions	Pamela Leigh Starr	$8.95
Indiscretions	Donna Hill	$8.95
Interlude	Donna Hill	$8.95
Intimate Intentions	Angie Daniels	$8.95
Just an Affair	Eugenia O'Neal	$8.95
Kiss or Keep	Debra Phillips	$8.95
Love Always	Mildred E. Riley	$10.95
Love Unveiled	Gloria Greene	$10.95
Love's Deception	Charlene Berry	$10.95
Mae's Promise	Melody Walcott	$8.95
Meant to Be	Jeanne Sumerix	$8.95
Midnight Clear	Leslie Esdaile	$10.95
(Anthology)	Gwynne Forster	
	Carmen Green	
	Monica Jackson	
Midnight Magic	Gwynne Forster	$8.95
Midnight Peril	Vicki Andrews	$10.95
My Buffalo Soldier	Barbara B. K. Reeves	$8.95
Naked Soul	Gwynne Forster	$8.95
No Regrets	Mildred E. Riley	$8.95
Nowhere to Run	Gay G. Gunn	$10.95

Object of His Desire	A. C. Arthur	$8.95
One Day at a Time	Bella McFarland	$8.95
Passion	T.T. Henderson	$10.95
Past Promises	Jahmel West	$8.95
Path of Fire	T.T. Henderson	$8.95
Picture Perfect	Reon Carter	$8.95
Pride & Joi	Gay G. Gunn	$8.95
Quiet Storm	Donna Hill	$8.95
Reckless Surrender	Rochelle Alers	$8.95
Rendezvous with Fate	Jeanne Sumerix	$8.95
Revelations	Cheris F. Hodges	$8.95
Rivers of the Soul	Leslie Esdaile	$8.95
Rooms of the Heart	Donna Hill	$8.95
Shades of Brown	Denise Becker	$8.95
Shades of Desire	Monica White	$8.95
Sin	Crystal Rhodes	$8.95
So Amazing	Sinclair LeBeau	$8.95
Somebody's Someone	Sinclair LeBeau	$8.95
Someone to Love	Alicia Wiggins	$8.95
Soul to Soul	Donna Hill	$8.95
Still Waters Run Deep	Leslie Esdaile	$8.95
Subtle Secrets	Wanda Y. Thomas	$8.95
Sweet Tomorrows	Kimberly White	$8.95
The Color of Trouble	Dyanne Davis	$8.95
The Price of Love	Sinclair LeBeau	$8.95
The Reluctant Captive	Joyce Jackson	$8.95
The Missing Link	Charlyne Dickerson	$8.95
Three Wishes	Seressia Glass	$8.95
Tomorrow's Promise	Leslie Esdaile	$8.95
Truly Inseperable	Wanda Y. Thomas	$8.95
Twist of Fate	Beverly Clark	$8.95
Unbreak My Heart	Dar Tomlinson	$8.95
Unconditional Love	Alicia Wiggins	$8.95
When Dreams A Float	Dorothy Elizabeth Love	$8.95

Whispers in the Night	Dorothy Elizabeth Love	$8.95
Whispers in the Sand	LaFlorya Gauthier	$10.95
Yesterday is Gone	Beverly Clark	$8.95
Yesterday's Dreams, Tomorrow's Promises	Reon Laudat	$8.95
Your Precious Love	Sinclair LeBeau	$8.95

ESCAPE WITH INDIGO !!!!

Join Indigo Book Club©
It's simple, easy and secure.

Sign up and receive the new releases
every month + Free shipping and
20% off the cover price.

Go online to www.genesis-press.com
and click on Bookclub or
call 1-888-INDIGO-1

Order Form

Mail to: Genesis Press, Inc.
P.O. Box 101
Columbus, MS 39703

Name _____
Address _____
City/State _____ Zip _____
Telephone _____

Ship to (if different from above)
Name _____
Address _____
City/State _____ Zip _____
Telephone _____

Credit Card Information
Credit Card # _____   ☐ Visa   ☐ Mastercard
Expiration Date (mm/yy) _____   ☐ AmEx   ☐ Discover

Qty.	Author	Title	Price	Total

Use this order form, or call
1-888-INDIGO-1

Total for books _____
Shipping and handling:
  $5 first two books,
  $1 each additional book _____
Total S & H _____
Total amount enclosed _____
Mississippi residents add 7% sales tax